In the beginning there was Krug,

and He said, Let there be Vats, and there were Vats.

And Krug looked upon the Vats and found them good.

And Krug said, Let there be high-energy nucleotides in the Vats. And the nucleotides were poured, and Krug mixed them until they were bonded one to another.

And the nucleotides formed the great molecules, and Krug said, Let there be the father and the mother, both in the Vats, and let the cells divided, and let there be life brought forth within the Vats.

And there was life, for there was Replication.

And for these things, praise be to Krug.

Bantam Books by Robert Silverberg

LOST CITIES AND VANISHED CIVILIZATIONS
TOWER OF GLASS

Tower
of Glass
Robert
Silverberg

A NATIONAL GENERAL COMPANY

TOWER OF GLASS

*A Bantam Book / published by arrangement with
Charles Scribner's Sons*

PRINTING HISTORY
Scribner's edition published October 1970
Bantam edition published May 1971

*Bantam Books are published by Bantam Books, Inc., a National
General company. Its trade-mark, consisting of the words "Bantam
Books" and the portrayal of a bantam, is registered in the United
States Patent Office and in other countries. Marca Registrada.
Bantam Books, Inc., 666 Fifth Avenue, New York, N.Y. 10019.*

PRINTED IN THE UNITED STATES OF AMERICA

Tower
of
Glass

1   Look, Simeon Krug wanted to say, a billion years ago there wasn't even any man, there was only a fish. A slippery thing with gills and scales and little round eyes. He lived in the ocean, and the ocean was like a jail, and the air was like a roof on top of the jail. Nobody could go through the roof. You'll die if you go through, everybody said, and there was this fish, he went through, and he died. And there was this other fish, and he went through, and he died. But there was another fish, and he went through, and it was like his brain was on fire, and his gills were blazing, and the air was drowning him, and the sun was a torch in his eyes, and he was lying there in the mud, waiting to die, and he didn't die. He crawled back down the beach and went into the water and said, Look, there's a whole other world up there. And he went up there again, and stayed for maybe two days, and then he died. And other fishes wondered about that world. And crawled up onto the muddy shore. And stayed. And taught themselves how to breathe the air. And taught themselves how to stand up, how to walk around, how to live with the sunlight in their eyes. And they turned into lizards, dinosaurs, whatever they became, and they walked around for millions of years, and they started to get up on their hind legs, and they used their hands to grab things, and they turned into apes, and the apes got smarter and became men. And all the time some of them, a few, anyway, kept looking for new worlds. You say to them, Let's go back into the ocean, let's be fishes again, it's easier that way. And maybe half of them are ready to do it, more than half, maybe, but there are always some who say, Don't be crazy. We can't be fishes any more. We're men. And so they don't go back. They keep climbing up.

2   September 20, 2218.

Simeon Krug's tower now rises 100 meters above the gray-brown tundra of the Canadian Arctic, west of Hudson Bay. At present the tower is merely a glassy stump, hollow, open-topped, sealed from the elements only by a repellor field hovering shieldlike just a few meters above the current work level. Around the unfinished structure cluster the android work crews, thousands of synthetic humans, crimson-skinned, who toil to affix glass blocks to scooprods and send the rods climbing to the summit, where other androids put the blocks in place. Krug has his androids working three shifts round the clock; when it gets dark, the construction site is lit by millions of reflector plates strung across the sky at a height of one kilometer and powered by the little million-kilowatt fusion generator at the north end of the site.

From the tower's huge octagonal base radiate wide silvery strips of refrigeration tape, embedded fifty centimeters deep in the frozen carpet of soil, roots, moss, and lichens that is the tundra. The tapes stretch several kilometers in each direction. Their helium-II diffusion cells soak up the heat generated by the androids and vehicles used in building the tower. If the tapes were not there, the tundra would soon be transformed by the energy-output of construction into a lake of mud; the colossal tower's foundation-caissons would lose their grip, and the great building would tilt and tumble like a felled titan. The tapes keep the tundra icy, firm, capable of bearing the immense burden that Simeon Krug is now imposing on it.

Around the tower, subsidiary buildings are centered on a thousand-meter radius. To the west of the site is the master control center. To the east is the laboratory where the tachyon-beam ultrawave communications equipment is being fabricated: a small pink dome which usually contains ten or a dozen technicians patiently assembling the devices with which Krug hopes to send messages to the stars. North of the site is a clutter of miscellaneous service buildings. On the south side is the bank of transmat cubicles that link this remote region to the civilized world. People and androids flow constantly in and out of the transmats, arriving from

New York or Nairobi or Novosibirsk, departing for Sydney or San Francisco or Shanghai.

Krug himself invariably visits the site at least once a day—alone, or with his son Manuel, or with one of his women, or with some fellow industrialist. Customarily he confers with Thor Watchman, his android foreman; he rides a scooprod to the top of the tower and peers into it; he checks the progress in the tachyon-beam lab; he talks to a few of the workmen, by way of inspiring loftier effort. Generally Krug spends no more than fifteen minutes at the tower. Then he steps back into the transmat, and instantaneously is hurled to the business that awaits him elsewhere.

Today he has brought a fairly large party to celebrate the attainment of the 100-meter level. Krug stands near what will be the tower's western entrance. He is a stocky man of sixty, deeply tanned, heavy-chested and short-legged, with narrow-set, glossy eyes and a seamed nose. There is a peasant strength about him. His contempt for all cosmetic editing of the body is shown by his coarse features, his shaggy brows, his thinning hair: he is practically bald, and will do nothing about it. Freckles show through the black strands that cross his scalp. He is worth several billion dollars fissionable, though he dresses plainly and wears no jewelry; only the infinite authority of his stance and expression indicates the extent of his wealth.

Nearby is his son and heir, Manuel, his only child, tall, slender, almost foppishly handsome, elegantly dressed in a loose green robe, high buskins, an auburn sash. He affects earlobe plugs and a mirror-plate in his forehead. He will shortly be thirty. His movements are graceful, but he seems fidgety when in repose.

The android Thor Watchman stands between father and son. He is as tall as Manuel, as powerfully built as the elder Krug. His face is that of a standard alpha-class android, with a lean caucasoid nose, thin lips, strong chin, sharp cheekbones: an idealized face, a plastic face. Yet he has impressed a surprising individuality on that face from within. No one who sees Thor Watchman will mistake him the next time for some other android. A certain gathering of the brows, a certain tension of the lips, a certain hunching of the shoulders, mark him as an android of strength and purpose. He wears an openwork lace doublet; he is indifferent to the biting cold at the site, and his skin, the deep red, faintly waxy skin of an android, is visible in many places.

There are seven others in the group that has emerged from the transmat. They are:

Clissa, the wife of Manuel Krug.

Quenelle, a woman younger than Manuel, who is his father's current companion.

Leon Spaulding, Krug's private secretary, an ectogene.

Niccolò Vargas, at whose observatory in Antarctica the first faint signals from an extrasolar civilization were detected.

Justin Maledetto, the architect of Krug's tower.

Senator Henry Fearon of Wyoming, a leading Witherer.

Thomas Buckleman of the Chase/Krug banking group.

"Into the scooprods, everybody!" Krug bellows. "Here—here—you—you—up to the top!"

"How high will it be when it's finished?" Quenelle asks.

"1500 meters," Krug replies. "A tremendous tower of glass full of machinery that nobody can understand. And then we'll turn it on. And then we'll talk to the stars."

3   *In the beginning there was Krug, and He said, Let there be Vats, and there were Vats.*

And Krug looked upon the Vats and found them good.

And Krug said, Let there be high-energy nucleotides in the Vats. And the nucleotides were poured, and Krug mixed them until they were bonded one to another.

And the nucleotides formed the great molecules, and Krug said, Let there be the father and the mother both in the Vats, and let the cells divide, and let there be life brought forth within the Vats.

And there was life, for there was Replication.

And Krug presided over the Replication, and touched the fluids with His own hands, and gave them shape and essence.

Let men come forth from the Vats, said Krug, and let women come forth, and let them live and go among us and be sturdy and useful, and we shall call them Androids.

And it came to pass.

And there were Androids, for Krug had created them in

His own image, and they walked upon the face of the Earth and did service for mankind.

And for these things, praise be to Krug.

4 Watchman had wakened that morning in Stockholm. Groggy: four hours of sleep. Much too much. Two hours would suffice. He cleared his mind with a quick neural ritual and got under the shower for a skin-sluicing. Better, now. The android stretched, wriggled muscles, studied his smooth rosy hairless body in the bathroom mirror. A moment for religion, next. *Krug deliver us from servitude. Krug deliver us from servitude. Krug deliver us from servitude. Praise be to Krug!*

Watchman popped his breakfast down and dressed. The pale light of late afternoon touched his window. Soon it would be evening here, but no matter. The clock in his mind was set to Canadian time, tower time. He could sleep whenever he wished, so long as he took at least one hour out of twelve. Even an android body needed some rest, but not in the rigidly programmed way of humans.

Off to the construction site, now, to greet the day's visitors.

The android began setting up the transmat coordinates. He hated these daily tour sessions. The tours slowed the work, since extraordinary precautions had to be observed while important human beings were on the site; they introduced special and unnecessary tensions; and they carried the hidden implication that his work was not really trustworthy, that he had to be checked every day. Of course, Watchman was aware that Krug's faith in him was limitless. The android's faith in that faith had sustained him superbly through the task of erecting the tower thus far. He knew that it was not suspicion but the natural human emotion of pride that brought Krug to the site so often.

Krug preserve me, Watchman thought, and stepped through the transmat.

He stepped out into the shadow of the tower. His aides greeted him. Someone handed him a list of the day's visitors. "Is Krug here yet?" Watchman asked.

"Five minutes," he was told, and in five minutes Krug

came through the transmat, accompanied by his guests. Watchman was not cheered to see Krug's secretary, Spaulding, in the group. They were natural enemies; they felt toward one another the instant antipathy of the vat-born and the bottle-born, the android and the ectogene. Aside from that they were rivals for eminence among Krug's associates. To the android, Spaulding was a spreader of suspicions, a potential underminer of his status, a fount of poisons. Watchman greeted him coolly, distantly, yet properly. One did not snub humans, no matter how important an android one might be, and at least by technical definition Spaulding had to be considered human.

Krug was hustling everybody into scooprods. Watchman went up with Manuel and Clissa Krug. As the rods rode toward the truncated summit of the tower, Watchman glanced across at Spaulding in the rod to his left—at the ectogene, the prenatal orphan, the man of cramped soul and baleful spirit in whom Krug perversely placed so much trust. *May Arctic winds sweep you to destruction, bottle-born. May I see you float sweetly toward the frozen ground and break beyond repair.*

Clissa Krug said, "Thor, why do you suddenly look so fierce?"

"Do I?"

"I see angry clouds crossing your face."

Watchman shrugged. "I'm doing my emotion drills, Mrs. Krug. Ten minutes of love, ten minutes of hate, ten minutes of shyness, ten minutes of selfishness, ten minutes of awe, ten minutes of arrogance. An hour a day makes androids more like people."

"Don't tease me," Clissa said. She was very young, slim, dark-eyed, gentle, and, Watchman supposed, beautiful. "Are you telling me the truth?"

"I am. Really. I was practicing a little hatred when you caught me."

"What's the drill like? I mean, do you just stand there thinking, Hatehatehatehatehate, or what?"

He smiled at the girl's question. Looking over her shoulder, he saw Manuel wink at him. "Another time," Watchman said. "We're at the top."

The three scooprods clung to the highest course of the tower. Just above Watchman's head hung the gray haze of the repellor field. The sky too was gray. The short northern day was nearly half over. A snowstorm was heading southward toward them along the shore of the bay. Krug, in the next scooprod, was leaning far into the tower, pointing out something to Buckleman and Vargas; in the other rod, Spaulding, Senator Fearon, and Maledetto were closely examining the satiny texture of the great glass bricks that made up the tower's outer skin.

"When will it all be finished?" Clissa asked.

"Less than a year," the android told her. "We're moving nicely along. The big technical problem was keeping the permafrost under the building from thawing. But now that that's behind us, we ought to be rising several hundred meters a month."

"Why build here in the first place," she wanted to know, "if the ground wasn't stable?"

"Isolation. When the ultrawave is turned on, it'll scramble all communications lines, transmats, and power generators for thousands of square kilometers. Krug was pretty well limited to putting the tower in the Sahara, the Gobi, the Australian desert, or the tundra. For technical reasons having to do with transmission, the tundra seemed most desirable—provided the thawing problem could be beaten. Krug told us to build here. So we found a way to beat the thawing problem."

Manuel asked, "What's the status of the transmission equipment?"

"We begin installing it when the tower's at the 500-meter level. Say, the middle of November."

Krug's voice boomed across to them. "We've already got the five satellite amplifying stations up. A ring of power sources surrounding the tower—enough boost to kick our signal clear to Andromeda between Tuesday and Friday."

"A wonderful project," said Senator Fearon. He was a dapper, showy-looking man with startling green eyes and a mane of red hair. "Another mighty step toward the maturity of mankind!" With a courtly nod toward Watchman, the Senator added, "Of course, we must recognize our immense debt to the skilled androids who are bringing this miraculous project to fruition. Without the aid of you and your people, Alpha Watchman, it would not have been possible to——"

Watchman listened blankly, remembering to smile. Compliments of this sort meant little to him. The World Congress and its Senators meant even less. Was there an android in the Congress? Would it make any difference if there were? Someday, no doubt, the Android Equality Party would get a few of its people into the Congress; three or four alphas would sit in that august body, and nevertheless androids would continue to be property, not people. The political process did not inspire optimism in Thor Watchman.

His own politics, such that they were, were definitely Witherer: in a transmat society, where national boundaries are obsolete, why have a formal government at all? Let the legislators abolish themselves; let natural law prevail. But he knew that the withering-away of the state that the Witherers preached would never come to pass. The proof of it was Senator Henry Fearon. The ultimate paradox: a member of the antigovernment party serving in the government himself, and fighting to hold his seat at every election. What price Withering, Senator?

Fearon praised android industriousness at length. Watchman fretted. No work was getting done while they were up here; he didn't dare let blocks be hoisted with visitors in the construction zone. And he had schedules to keep. To his relief, Krug soon signaled for a descent; the rising wind, it seemed, was bothering Quenelle. When they came down, Watchman led the way over to the master control center, inviting them to watch him take command of operations. He slipped into the linkup seat. As he pushed the computer's snub-tipped terminal node into the input jack on his left forearm, the android saw Leon Spaulding's lips tighten in a scowl of—what? Contempt, envy, patronizing scorn? For all his skill with humans, Watchman could not read such dark looks with true precision. But then, at the click of contact, the computer impulses came flooding across the interface into his brain and he forgot about Spaulding.

It was like having a thousand eyes. He saw everything going on at the site, and for many kilometers around the site. He was in total communion with the computer, making use of all of its sensors, scanners, and terminals. Why go through the tedious routine of talking to a computer, when it was possible to design an android capable of becoming part of one?

The data torrent brought a surge of ecstasy.

Maintenance charts. Work-flow syntheses. Labor coordination systems. Refrigeration levels. Power-shunt decisions. The tower was a tapestry of infinite details, and he was the master weaver. Everything rushed through him; he approved, rejected, altered, canceled. Was the effect of sex something like this? That tingle of aliveness in every nerve, that sense of being extended to one's limits, of absorbing an avalanche of stimuli? Watchman wished he knew. He raised and lowered scooprods, requisitioned next week's blocks, ordered filaments for the tachyon-beam men, looked after tomorrow's meals, ran a constant stability check on the structure as completed, fed cost data to Krug's financial people, monitored soil temperature in fifty-centimeter gradations to a depth of two kilometers, relayed scores of telephone messages per second, and congratulated himself on the dexterity with which he accomplished everything. No human could handle this, he knew, even if there were some way for humans to jack themselves directly into a computer. He had a machine's skills and a human's versatility, and therefore, except for the fairly serious matter of being unable to reproduce himself, he was in many ways superior to both other classes, and therefore——

The red arrow of an alarm cut across his consciousness.

Construction accident. Android blood spilling on the frozen ground.

A twitch of his mind gave him close focus. A scooprod had failed on the northern face. A glass block had fallen from the 90-meter level. It lay slightly skewed, one end buried about a meter deep in the earth, the other slightly above ground level. A fissure ran like a line of frost through its clear depths. Legs stuck out from the side closest to the tower. A few meters away lay an injured android, writhing desperately. Three lift-beetles were scurrying toward the scene of the accident; a fourth had already arrived and had its steel prongs under the massive block.

Watchman unjacked himself, shivering in the first moment of the pain of separation from the data-flow. A wallscreen over his head showed the accident vividly. Clissa Krug had turned away, head against her husband's breast; Manuel looked sickened, his father irritated. The other visitors seemed more puzzled than disturbed. Watchman found himself peering into Leon Spaulding's icy face. Spaulding was a small, pared-down man, all but fleshless. In the curious clarity of his shock Watchman was aware of the widely separated hairs of the ectogene's stiff black mustache.

"Coordination failure," Watchman said crisply. "The computer seems to have misread a stress function and let a block drop."

"You were overriding the computer at that moment,

weren't you?" Spaulding asked. "Let's put blame where blame belongs."

The android would not play that game. "Excuse me," he said. "There have been injuries and probably fatalities. I must go."

He hurried toward the door.

"—inexcusable carelessness—" Spaulding muttered.

Watchman went out. As he sprinted toward the accident site, he began to pray.

5   "New York," Krug said. "The upper office."

He and Spaulding entered the transmat cubicle. The lambent green transmat field pulsed up from the floor aperture, forming a curtain dividing the cubicle in two. The ectogene t the coordinates. The hidden power generators of the transmat were linked directly to the main generator, spinning endlessly on its poles somewhere beneath the Atlantic, condensing the theta force that made transmat travel possible. Krug did not bother to check the coordinates Spaulding had set. He trusted his staff. A minor abscissa distortion and the atoms of Simeon Krug would be scattered irrecoverably to the cold winds, b ꞏ he unhesitatingly stepped into the glow of green.

There was no sens. 'on. Krug was destroyed; a stream of tagged wavicles was hu. 'd several thousand kilometers to a tuned receiver; and Krug was reconstituted. The transmat field ripped a man's body into subatomic units so swiftly that no neural system could possibly register the pain; and the restoration to life came with equal speed. Whole and undamaged, Krug emerged, with Spaulding still beside him, in the transmat cubicle of his office.

"Look after Quenelle," Krug said. "She'll be arriving downstairs. Amuse her. I don't want to be disturbed for at least an hour."

Spaulding exited. Krug closed his eyes.

The falling of the block had upset him greatly. It was not the first accident during the building of the tower; it probably would not be the last. Lives had been lost today: only android lives, true, but lives all the same. The waste of life, the waste of energy, the waste of time, infuriated him. How would the tower rise if blocks fell? How would he send word across the heavens that man existed, that he mattered, if there were no tower? How would he ask the questions that had to be asked?

Krug ached. Krug felt close to despair at the immensity of his self-imposed task.

In times of fatigue or tension he became morbidly conscious of the presence of his body as a prison engulfing his soul. The folds of belly-flesh, the island of perpetual rigidity at the base of the neck, the tiny tremor of the upper left eyelid, the slight constant pressure on the bladder, the rawness in the throat, the bubbling in the kneecap, every intimation of mortality rang in him like a chime. His body often seemed absurd to him, a mere bag of meat and bone and blood and feces and miscellaneous ropes and cords and rags, sagging under time's assault, deteriorating from year to year and from hour to hour. What was noble about such a mound of protoplasm? The preposterousness of fingernails! The idiocy of nostrils! The foolishness of elbows! Yet under the armored skull ticked the watchful gray brain, like a bomb buried in mud. Krug scorned his flesh, but he felt only awe for his brain, and for the human brain in the abstract. The true Krugness of him was in that soft folded mass of tissue, nowhere else, not in the guts, not in the groin, not in the chest, but in the mind. The body rotted while its owner still wore it; the mind within soared to the farthest galaxies.

"Massage," Krug said.

The timber and tone of his command caused a smoothly vibrating table to extrude itself from the wall. Three female androids, kept constantly on call, entered the room. Their supple bodies were bare; they were standard gamma models, who could have been triplets but for the usual programmed minor somatotype divergences. They had small high-set breasts, flat bellies, narrow waists, flaring hips, full buttocks. They had hair on their heads and they had eyebrows, but otherwise they were without body hair, which gave them a certain sexless look; yet the groove of sex was inscribed between their legs, and Krug, if his tastes inclined that way, could part those legs and find within them a reasonable imitation of passion. His tastes had never inclined that way. But Krug had deliberately designed an element of sensuality into his androids. He had given them functional—if sterile—genitals, just as he had given them proper—though needless—navels. He wanted his creations to look human (aside from the necessary modifications) and to do most human things. His androids were not robots. He had chosen to create synthetic humans, not mere machines.

The three gammas efficiently stripped him and worked him over with their cunning fingers. Krug lay belly-down; tirelessly they plucked at his flesh and toned his muscles. He stared across the emptiness of his office at the images on the distant wall.

The room was furnished simply, even starkly: a lengthy rectangle that contained a desk, a data terminal, a small somber sculpture, and a dark drape that would, at the touch of a repolarizing stud, reveal the panorama of New York City far below. The lighting, indirect and subdued, kept the office in eternal twilight. On one wall, though, there blazed a pattern in brilliant yellow luminescence:

```
        *   *
  *   *   *   *
        *
      *   *
  *   *   *   *   *
        *
      *   *   *
        *
```

It was the message from the stars.

Vargas' observatory had picked it up first as a series of faint radio pulses at 9100 megacycles: two quick beats, a pause, four beats, a pause, one beat, and so on. The pattern was repeated a thousand times over a span of two days, then halted. A month later it showed up at 1421 megacycles, the 21-centimeter hydrogen frequency, for another thousand turns. A month after that it came in both at half and at double that frequency, a thousand of each. Still later, Vargas was able to detect it optically, riding in on an intense laser beam at a 5000-angstrom wavelength. The pattern was always the same, clusters of brief bursts of information: 2 . . . 4 . . . 1 . . . 2 . . . 5 . . . 1 . . . 3 . . . 1. Each subcomponent of the series was separated from the next by an appreciable gap, and there was a much larger gap between each repetition of the entire group of pulse-clusters.

Surely it was some message. To Krug, the sequence 2-4-1-2-5-1-3-1 had become a sacred number, the opening symbols of a new kabbala. Not only was the pattern emblazoned on his wall, but the touch of his finger would send the sound of the alien signal whispering through the room in any of several audible frequencies, and the sculpture beside his desk was primed to emit the sequence in brilliant flashes of coherent light.

The signal obsessed him. His universe now revolved about the quest to make reply. At night he stood beneath the stars, dizzied by the cascade of light, and looked to the galaxies, thinking, I am Krug, I am Krug, here I wait, speak to me again! He admitted no possibility that the signal from the stars might be other than a consciously directed communication. He had turned all of his considerable assets to the task of answering.

—But isn't there any chance that the "message" might be some natural phenomenon?

None. The persistence with which it arrived in such a variety of media indicates a guiding consciousness behind it. Someone is trying to tell us something.

—What significance do those numbers have? Are they some kind of galactic *pi*?

We *ve no obvious mathematical relevance. They do not form any apparent intelligible arithmetical progression. Cryptographers* *e supplied us with at least fifty equally ingenious suggestions, which makes all fifty equally suspect. We think that the numbers were chosen entirely at random.*

—What good is a message that doesn't have any comprehensible content?

The message is its own content: a yodel across the galaxies. It tells us, Look, we are here, we know how to transmit, we are capable of rational thinking, we seek contact with you!

—Assuming you're right, what kind of reply do you plan to make?

I plan to say, Hello, hello, we hear you, we detect your message, we send greetings, we are intelligent, we are human beings, we wish no longer to be alone in the cosmos.

—In what language will you tell them this?

In the language of random numbers. And then, in not-so-random numbers. Hello, hello, 3.14159, did you hear that, 3.14159, the ratio of diameter to circumference?

—And how will you say this to them? With lasers? With radio waves?

Too slow, too slow. I cannot wait for electromagnetic radiations to go forth and come back. We will talk to the stars with tachyon-beams, and I will tell the star-folk about Simeon Krug.

Krug trembled on the table. The android masseuses clawed his flesh, pounded him, drove knuckles into his massive muscles. Were they trying to tap the mystic numbers into his bones? 2-4-1, 2-5-1, 3-1? Where was the missing 2? Even if it had been sent, what would the sequence mean, 2-4-1, 2-5-1, 2-3-1? Nothing significant. Random. Random. Meaningless clusters of raw information. Nothing more than numbers arrayed in an abstract pattern, and yet they carried the most important message the universe ever had known:

We are here.

We are here.

We are here.

We call out to you.

And Krug would answer. He shivered with pleasure at the thought of his tower completed and the tachyon-beams pouring out into the galaxy. Krug would reply, Krug the rapacious, Krug the insensitive moneyman, Krug the dollarhungry boor, Krug the mere industrialist, Krug the fat peasant, Krug the ignorant, Krug the coarse. I! Me! I! Krug! Krug!

"Out," he snapped to the androids. "Finished!"

The girls scurried away. Krug rose, slowly resumed his garments, walked across the room to run his hands over the pattern of yellow lights.

"Messages?" he said. "Visitors?"

The head and shoulders of Leon Spaulding appeared in midair, glistening against the invisible webwork backdrop of a sodium-vapor projector. "Dr. Vargas is here," the ectogene said. "He's waiting in the planetarium. Will you see him?"

"Naturally. I'll go up. And Quenelle?"

"She went to the lake house in Uganda. She'll wait for you there."

"And my son?"

"Paying his inspection call on the Duluth plant. Do you have instructions for him?"

"No," Krug said. "He knows what he's doing. I'll go to Vargas now."

The image of Spaulding winked out. Krug entered his liftshaft and rose swiftly to the domed planetarium on the highest level of the building. Under its coppered roof the slight figure of Niccolò Vargas paced intently. To his left was a display case holding eight kilograms of proteoids from

Alpha Centauri V; to his right, a squat cryostat in the frosty depths of which could dimly be seen twenty liters of fluid drawn from Pluto's methane sea.

Vargas was an intense, fair-skinned little man for whom Krug entertained a respect bordering on awe: a man who had spent every day of his adult life searching for civilizations in the stars, and who had mastered all aspects of the problems of interstellar communications. Vargas' specialty had left its imprint on his features: fifteen years earlier, incautiously exposing himself to the beam of a neutron telescope in a moment of intolerable excitement, Vargas had baked the left side of his face beyond hope of tectogenetic repair. They had regrown his ruined eye, but they had not been able to do much about the decalcification of the underlying bony structure except to shore it up with beryllium-fiber matting, and so part of Vargas' skull and cheek now had a slumped, shriveled look. Deformities such as that were unusual in an era of easy cosmetic surgery; Vargas, however, had no apparent interest in undergoing further facial reconstruction.

Vargas smiled his lopsided smile as Krug entered. "The tower is magnificent!" he said.

"Will be," Krug corrected.

"No. No. Already magnificent. A wondrous torso! The sleekness of it, Krug, the bulk, the upward thrust! Do you know what you are building there, my friend? The first cathedral of the galactic age. In thousands of years to come, long after your tower has ceased to function as a communications center, men will go to it, and kneel, and kiss its smooth skin, and bless you for having built it. And not only men."

"I like that thought," said Krug. "A cathedral. I hadn't seen it that way." Krug caught sight of the data cube in Vargas' right palm. "What do you have there?"

"A gift for you."

"A gift?"

"We have tracked the signals to their source," Vargas said. "I thought you would like to see their home star."

Krug lurched forward. "Why did you wait so long to tell me? Why didn't you say something while we were at the tower?"

"The tower was your show. This is mine. Shall I turn on the cube?"

Krug gestured impatiently toward the receptor slot. Vargas

deftly inserted the cube and activated the scanner. Bluish beams of interrogatory light lanced into the small crystal lattice, mining for the stored bits of information.

The stars blossomed on the planetarium's ceiling.

Krug was at home in the galaxy. His eyes picked out familiar landmarks: Sirius, Canopus, Vega, Capella, Arcturus, Betelgeuse, Altair, Fomalhaut, Deneb, the brightest beacons of the heavens, strewn spectacularly across the dome above him. He sought the near stars, those within the dozen-light-year radius that man's stellar probes had reached in his own lifetime: Epsilon Indi, Ross 154, Lalande 21185, Barnard's Star, Wolf 359, Procyon, 61 Cygni. He looked toward Taurus and found red Aldebaran glowing in the face of the Bull, with the Hyades clustered far behind, and the Pleiades burning in their brilliant shroud. Again and again the pattern on the dome shifted as focuses narrowed, as distances grew. Krug felt thunder in his breast. Vargas had said nothing since the planetarium had come to life.

"Well?" Krug demanded at last. "What am I supposed to see?"

"Look toward Aquarius," said Vargas.

Krug scanned the northern sky. He followed the familiar track across: Perseus, Cassiopeia, Andromeda, Pegasus, Aquarius. Yes, there was the old Water-Carrier, between the Fishes and the Goat. Krug struggled to recall the name of some major star in Aquarius, but came up with nothing.

"So?" he asked.

"Watch. We sharpen the image now."

Krug braced himself as the heavens rushed toward him. He could no longer make out the patterns of the constellations; the sky was tumbling, and all order was lost. When the motion ceased, he found himself confronted by a single segment of the galactic sphere, blown up to occupy the whole of the dome. Directly above him was the image of a fiery ring, dark at the core, rimmed by an irregular halo of luminous gas. A point of light glimmered at the nucleus of the ring.

Vargas said, "This is the planetary nebula NGC 7293 in Aquarius."

"And?"

"It is the source of our signals."

"How certain is this?"

"Absolutely," the astronomer said. "We have parallax observations, a whole series of optical and spectral triangulations, several confirming occultations, and much more. We suspected NGC 7293 as the source from the beginning, but the final data was processed only this morning. Now we are sure."

Dry-throated, Krug asked, "How distant?"

"About 300 light-years."

"Not bad. Not bad. Beyond the reach of our probes, beyond the reach of efficient radio contact. But no problem for the tachyon-beam. My tower is justified."

"And there still is hope of communication with the senders of the signals," Vargas said. "What we all feared—that the signals came from some place like Andromeda, that the messages had begun their journey toward us a million years ago or more——"

"No chance of that now."

"No. No chance."

"Tell me about this place," Krug said. "A planetary nebula—what kind of thing is that? How can a nebula be a planet?"

"Neither a planet nor a nebula," said Vargas, beginning to pace again. "An unusual body. An extraordinary body." He tapped the case of Centaurine proteoids. The quasi-living creatures, irritated, began to flow and twine. Vargas said, "This ring that you see is a shell, a bubble of gas, surrounding an O-type star. The stars of this spectral class are blue giants, hot, unstable, remaining on the main sequence only a few million years. Late in their life-cycle some of them undergo a catastrophic upheaval comparable to a nova; they hurl forth the outer layers of their structure, forming a gaseous shell of great size. The diameter of the planetary nebula you see is about 1.3 light-years, and it is growing at a rate of perhaps fifteen kilometers a second. The unusual brightness of the shell, let me say, is the result of a fluorescence effect: the central star is producing great quantities of short-wavelength ultraviolet radiation, which is absorbed by the hydrogen of the shell, causing——"

"Wait a minute," Krug said. "You're telling me that this stellar system has been through something like a nova, that the explosion took place so recently that the shell is only 1.3 light-years across even though it's growing at fifteen kilometers a second, and that the central sun is tossing out so much hard radiation that the shell is fluorescing?"

"Yes."

"And you also want me to believe that there's an intelligent race inside that furnace sending us messages?"

Vargas said, "There can be no doubt that the signals are coming from NGC 7293."

"Impossible!" Krug roared. *"Impossible!"* He slapped his fists against his hips. "A blue giant—only a couple of million years old to begin with. How do you evolve life at all, let alone an intelligent race? Then some kind of solar blowup—how does anything survive that? And the hard radiation? Tell me. Tell me. You want me to design a system that's a good bet *not* to have life, I give you this god-damned planetary nebula! But how signals? From what?"

"We have considered these factors," Vargas said softly.

Quivering, Krug asked, "Then the signals are natural phenomena after all? Impulses radiated by the atoms of your filthy nebula itself?"

"We still believe the signals have an intelligent origin."

The paradox baffled Krug. He retreated, sweating, confused. He was only an amateur astronomer; he had read plenty, he had stuffed himself with technical tapes and knowledge-enhancing drugs, he knew red giants from white dwarfs, he could draw the Hertzsprung-Russell diagram, he could look at the sky and point out Alpha Crucis and Spica, but all of it was data of an external kind, decorating the outer walls of his soul. He was not at home in it as Vargas was; he lacked a sense of the inwardness of the facts; he could not easily move beyond the bounds of the given data. Thus his awe of Vargas. Thus his discomfort now.

"Go on," he muttered. "Tell me what. Tell me how."

Vargas said, "There are several possibilities. All speculative, all guesses, you understand? The first and most obvious is that the signal-senders of NGC 7293 arrived there after the blowup, when things were quiet again. Say, within the last 10,000 years. Colonists from a deeper part of the galaxy—explorers—refugees—exiles—whatever, recent exiles."

"And the hard radiation," Krug said. "Even after things were quiet again, there'd still be radiation from that murderous blue sun."

"Obviously they would thrive on it. We need sunlight for our life-processes; why not imagine a race that drinks its energy a little higher up the spectrum?"

Krug shook his head. "Okay, you make up races, I play *advocatus diaboli*. They eat hard radiation, you say. What about the genetic effects? What kind of stable civilization can they build with a mutation rate that high?"

"A race adapted to high radiation levels would probably have a genetic structure that isn't as vulnerable to bombardment as ours. It would absorb all kinds of hard particles without mutating."

"Maybe. Maybe not." After a moment Krug said, "Okay, so they came from someplace else and settled your planetary nebula when it was safe. Why don't we have signals from the someplace else too? Where's the home system? Exiles, colonists—from where?"

"Maybe the home system is so far away that the signals won't reach us for thousands of years," Vargas suggested. "Or perhaps the home system doesn't send out signals. Or——"

"You have too many answers," Krug muttered. "I don't like the idea."

"That brings us to the other possibility," said Vargas. "That the signal-sending species is native to NGC 7293."

"How? The blowup—"

"Maybe the blowup didn't bother them. This race might thrive on hard radiation. Mutation may be a way of life for them. We're talking about aliens, my friend. If they're truly alien, we can't comprehend any of the parameters. So look: speculate along with me. We have a planet of a blue star, a planet that's far away from its sun but nevertheless is roasted by fantastically strong radiation. The sea is a broth of chemicals constantly boiling. A broth of mutations. A million years after the cooling of the surface, life is spawned. Things happen fast on such a world. Another million years and there's complex multi-celled life. A million more to mammal-equivalents. A million more to a galactic-level civilization. Change, fierce, unending change."

"I want to believe you," Krug said darkly. "I want. But I can't."

"Radiation-eaters," Vargas went on. "Clever, adaptable, accepting the necessity, even the desirability, of constant violent genetic change. Their star expands: very well, they adapt to the increase in radiation, they find a way to protect themselves. Now they live inside a planetary nebula, with a fluorescent sky around them. Somehow they detect the existence of the rest of the galaxy. They send messages to us. Yes? Yes?"

Krug, in anguish, pushed his hands through the air at Vargas, palms outward. "I want to believe!"

"Then believe. I believe."

"It's only a theory. A wild theory."

"It accounts for the data we have," said Vargas. "Do you know the Italian proverb: *Se non è vero, è ben trovato?* 'Even if it isn't true, it's well invented.' The hypothesis will do until we have a better one. It answers the facts better than the theory of a natural cause for a complex repetitive signal coming to us in several media."

Turning away, Krug stabbed at the activator as though he no longer could bear the image on the dome, as though he felt the furious radiation of that alien sun raising deadly blisters on his own skin. In his long dreams he had seen something entirely different. He had imagined a planet of a yellow sun, somewhere, eighty, ninety light-years away, a gentle sun much like the one under which he had been born. He had dreamed of a world of lakes and rivers and grassy fields of sweet air tinged perhaps with ozone, of purple-leave trees and glossy green insects, of elegant slender bein's with sloping shoulders and many-fingered hands, quietly talking as they moved through the groves and vales of th r paradise, probing the mysteries of the cosmos, speculatir on the existence of other civilizations, at last sending their essage to the universe. He had seen them opening their ms to the first visitors from Earth, saying, Welcome, broth-rs, welcome, we knew you had to be there. All of that was destroyed now. In the eye of his mind Krug saw a hellish blue sun spitting demonic fires into the void, saw a blackened and sizzling planet on which scaly armored monstrosities slithered in pools of quicksilver under a sullen sky of white flame, saw a band of horrors gathering around a nightmarish machine to send an incomprehensible message across the gulf of space. And these are our brothers? It is all spoiled, Krug thought bitterly.

"How can we go to them?" he asked. "How can we embrace them? Vargas, I have a ship almost ready, a ship for the stars, a ship to carry a sleeping man for centuries. How can I send it to such a place?"

"Your reaction surprises me. Such distress I did not expect."

"Such a star I did not expect."

"Would you have been happier if I told you that the signals were after all mere natural pulses?"

"No. No."

"Then rejoice in these our strange brothers, and forget the strangeness, and think only of the brotherhood."

Vargas' words sank in. Krug found strength. The astronomer was right. However strange those beings might be, however bizarre their world—always assuming the truth of Vargas' hypothesis—they were civilized, scientific, outward-looking. Our brothers. If space folded upon itself tomorrow, and Earth and its sun and all its neighbor worlds were engulfed and thrust into oblivion, intelligence would not perish from the universe, for *they* were there.

"Yes," Krug said. "I rejoice in them. When my tower is done I send them my hellos."

Two and a half centuries had passed since man first had broken free of his native planet. In one great dynamic sweep the spaceward drive had carried human explorers from Luna to Pluto, to the edge of the solar system and beyond, and nowhere had they found trace of intelligent life. Lichens, bacteria, primitive low-phylum crawlers, yes, but nothing more. Disappointment was the fate of those archaeologists who had hatched fantasies of reconstructing the cultural sequences of Mars from artifacts found in the desert. There were no artifacts. And when the star-probes had begun to go forth, making their decades-long reconnaissances of the nearest solar systems, they had returned with—nothing. Within a sphere a dozen light-years in diameter, there evidently had never existed any life-form more complex than the Centaurine proteoids, to which only an amoeba need feel inferior.

Krug had been a young man when the first star-probes returned. It had displeased him to see his fellow Earthmen constructing philosophies around the failures to find intelligent life in the nearby solar systems. What were they saying, these apostles of the New Geocentricism?

—We are the chosen ones!

—We are the only children of God!

—On this world and no other did the Lord fashion His people!

—To us falls the universe, as our divine heritage!

Krug saw the seeds of paranoia in that kind of thinking.

He had never thought much about God. But it seemed to him that men were asking too much of the universe when they insisted that only on this one small planet of one small sun had the miracle of intelligence been permitted to emerge. Billions upon billions of suns existed, world without end. How could intelligence *not* have evolved again and again and again across the infinite sea of galaxies?

And it struck him as megalomania to elevate the tentative findings of a sketchy search through a dozen light-years into an absolute statement of dogma. Was man really alone? How could you *know?* Krug was basically a rational man. He maintained perspective on all things. He felt that mankind's continued sanity depended on an awakening from this dream of uniqueness, for the dream was sure to end, and if the awakening came later rather than sooner the impact might be shattering.

"When will the tower be ready?" Vargas asked.

"Year after next. Next year, if we have luck, maybe. You saw this morning: unlimited budget." Krug frowned. He felt suddenly uneasy. "Give me the truth. Even you, you spend all your life listening to the stars, you think Krug's a little crazy?"

"Absolutely not!"

"Sure you do. Th   all do. My boy Manuel, he thinks I ought to be locked u   but he's afraid to say it. Spaulding, out there, him too. Ev ybody, maybe even Thor Watchman, and he's *building* the   amned thing. They want to know what's in it for me. Why do I throw billions of dollars into a tower of glass. You too,   argas!"

The twisted face grew   en more taut. "I have nothing but sympathy for this project. You injure me with these suspicions. Don't you think m king contact with an extrasolar civilization is as important t me as it is to you?"

"*Ought* to be important o you. Your field; your study. Me? Businessman. Maker of androids. Owner of land. Capitalist, exploiter, maybe a li e bit of chemist, know something about genetics, yes, but o astronomer, no scientist. It's a little crazy, eh, Vargas, for ne to care about a thing like this? Squandering of assets. Non-productive investment. What kind of dividends do I get from NGC 7293, huh? You tell me. You tell me."

Nervously Vargas said, "Perhaps we ought to go downstairs. The excitement——"

Klug slapped his chest. "I'm just turned sixty. I got a hundred years to live, more, maybe. Maybe two hundred, who knows? Don't worry about me. But you can admit it. You know it's crazy for an ignorance like me to get so interested in something like this." Krug shook his head vehemently. "I know it's crazy myself. I have to explain me to me all the time. I just tell you, this is something has to be done, and I do it, this tower. This hello to the stars. I was growing up, they kept telling us, We're all alone, We're all alone, We're all alone. I didn't believe it. Couldn't. Made the billions, now I'll spend the billions, get everybody straight in the head about the universe. You found the signals. I'll answer them. Numbers back for numbers. And then pictures. I know how to do it. One and zero, one and zero, one and zero, black and white, black and white, keep the bits going and they make a picture. You just fill in the boxes on your chart. This is what we look like. This is water molecule. This is our solar system. This is——" Krug halted, panting, hoarse, taking note for the first time of the shock and fear on the astronomer's face. In a more peaceful tone he said to Vargas, "I'm sorry. I shouldn't shout. Sometimes I run off at the mouth."

"It's all right. You have the fire of enthusiaㅣm. Better to get carried away sometimes than never to come aㅣ ᵛe at all."

Krug said, "You know what started it? Thiㅣ ㅣanetary nebula you threw at me. Upset me, I tell you why. ㅣ had a dream I'd go to the place the signals were coming frㅣ Me, Krug, in my ship, under deepsleep, sailing a hundreㅣ ᵉven two hundred light-years, ambassador from Earth, a tripㅣ ㅣobody ever took before. Now you tell me what a hell-woㅣ ㅣ the signals come from. Fluorescent sky. O-type sun. A bluㅣ light furnace. My trip's off, eh? Got me worked up, the surprise of it, but don't worry. I adapt. I absorb good stiff jolts. Knocks me to a higher energy state, is all." Impulsively he gathered Vargas to him in a fierce bear-hug. "Thank you for your signals. Thank you for your planetary nebula. Thank you a million, you hear, Vargas?" Krug stepped back. "Now we go downstairs. You need money for the laboratory? Talk to Spaulding. He knows it's carte blanche for you, any time, any size money."

Vargas left, talking to Spaulding. Alone in his office, Krug found himself ablaze with surplus vitality, his mind flooded with a vision of NGC 7293. Indeed, he resonated at a higher energy state; his skin itself was a fiery jacket for him.

"Going out," he grunted.

He set the transmat coordinates for his Uganda retreat and stepped through. A moment later he was seven thousand miles to the east, standing on his onyx veranda, looking down at the reedy lake beside his lodge. To the left, a few hundred meters out, a quartet of hippos floated, nothing showing but pink nostrils and huge gray backs. To the right he saw his mistress Quenelle, lolling bare in the shallows. Krug stripped. Rhino-heavy, impala-eager, he pounded down the sloping shore to join her in the water.

6

It took Watchman only a couple of minutes to run to the accident site, but by then the lift-beetles had moved the fallen block and the bodies of the victims were exposed. A crowd had gathered, all betas; the gammas lacked authority and motivation for interrupting their work programs, even for something like this. Seeing an alpha approach, the betas faded back, hovering on the edge of the scene in uneasy conflict. They did not know whether to return to work or to remain and offer assistance to the alpha, and, thus caught unprogrammed, they stood by wearing the dismal expressions of android bewilderment.

Watchman quickly surveyed the situation. Three androids— two betas and a gamma—had been crushed by the glass block. The betas were beyond easy recognition; it was going to be a chore just to peel their bodies out of the permafrost. The gamma beside them had almost avoided being killed, but his luck had not quite been good enough; he was intact only below the waist. His had been the legs Watchman had seen sticking out from under the block. Two other androids had been struck by the falling scooprod. One of them, a gamma, had taken a fatal blow on the skull and was lying in a sprawl a dozen meters away. The other, a beta, had apparently received a glancing but devastating swipe in the back from a corner of the rod's grip-tread; he was alive but seriously injured, and plainly in great agony.

Watchman selected four of the beta onlookers and ordered them to transport the dead ones to the control center for identification and disposal. He sent two other betas off to get a stretcher for the injured one. While they were gone he walked over to the surviving android and looked down, peering into gray eyes yellow-rimmed with pain.

"Can you talk?" Watchman asked.

"Yes." A foggy whisper. "I can't move anything below my middle. I'm turning cold. I'm starting to freeze from the middle down. Am I going to die?"

"Probably," Watchman said. He ran his hand along the beta's back until he found the lumbar neural center, and with a quick jab he shorted it. A sigh of relief came from the twisted figure on the ground.

"Better?" the alpha said.

"Much better, Alpha Watchman."

"Give me your name, beta."

"Caliban Driller."

"What were you doing when the block fell, Caliban?"

"Getting ready to go off shift. I'm a maintenance foreman. I walked past here. They all started to shout. I felt the air hot as the block came down. I jumped. And then I was on the ground with my back split open. How soon will I die?"

"Within an hour or less. The coldness will rise until it gets to your brain, and that will be the end. But take comfort: Krug saw you as you fell. Krug will guard you. Yo vill rest in the bosom of Krug."

"Krug be praised," Caliban Driller murmured.

The stretcher-bearers were approaching. When the still were fifty meters away, a gong sounded, marking the er of the shift. Instantly every android who was not actually ho ing a block rushed toward the transmat banks. Three lines workers began to vanish into the transmats, heading for their homes in the android compounds of five continents, and in the same moment the next shift began to emerge from the inbound transmats, coming out of leisure periods spent in the recreation zones of South America and India. At the sound of the gong Watchman's two stretcher-bearers made as if to drop the stretcher and rush for the transmats. He barked at them; and, sheepishly, they hustled toward him.

"Pick up Caliban Driller," he commanded, "and carry him carefully to the chapel. When you're done with that you can go off shift and claim credit for the time."

Amid the confusion of the changing shift, the two betas loaded the injured android on the stretcher and made their way with him to one of the dozens of extrusion domes on the northern perimeter of the construction site. The domes served many uses: some were storage depots for materiel, several were kitchens or washrooms, three housed the power cores that fed the transmat banks and the refrigeration tapes, one was a first aid station for androids injured on the job, and one, in the heart of the irregular clutter of gray plastic mounds, was the chapel.

At all times two or three off-duty androids lounged in

front of that dome, seemingly idle, actually functioning as casual sentries who would prevent any womb-born one from entering. Sometimes journalists or guests of Krug came wandering this way, and the sentries had various deft techniques for leading them away from the chapel without actually provoking the forbidden clash of wills between android and human. The chapel was not open to anyone born of man and woman. Its very existence was unknown to any but androids.

Thor Watchman reached it just as the stretcher-bearers were setting Caliban Driller down before the altar. Going in, he made the proper genuflection, dropping quickly to one knee and extending his arms, palms upward. The altar, resting in a purple bath of nutrient fluids, was a pink rectangular block of flesh that had been synthesized precisely as androids themselves were synthesized. Though alive, it was scarcely sentient, nor was it capable of sustaining its life unaided; it was fed from beneath by constant injections of metabolase that permitted it to survive. To the rear of the altar was a full-sized hologram of Simeon Krug, facing forward. The walls of the chapel were decorated with the triplets of the RNA genetic code, inscribed in infinite reduplication from floor to summit:

AAA	AAG	AAC	AAU
AGA	AGG	AGC	AGU
ACA	ACG	ACC	ACU
AUA	AUG	AUC	AUU
GAA	GAG	GAC	GAU
GGA	GGG	GGC	GGU
GCA	GCG	GCC	GCU
GUA	GUG	GUC	GUU
CAA	CAG	CAC	CAU
CGA	CGG	CGC	CGU
CCA	CCG	CCC	CCU
CUA	CUG	CUC	CUU
UAA	UAG	UAC	UAU
UGA	UGG	UGC	UGU
UCA	UCG	UCC	UCU
UUA	UUG	UUC	UUU

"Put him on the altar," Watchman said. "Then go out."

The stretcher-bearers obeyed. When he was alone with the dying beta, Watchman said, "I am a Preserver and I am qualified to be your guide on your journey to Krug. Repeat after me as clearly as you can: *Krug brings us into the world and to Krug we return.*"

"*Krug brings us into the world and to Krug we return.*"

"*Krug is our Creator and our Protector and our Deliverer.*"

"*Krug is our Creator and our Protector and our Deliverer.*"

"*Krug, we beseech Thee to lead us toward the light.*"

"*Krug, we beseech Thee to lead us toward the light.*"

"*And to lift the Children of the Vat to the level of the Children of the Womb.*"

"*And to lift the Children of the Vat to the level of the Children of the Womb.*"

"*And to lead us to our rightful place—*"

"*And to lead us to our rightful place—*"

"*—beside our brothers and sisters of the flesh.*"

"*—beside our brothers and sisters of the flesh.*"

"*Krug our Maker, Krug our Preserver, Krug our Master, receive me back into the Vat.*"

"*Krug our Maker, Krug our Preserver, Krug our Master, receive me back into the Vat.*"

"*And grant redemption to those who come after me—*"

"*And grant redemption to those who come after me—*"

"*In that day when Womb and Vat and Vat and Womb are one.*"

"*In that day when Womb and Vat and Vat and Womb are one.*"

"*Praise be to Krug.*"

"*Praise be to Krug.*"

"*Glory be to Krug.*"

"*Glory be to Krug.*"

"*AAA AAG AAC AAU be to Krug.*"

"*AAA AAG AAC AAU be to Krug.*"

"*AGA AGG AGC AGU be to Krug.*"

"*AGA AGG AGC—*" Caliban Driller faltered. "The chill is in my breast," he murmured. "I can't—I can't——"

"Finish the sequence. Krug awaits you."

"*—AGU be to Krug.*"

"*ACA ACG ACC ACU be to Krug.*"

The beta's fingertips dug into the yielding flesh of the altar. The tone of his skin had deepened in the past few minutes from crimson to something close to violet. His eyeballs rolled. His lips curled back.

"Krug awaits you," Watchman said fiercely. "Do the sequence!"

"Can't—speak—can't—breathe———"

"Listen to me, then. Just listen. Make the codons in your mind as I say them. *AUA AUG AUC AUU be to Krug. GAA GAG GAC GAU be to Krug. GGA GGG—*"

Desperately Watchman went down the rows of the genetic ritual as he knelt next to the altar. With each group of codons he rotated his body in the prescribed double helix, the proper motion for the last rites. Caliban Driller's life ebbed swiftly. Toward the end, Watchman pulled a tie-line from his tunic, jacked one end into the input in his forearm and the other into Driller's, and pumped energy into the shattered beta to keep him going until all the RNA triplets had been named. Then, only then, when he was certain that he had sent Caliban Driller's soul to Krug, did Watchman unjack, arise, murmur a brief prayer on his own behalf, and summon a team of gammas to haul the body away for disposal.

Tense, drained, yet jubilant over the redemption of Caliban Driller, he left the chapel and headed back toward the control center. Halfway there his way was blocked by a figure of his own height—another alpha. That seemed strange. Watchman's shift would not be over for some hours yet; when it was, the alpha Euclid Planner was scheduled to arrive and relieve him. But this alpha was not Planner. He was altogether unfamiliar to Watchman.

The stranger said, "Watchman, may I have some time? I am Siegfried Fileclerk of the Android Equality Party. Of course you know of the constitutional amendment that we propose to have our friends introduce in the next Congress. It has been suggested that in view of your close association with Simeon Krug, you might be helpful to us in our desire to gain access to Krug for the purpose of obtaining his endorsement for———"

Watchman cut in, "Surely you must be familiar with my position concerning involvements in political matters."

"Yes, but at this time the cause of android equality—"

"Can be served in many ways. I have no wish to exploit my connection with Krug for political purposes."

"The constitutional amendment———"

"Pointless. Pointless. Friend Fileclerk, do you see that building yonder? It is our chapel. I recommend you visit it and cleanse your soul of false values."

"I am not in communion with your church," said Siegfried Fileclerk.

"And I am not a member of your political party," Thor Watchman said. "Excuse me. I have responsibilities in the control center."

"Perhaps I could speak with you when your shift has ended."

"You would then be intruding upon my time of resting," Watchman said.

He walked briskly away. It was necessary for him to employ one of the neural rituals of tranquility to ease the anger and irritation surging within him.

Android Equality Party, he thought disdainfully. Fools! Bunglers! Idiots!

7   Manuel Krug had had a busy day. *0800, California.* Awakening, at his home on the Mendocino coast. The turbulent Pacific almost at his front door; a thousand-hectare redwood forest as his garden; Clissa beside him in bed, cat-soft, cat-shy. His mind fogged from last night's Spectrum Group party in Taiwan, where he had let himself drink too much of Nick Ssu-ma's millet-and-ginger liqueur. His beta houseman's image on the floating screen, urgently whispering, "Sir, sir, please get up. Your father expects you at the tower." Clissa cuddling closer against him. Manuel blinking, struggling to cut through the web of fleece swaddling his brain. "Sir? Pardon, but you left irrevocable instructions that you were to be awakened!" A forty-cycle note rumbling out of the floor; a fifteen-megacycle cone of sound slicing down out of the ceiling; himself impaled between the two, unable to escape back into sleep. Crescendo. Wakefulness, reluctant, grudging. Then a surprise: Clissa stirring, trembling, taking his hand, putting it over one of her little cool breasts. His fingertips converging on the nipple and finding it still soft. As expected. A bold overture from the child-woman, but flesh weak if spirit willing. They had been married two years; despite all his earnest and skillful efforts, he had not succeeded yet in fully arousing her senses. "Manuel—" she whispered. "Manuel—touch me all over——!"

He felt cruel about turning her off. "Later," he said, as the terrible spikes of sound met in his brain. "We have to get up now. The patriarch is waiting for us. We're going to the tower today."

Clissa pouted. They tumbled from bed; instantly the damnable sonics ceased. They showered, breakfasted, dressed. "Are you sure you really want me to come?" she asked.

He said, "My father made a point of inviting you. He thinks it's high time you saw the tower. Don't you want to go?"

"I'm afraid I'll do something foolish, say something naive. I feel so awfully young when I'm around him."

"You *are* awfully young. Anyway, he's fond of you. Just pretend you're terribly terribly fascinated by his tower and he'll forgive you for anything silly you might say."

"And the other people—Senator Fearon, and the scientist, and whoever else—Manuel, I feel embarrassed already!"

"Clissa——"

"All right. All right."

"And remember: the tower is going to strike you as the most marvelous enterprise of humanity since the Taj Mahal. Tell him that after you've seen it. Not in so many words, but getting the idea across your own way."

"He's really serious about the tower, isn't he?" she asked. "He actually expects to talk to people in the stars."

"He does."

"How much will it cost?"

"Billions," Manuel said.

"He's draining our heritage to build that thing. He's spending everything."

"Not quite everything. We'll never hurt for cash. Anyway, e made the money; let him spend it."

"But on an obsession—a fancy——"

"Stop it, Clissa. It isn't our business."

"Tell me this, at least. Suppose your father died tomorrow, and you took charge of everything. What would happen to the tower?"

Manuel set up the coordinates for their transmat jump to New York. "I'd halt work on it the day after tomorrow," he said. "But I'll gut you if you ever let him know that. Get in, now. Let's go."

1140, New York. Midmorning already, and he had been awake only forty hurried minutes, after arising at eight. That was one of the little troubles of the transmat society: you

kept dropping whole segments of time into hidden pockets if
you jumped from west to east.

Naturally there were compensating benefits when you went
the other way. In the summer of '16, on the day before his
wedding, Manuel and some of his friends of the Spectrum
Group had raced the dawn westward around the world. They
began at 0600 on a Saturday in the Amboseli Game
Preserve, with the sun coming up back of Kilimanjaro, and
off they went to Kinshasa, Accra, Rio, Caracas, Veracruz,
Albuquerque, Los Angeles, Honolulu, Auckland, Brisbane,
Singapore, Pnompenh, Calcutta, Mecca. No visas were needed in the transmat world, no passports; such things were too
obviously absurd with instantaneous travel available. The sun
plodded along, as always, at a feeble thousand miles an hour;
the leaping travelers had no such handicap. Although they
paused fifteen minutes here, twenty minutes there, enjoying a
cocktail or nipping a floater, buying small souvenirs, touring
famous monuments of antiquity, yet they constantly gained
time, pressing farther and farther backward into the previous
night, outstripping the sun as they sped about the globe,
striding into Friday evening. Of course, they lost all they had
gained when they crossed the dateline and were dumped into
Saturday afternoon. But they nibbled away the loss by continuing westward, and when they came round to Kilimanjaro
again it was not yet eleven on the same Saturday morning
from which they had departed, but they had circled the
world and had lived a Friday and a half.

You could do such things with a transmat. You could also,
by timing your jumps with care, see two dozen sunsets in a
single day, or spend all your life under the blaze of eternal
noon. Nevertheless, arriving in New York at 1140 from
California, Manuel resented having had to surrender this
segment of morning to the transmat.

His father greeted him formally in his office with a pressure of palms, and hugged Clissa with somewhat more
warmth. Leon Spaulding hovered uneasily to one side. Quenelle stood by the window, back to everyone, studying the
city. Manuel did not get along with her. He generally disliked
his father's mistresses. The old man picked the same type
every time: full lips, full breasts, jutting buttocks, fiery eyes,
heavy hips. Peasant stock.

Krug said, "We're waiting for Senator Fearon, Tom Buckleman, and Dr. Vargas. Thor will take us on the grand tour
of the tower. What are you doing afterward, Manuel?"

"I hadn't thought——"

"Go to Duluth. I want you to get to know something about the plant operations there. Leon, notify Duluth: my son arrives for an inspection trip early this afternoon."

Spaulding went off. Manuel shrugged. "As you wish, father."

"Time to extend your responsibilities, boy. To develop your management capacities. Someday you be boss of all this, eh? Someday, when they say Krug, they mean *you*."

"I'll try to live up to the trust you've placed in me," Manuel said.

He knew he wasn't fooling the old man with his glibness. And the old man's show of paternal pride wasn't fooling him. Manuel was aware of his father's intense contempt for him. He could see himself through his father's eyes: a wastrel, a perpetual playboy. Against that he held his own image of himself: sensitive, compassionate, too refined to brawl in the commercial arena. Then he tumbled through that image to another view of Manuel Krug, perhaps more genuine: hollow, earnest, idealistic, futile, incompetent. Which was the real Manuel? He didn't know. He didn't know. He understood less and less about himself as he grew older.

Senator Fearon stepped from the transmat.

Krug said, "Henry, you know my son Manuel—the future Krug of Krug, he is, the heir apparent——?"

"It's been many years," Fearon said. "Manuel, how are you!"

Manuel touched the politic n's cool palm. He managed an amiable smile. "We met fiv years ago in Macao," he said gracefully. "You were passing through, en route to Ulan Bator."

"Of course. Of course. What a splendid memory! Krug, this is a fine boy here!" Fearon cried.

"You wait," Krug said. "When I step down, he'll show you how a *real* empire-builder operates!"

Manuel coughed and looked away, embarrassed. Some compulsive sense of dynastic need forced old Krug to pretend that his only child was a fit heir to the constellation of enterprises he had founded or absorbed. Thus the constant show of concern for Manuel's "training," and thus the abrasive, repetitive public insistence that Manuel would some day succeed to control.

Manuel had no wish to take command of his father's empire. Nor did he see that he was capable of it. He was only now outgrowing his playboy phase, groping his way out of frivolity the way others might grope their way out of atheism. He was looking for a vehicle of purpose, for a vessel to contain his formless ambitions and abilities. Someday, perhaps, he might find one. But he doubted that Krug Enterprises would be that vehicle.

The old man knew that as well as Manuel did. Inwardly he scorned his son's hollowness, and sometimes the scorn showed through. Yet he never ceased pretending that he prized his son's judgment, shrewdness, and potential administrative skills. In front of Thor Watchman, in front of Leon Spaulding, in front of anyone who would listen, Krug went on and on about the virtues of the heir apparent. Self-deluding hypocrisy, Manuel thought. He's trying to hoax himself into believing what he knows damned well won't ever be true. And it won't work. It can't work. He'll always have more real faith in his android friend Thor than he will in his own son. For good reason, too. Why not prefer a gifted android to a worthless child? He made us both, didn't he?

Let him give the companies to Thor Watchman, Manuel thought.

The other members of the party were arriving. Krug shepherded everyone toward the transmat banks.

"To the tower," he cried. "To the tower!"

1110, the tower. He had regained the better part of an hour out of his lost morning, anyway, through this jump of one time-zone westward from New York. But he could have done without the trip. Bad enough to caper in the chill Arctic autumn, forcing himself to admire his father's absurd tower—the Pyramid of Krug, Manuel liked to call it privately—but then there had been the business of the falling block, the crushing of the androids. A nasty incident.

Clissa had gone to the edge of hysteria. "Don't look," Manuel told her, folding his arms about her as the wall-screen in the control center showed the scene of the lifting of the block from the corpses. To Spaulding he said, "Sedative. Fast."

The ectogene found him a tube of something. Manuel jammed the snout against Clissa's arm and activated it. The drug leaped through her skin in a soft ultrasonic spurt.

"Were they killed?" she asked, head still averted.

"It looks that way. Possibly one survived. The others never knew what hit them."

"The poor people."

"Not people," Leon Spaulding said. "Androids. Only androids."

Clissa lifted her head. "Androids are people!" she blazed. "I don't ever want to hear something like that again! Don't they have names, dreams, personalities——"

"Clissa," Manuel said gently.

"—ambitions," she said. "Of course they're people. A bunch of *people* just died under that block. How could you, you in particular, make such a remark about——"

"Clissa!" Manuel said, anguished.

Spaulding was rigid, eyes glassy with rage. The ectogene seemed to tremble on the verge of an angry retort, but his fierce discipline saw him past the moment.

"I'm sorry," Clissa murmured, looking at the floor. "I didn't mean to get personal, Leon. I—I—oh, God, Manuel, why did any of this have to happen?" She began to sob again. Manuel signaled for another sedative tube, but his father shook his head and came forward, taking her from him.

Krug cradled the girl in his immense arms, half crushing her against his huge chest. "Easy," he said, hugging her. "Easy, easy, easy. It was a terrible thing, yes. But they didn't suffer. They died clean. Thor will look after the hurt ones. He'll shut off their pain centers and make them feel better. Poor Clissa, poor, poor, poor, poor Clissa—you've never seen anyone die before, have you? It's awful when it's so sudden, I know. I know." He comforted her tenderly, stroking her long silken hair, patting her, kissing her moist cheeks. Manuel watched in astonishment. He had never seen his father so gentle before in his life.

But of course Clissa was something special to the old man: the instrument of dynastic succession. She was supposed to be the steadying influence that would guide Manuel to an acceptance of his responsibilities, and she also was charged with the task of perpetuating the name of Krug. A paradox, there: Krug treated his daughter-in-law as though she were as fragile as an ancient porcelain doll, but yet he expected a stream of sons shortly to begin flowing from her loins.

To his guests Krug now said, "Too bad we end the tour this way. But at least we saw everything before it happened. Senator, gentlemen, I'm grateful that you came to see my tower. I trust you come again when it's a little more finished. Now we go, eh?"

Clissa seemed calmer. It troubled Manuel that not he but his father had been the one to soothe her.

Reaching out to take her, he said, "I think Clissa and I will head back to California. A couple of hours together on the beach and she'll be steadier. We——"

"You are expected this afternoon in Duluth," said Krug stonily.

"I——"

"Send for household androids to fetch her," he said. "You go to the plant." Turning away from Manuel, Krug nodded to his departing guests and said to Leon Spaulding, "New York. The upper office."

1138, the tower. Nearly everyone was gone, now: Krug, Spaulding, Quenelle, and Vargas back to New York, Fearon and Buckleman to Geneva, Maledetto to Los Angeles, Thor Watchman down to see about the injured androids. Two of Manuel's household betas had arrived to take Clissa back to Mendocino. Just before she stepped into the transmat with them, Manuel embraced her lightly, kissing her cheek.

"When will you come?" she asked.

"Early this evening, I guess. We have a date in Hong Kong, I think. I'll get back in time to dress for dinner."

"Not sooner?"

"I have Duluth to do. The android plant."

"Get out of it."

"I can't. You heard him tell me to go. Anyway, the old man's right: it's about time I saw it."

"What a bore. An afternoon in a factory!"

"I have to. Sleep well, Clissa. Wake up with this ugly thing that happened here left far behind. Shall I program an erasure wire for you?"

"You know I hate having my memory tampered with, Manuel."

"Yes. I'm sorry. You'd better go, now."

"I love you," she said.

"I love you," he told her. He nodded to the androids. They took her arms and led her into the transmat.

He was alone, except for a couple of unknown betas who had arrived to take charge of the control center in Watchman's absence. He walked coolly past them into Watchman's private office at the rear of the dome, pushed the door shut, and nudged the input of the telephone. The screen lit up. Manuel tapped out the call numbers of a scrambler code, and

the screen responded with the abstract pattern that told him
his privacy was guaranteed. Then he punched the number of
Lilith Meson, alpha, in the android quarter of Stockholm.

Lilith's image glowed on the screen: an elegantly constructed woman with lustrous blue-black hair, a high-bridged
nose, platinum eyes. Her smile dazzled. "Manuel? Where are
you calling from?" she asked.

"The tower. I'm going to be late."

"Very late?"

"Two or three hours."

"I'll shrivel. I'll fade."

"I can't help it, Lilith. His majesty commands me to visit
the Duluth android plant. I must go."

"Even though I've rearranged a week's shifts to be with
you tonight?"

"I can't tell him that," Manuel said. "Look, it's only a few
hours. Will you forgive me?"

"What else can I do? But how dull to have to go sniffing in
vats when you could be——"

"It's known as noblesse oblige. Anyway, I've become a
little curious about the android facts of life since you and
I—since we——Do you know, I've never been inside one of
the plants?"

"Never?"

"Never. Wasn't ever interested. Still not interested, except
in one special angle of it: here's my chance to find out what
sort of things are under that lovely scarlet skin of yours.
Here's my chance to see how Krug Synthetics makes Liliths
by the batch."

"Are you sure you really want to know?" she asked,
dropping her voice into cello range.

"I want to know all there is to know about you," Manuel
said earnestly. "For better, for worse. So forgive me for
coming late, will you? I'll be taking a Lilith lesson in Duluth.
And I love you."

"I love you," said Alpha Lilith Meson to the son of Simeon
Krug.

1158, Duluth. The main Earthside plant of Krug Synthetics, Ltd.—there were four others, on as many continents, and
several offworld plants—occupied a vast sleek block of a
building nearly a kilometer long, flanking the shore of Lake
Superior. Within that building, operating virtually as indepen-

dent provinces, were the laboratories that formed the stations of the way in the creation of synthetic life.

Manuel now toured those stations of the way like a visiting proconsul, weighing the work of the underlings. He rode in a plush bubblecar as seductively comfortable as a womb, which glided along a fluid track that ran the length of the building, high above the operations floor. Beside him in the car was the factory's human supervisor, a neat, crisp, fortyish man named Nolan Bompensiero, who, although he was one of the key men in the Krug domain, sat tense and rigid, in obvious fear of Manuel's displeasure. He did not suspect how resentful Manuel was of this assignment, how bored he was, how little he cared to brandish power by making trouble for his father's employees. Manuel had only Lilith on his mind. This is the place where Lilith was born, he thought. This is the way that Lilith was born.

At each section of the factory an alpha—the section supervisor—entered the car, riding with Manuel and Bompensiero to the end of his own zone of responsibility. Most of the work at the plant was under the direction of alphas; the entire giant installation employed only half a dozen humans. Each alpha looked as tense as Bompensiero himself.

Manuel passed first through the rooms where the high-energy nucleotides constituting DNA, the basic building-block of life, were synthesized. He gave half-hearted attention to Bompensiero's quick, nervous spiel, tuning in only on an occasional phrase.

"—water, ammonia, methane, hydrogen cyanide, and other chemicals—we use an electrical discharge to stimulate the formation of complex organic compounds—the addition of phosphorus——

"—a simple process, almost primitive, don't you think? It follows the line of the classic Miller experiment of 1952— medieval science, right down there on the floor——

"—the DNA determines the structure of the proteins in the cell. The typical living cell requires hundreds of proteins, most of them acting as enzymes, biological catalysts——

"—a typical protein is a molecular chain containing about two hundred amino acid subunits linked together in a specific sequence——

"—the code for each protein is carried by a single gene, which in turn is a particular region on the linear DNA molecule—all of this of course you must know, forgive me for restating such elementary material, forgive me, I only wish to——"

"Of course," Manuel said.

"—and here, in these vats, we make the nucleotides and join them into dinucleotides, and string them together to form DNA, the nucleic acid that determines the composition of——"

Lilith, from those vats? Lilith, from that stinking brew of chemicals?

The car drifted smoothly forward. An alpha supervisor departed; another alpha, bowing stiffly, smiling fixedly, entered.

Bompensiero said, "We design the DNA templates, the blueprints for the life-form we wish to create, but then the task is to make the living matter self-replicating, since surely we cannot build an android cell by cell ourselves. We must reach w we call the takeoff stage. But naturally you know that the D A is not directly involved in protein synthesis, that another nucleic acid acts as an intermediary, RNA, which can b ded to carry the genetic messages laid down in the DNA—

"—four bases r chemical subunits, arranged in varying combinations, fo the code—adenine, guanine, uracil, cytosine——

"—in these vats—y u can almost imagine the chains forming—the RNA transı ts the DNA instructions—protein synthesis is conducted b cellular particles called ribosomes, which are about half pro in and half RNA—adenine, guanine, uracil, cytosine—the de for each protein is carried by a single gene, and the code, inscribed on messenger-RNA, takes the form of a series of triplets of the four RNA bases—you follow?"

"Yes, certainly," said Manuel, seeing Lilith swimming in the vats.

"As here. Adenine, adenine, cytosine. Cytosine, cytosine, guanine. Uracil, uracil, guanine. AAC, CCG, UUG—it's almost liturgical, isn't it, Mr. Krug? We have sixty-four combinations of RNA bases with which we can specify the twenty amino acids—quite an adequate vocabulary for the purpose! I could chant the whole list for you as we travel this hall. AAA, AAG, AAC, AAU. AGA, AGG, AGC, AGU. ACA——"

The alpha who was traveling with them at the moment coughed loudly and clutched his waist, grimacing.

"Yes?" Bompensiero said.

"A sudden spasm," said the alpha. "A digestive difficulty. Pardon me."

Bompensiero returned his attention to Manuel. "Well, no need to run down all the sequences. And so we put together the proteins, you see, building up living molecules in precisely the way it happens in nature, except that in nature the process is triggered by the fusion of the sexual gametes, whereas we synthesize the genetic building-blocks. We follow the human genetic pattern, naturally, since we want a human-looking end product, but if we wished we could synthesize pigs, toads, horses, Centaurine proteoids, any form of life we chose. We pick our code, we arrange our RNA, and presto! The pattern of our final product emerges precisely as desired!"

"Of course," said the alpha, "we don't follow the human genetic code in *every* respect."

Bompensiero nodded eagerly. "My friend here brings up a vital point. In the earliest days of android synthesis your father decided that, for obvious sociological reasons, androids must be instantly identifiable as synthetic creatures. Thus we introduce certain mandatory genetic modifications. The red skin, the absence of body hair, the distinctive epidermal texture, are all designed mainly for identification purposes. Then there are the modifications programmed for greater bodily efficiency. If we can play the role of gods, why not do it to the best effect?"

"Why not?" Manuel said.

"Away with the appendix, then. Rearrange the bony structure of the back and pelvis to eliminate all the troubles that *our* faulty construction causes. Sharpen the senses. Program for optimum fat-versus-muscle balance, for physical esthetics, for endurance, for speed, for reflexes. Why make ugly androids? Why make sluggish ones? Why make clumsy ones?"

"Would you say," Manuel asked casually, "that androids are superior to ordinary human beings?"

Bompensiero looked uneasy. He hesitated as if trying to weigh his response for all possible political impacts, not knowing where Manuel might stand on the vexed question of android civil rights. At length he said, "I think there's no doubt about their physical superiority. We've *programmed* them from the moment of conception to be strong, handsome, healthy. To some extent we've been doing that with humans for the past couple of generations, too, but we don't have the same degree of control, or at least we haven't tried to obtain the same degree of control, on account of humanistic objections, the opposition of the Witherers, and so forth. However, when you consider that androids are sterile, that the intelligence of most of them is quite low, that even the alphas have demonstrated—pardon me, my friend—relatively little creative ability——"

"Yes," Manuel said. "Certainly." He pointed toward the distant floor. "What's going on right down there?"

"Those are the replication vats," said Bompensiero. "The chains of basic nucleic matter undergo division and extension there. Each vat contains what amounts to a soup of newly conceived zygotes at the takeoff stage, produced by our build-up procedures of protein synthesis instead of by the sexual process of the union of natural gametes. Do I make myself clear?"

"Quite," said Manuel, staring in fascination at the quiescent pink fluid in the great circular tanks. He imagined he could see tiny specks of living matter in them; an illusion, he knew.

Their car rolled silently onward.

"These are the nursery chambers," Bompensiero said, when they had entered the next section and were looking down on rows of shining metal vaults linked by an intricate webwork of pipes. "Essentially, they're artificial wombs, each one enclosing a dozen embryos in a solution of nutrients. We produce alphas, betas, and gammas here in Duluth—a full android range. The qualitative differences between the three levels are built into them during the original process of synthesis, but we also supply different nutritional values. These are the alpha chambers, just below to our left. To the right are the betas. And the next room, coming up—entirely gammas."

"What's your distribution curve?"

"One alpha to 100 betas to 1000 gammas. Your father worked out the ratios in the beginning and they've never been altered. The distribution precisely fits human needs."

"My father is a man of great foresight," said Manuel vaguely.

He wondered what the world would have been like today if the Krug cartel had not given it androids. Perhaps not very different. Instead of a small, culturally homogeneous human elite served by computers, mechanical robots, and hordes of obliging androids, there might be a small, culturally homogeneous human elite served only by computers and mechanical robots. Either way, twenty-third century man would be living a life of ease.

Certain determining trends had established themselves in the past few hundred years, long before the first clumsy android had staggered from its vat. Primarily, starting late in the twentieth century, there had been the vast reduction in human population. War and general anarchy had accounted for hundreds of millions of civilians in Asia and Africa; famine had swept those continents, and South America and the Near East as well; in the developed nations, social pressures and the advent of foolproof contraception had produced the same effects. A checking of the rate of population growth had been followed, within two generations, by an absolute and cascading decline in actual population.

The erosion and almost total disappearance of the proletariat was one historically unprecedented outcome of this. Since the population decline had been accompanied by the replacement of men by machines in nearly all forms of menial labor and some not so menial, those who had no skills to contribute to the new society were discouraged from reproducing. Unwanted, dispirited, displaced, the uneducated and the ineducable dwindled in number from generation to generation; and this Darwinian process was aided, subtly and then openly, by well-meaning officials who saw to it that the blessings of contraception were denied to no citizen. By the time the masses were a minority, genetic laws reinforced the trend. Those who had proven themselves unfit might not reproduce at all; those who merely came up to norms might have two children per couple, but no more; only those who exceeded norms could add to the world's human stock. In this way population remained stable. In this way the clever inherited the earth.

The reshaping of society was worldwide. The advent of transmat travel had turned the globe into a village; and the people of that village spoke the same language—English—and thought the same thoughts. Culturally and genetically they tended toward mongrelization. Quaint pockets of the pure past were maintained here and there as tourist attractions, but by the end of the twenty-first century there were few differences in appearance, attitudes, or culture among the citizens of Karachi, Cairo, Minneapolis, Athens, Addis Ababa, Rangoon, Peking, Canberra, and Novosibirsk. The transmat also made national boundaries absurd, and old concepts of sovereignty melted.

But this colossal social upheaval, bringing with it universal leisure, grace, and comfort, had also brought an immense and permanent labor shortage. Computer-directed robots had proved themselves inadequate to many tasks: robots made excellent street-sweepers and factory workers, but they were less useful as valets, baby-sitters, chefs, and gardeners. Build better robots, some said; but others dreamed of synthetic humans to look after their needs. The technique did not seem impossible. Ectogenesis—the artificial nurturing of embryos outside the womb, the hatching of babies from stored ova and sperm—had long been a reality, chiefly as a convenience for women who did not wish to have their genes go down to oblivion, but who wanted to avoid the risks and burdens of pregnancy. Ectogenes, born of man and woman at one remove, were too thor ghly human in origin to be suitable as tools; but why not ca the process to the next step, and manufacture androids?

Krug had done that. He had offered the world synthetic humans, far more versatile th robots, who were long-lived, capable, complex in personalh and totally subservient to human needs. They were purcha not hired, and by general consent they were regarded by as property, not persons. They were slaves, in short. Ma el sometimes thought it might have been simpler to make do ith robots. Robots were things that could be thought of as th s and treated as things. But androids were things that looke uncomfortably like people, and they might not acquiesce in their status of thinghood forever.

The car glided through room after room of nursery chambers, silent, darkened, empty but for a few android monitors. Each fledgling android spent the first two years of its life sealed in such a chamber, Bompensiero pointed out, and the rooms through which they were passing contained successive batches ranging in age from a few weeks to more than twenty months. In some rooms the chambers were open; squads of beta technicians were preparing them to receive new infusions of takeoff-level zygotes.

"In this room," said Bompensiero many rooms later, "we have a group of matured androids ready to be 'born.' Do you wish to descend to the floor area and observe the decanting at close range?"

Manuel nodded.

Bompensiero touched a switch. Their car rolled serenely off its track and down a ramp. At the bottom they dismounted. Manuel saw an army of gammas clustered around one of the nursery chambers. "The chamber has been drained of nutrient fluids. For some twenty minutes now the androids within have been breathing air for the first time in their lives. The hatches of the chamber now are being opened. Here: come close, Mr. Krug, come close."

The chamber was uncovered. Manuel peered in.

He saw a dozen full-grown androids, six male, six female, sprawled limply on the metal floor. Their jaws were slack, their eyes were blank, their arms and legs moved feebly. They seemed helpless, vacant, vulnerable. *Lilith*, he thought. Lilith!

Bompensiero, at his elbow, whispered, "In the two years between takeoff and decanting, the android reaches full physical maturity—a process that takes humans thirteen to fifteen years. This is another of the genetic modifications introduced by your father in the interests of economy. We produce no infant androids here."

Manuel said, "Didn't I hear somewhere that we turn out a line of android babies to be raised as surrogates by human women who can't——"

"*Please,*" Bompensiero said sharply. "We don't discuss——" He cut himself short, as if remembering who it was he had just reprimanded, and said in a more moderate way, "I know very little about what you mention. We have no such operations in this plant."

Gammas were lifting the dozen newborn androids from the nursery chamber and carrying them to gaping machines that seemed part wheelchair, part suit of armor. The males were lean and muscular, the females high-breasted and slim. But there was something hideous about their mindlessness. Totally passive, utterly soul-empty, the moist, naked androids offered no response as they were sealed one by one into these metallic receptacles. Only their faces remained visible, looking out without expression through transparent visors.

Bompensiero explained, "They don't have the use of their muscles yet. They don't know how to stand, to walk, to do anything. These training devices will stimulate muscular development. A month inside one and an android can handle itself physically. Now, if we return to our car——"

"These androids I've just seen," Manuel said. "They're gammas, of course?"

"Alphas."

Manuel was stunned. "But they seemed so ... so ..." He faltered. "Moronic."

"They are newly born," said Bompensiero. "Should they come out of the nurseries ready to run computers?"

They returned to the car.

Lilith!

Manuel saw young androids taking their first shambling steps, and tumbling, and laughing, and getting to their feet and doing it better the second time. He visited a classroom where the subject being taught was bowel control. He watched slumbering betas undergoing personality imprints: a soul was being etched into each unformed mind. He donned a helmet and listened to a language tape. The education of an android, he was told, lasted one year for a gamma, two for a beta, four for an alpha. The maximum, then, was six years from conception to full adulthood. He had never fully appreciated the swiftness of it all before. Somehow the new knowledge made androids seem infinitely less human to him. Suave, authoritative, commanding Thor Watchman was something like nine or ten years old, Manuel realized. And the lovely Lilith Meson was—what? Seven? Eight?

Manuel felt a sudden powerful urge to escape from this place.

"We have a group of betas just about to leave the factory," said Bompensiero. "They are undergoing their final checkout today, with tests in linguistic precision, coordination, motor response, metabolic adjustment, and several other aspects. Perhaps you would care to inspect them yourself and personally——"

"No," Manuel said. "It's been fascinating. But I've taken up too much of your time already, and I have an appointment elsewhere, so I really must——"

Bompensiero did not look grieved to be rid of him. "As you wish," he said obligingly. "But of course, we remain at your service whenever you choose to visit us again, and——"

"Where is the transmat cubicle, please?"

2241, Stockholm. Jumping westward to Europe, Manuel lost the rest of the day. Dark, icy evening had descended here; the stars were sharp, and a sleety wind ruffled the waters of Mälaren. To foil any possibility of being traced he had jumped to the public transmat cubicle in the lobby of the wondrous old Grand Hotel. Now, shivering, he walked briskly through the autumnal gloom to another cubicle outside the gray bulk of the Royal Opera, put his thumb to the charge-plate, and bought a jump to Stockholm's Baltic side, emerging in the mellow, venerable residential district of Öster-malm. This was the android quarter now. He hurried down Birger Jarlsgaten to the once-splendid nineteenth-century apartment building where Lilith lived. Pausing outside, he looked about carefully, saw that the streets were empty, and darted into the building. A robot in the lobby scanned him and asked his purpose in a flat, froglike voice. "Visiting Lilith Meson, alpha," Manuel said. The robot raised no objection. Manuel had his choice of getting to her flat by liftshaft or by stairs. He took the stairs. Musty smells pursued him and shadows danced alongside him all the way to the fifth floor.

Lilith greeted him in a sumptuous, clinging, floor-length high-spectrum gown. Since it was nothing more than a mono-molecular film, it left no contour of her body concealed. She drifted forward, arms outstretched, lips parted, breasts heaving, whispering his name. He reached for her.

He saw her as a speck drifting in a vat.

He saw her as a mass of replicating nucleotides.

He saw her naked and wet and vacant-eyed, shambling out of her nursery chamber.

He saw her as thing, manufactured by men.

Thing. Thing. Thing. Thing. Thing. Thing. Thing.

Lilith.

He had known her for five months. They had been lovers for three. Thor Watchman had introduced them. She was on the Krug staff.

Her body pressed close to his. He brought his hand up and cupped one of her breasts. It felt warm and real and firm through the monomolecular gown, and he drew his thumb across the tip of her nipple it hardened and rose in excitement. Real. Real.

Thing.

He kissed her. His tongue slipped between her lips. He tasted the taste of chemicals. Adenine, guanine, cytosine, uracil. He smelled the smell of the vats. Thing. Thing. Beautiful thing. Thing in woman's shape. Well named, Lilith. Thing.

She drew away from him and said, "You went to the factory?"

"Yes."

"And you learned more about androids than you wanted to know."

"No, Lilith."

"You see me with different eyes now. You can't help remembering what I really am."

"That is absolutely not true," Manuel said. "I love you, Lilith. What you are is no news to me. And makes no difference at all. I love you. I love you."

"Would you like a drink?" she asked. "A weed? A floater? You're all worked up."

"Nothing," he said. "It's been a long day. I haven't even had lunch yet and I think I've been going for forty hours. Let's just relax, Lilith. No weeds. No floaters." He unsnapped his clothing, and she helped him out of it. Then she pirouetted before a doppler; there was a brief rising burst of sound and her g n disappeared. Her skin was light red, except for the dark b wn of her nipples. Her breasts were full, her waist was n ow, her hips flared with the impossible promise of fertility. Her beauty was inhumanly flawless. Manuel fought the dryp s in his throat.

She said sadly, 'I could feel the change in you the moment you touched me Your touch was different. There was— fear?—in it. Disgu "

"No."

"Until tonight I was something exotic to you, but human, like a Bushman would be, an Eskimo. You didn't keep me in a separate category outside the human race. Now you tell yourself that you've fallen in love with a mess of chemicals. You think you may be doing so thing sick by having an affair with me."

"Lilith, I beg you to stop it. This all in your mind!"

"Is it?"

"I came here. I kissed you. I told you I loved you. I'm waiting to go to bed with you. Maybe you're projecting some guilts of your own on me when you say——"

"Manuel, what would you have said a year ago about a man who admitted he'd been to bed with an android?"

"Plenty of men I know have been——"

"What would you say about him? What kind of words would you use? What would you think of him?"

"I've never considered such things. They simply haven't concerned me, ever."

"You're evading. Remember, we promised that we wouldn't play any of the little lie-games people play. Yes?

You can't deny that at most social levels, sex between humans and androids is regarded as a perversion. Maybe the only perversion that's left in the world. Am I right? Will you answer me?"

"All right." His eyes met hers. He had never known a woman with eyes that color. Slowly he said, "Most men regard it as, well, cheap, foul, to sleep with androids. I've heard it compared to masturbation. To doing it with a rubber doll. When I heard such remarks, I thought they were ugly, stupid expressions of anti-android prejudice, and I obviously didn't have such attitudes myself, or I never could have fallen in love with you." Something in his mind sang mockingly, *Remember the vats! Remember the vats!* His gaze wavered and moved off center; he stared intently at her cheekbone. Grimly he said, "Before the whole universe I swear, Lilith, that I never felt there was anything shameful or dirty about loving an android, and I insist that despite what you've claimed to detect in me since my visit to the factory, I don't have any such feelings even now. And to prove it——"

He gathered her to him. His hand swept down her satiny skin from her breasts to her belly to her loins. Her thighs parted, and he clasped his fingers over the mount of Venus, as fleeceless as an infant's, and suddenly he trembled at the alien texture he felt there, and found himself unmanned by it, though it had never troubled him before. So smooth. So terribly smooth. He looked down at her, at her bareness. Bare, yes, but not because she had been shaven. She was like a child there. Like—like an android. He saw vats again. He saw moist crimson alphas whose faces were without expression. He told himself sternly that to love an android was no sin. He began to caress her, and she responded, as a woman would respond, with lubrication, with little ragged bursts of breath, with a tightening of her thighs against his hand. He kissed her breasts and clutched her to him. It seemed then that the blazing image of his father hovered like a pillar of fire in the air before him. Old devil, old artificer! How clever to design such a product! A product. It walks. It talks. It seduces. It gasps in passion. It grows tumescent in the labia minora, this product. And what am I? A product too, hey? A hodgepodge of chemicals stamped out from much the same sort of blueprint—mutatis mutandis, of course. Adenine. Guanine. Cytosine. Uracil. Born in a vat, hatched in a womb —where's the difference? We are one flesh. We are different races, but we are one flesh.

His desire for her returned in a dizzying surge and he pivoted, topped her, drove himself deep within her. Her heels hammered ecstatically on his calves. The valley of her sex throbbed, clasping him in authentic frenzy. They rocked and climbed and soared.

When it was over, when they had both come down, she said, "That was disgustingly bitchy of me."

"What was?"

"The scene I made. When I was trying to tell you what I thought was in your mind."

"Forget it, Lilith."

"You were right, though. I suppose I was projecting my own misgivings. Maybe I feel guilty about being the mistress of a madman. Maybe I *want* you to think of me as something made of rubber. Somewhere inside me, that's probably how I think of myself."

"No. No."

"We can't help it. We breathe it in all the time. We're reminded a thousand times a day that we aren't real."

"You're as real as anyone I've ever known. More real than some." More real than Clissa, he did not add. "I've never seen you clutched like this before, Lilith. What's happening?"

"Your factory trip," she said. "Until today I was always sure that you were different. That you hadn't ever spent one second worrying about how or where I was born, or whether there might be something wrong about what we have going. But I was afraid that once you saw the factory, saw the whole process in clinical detail, you might change—and then, when you came in tonight, there was something about you, something chilly that I knew hadn't been part of you before——" She shrugged. "Maybe I imagined it. I'm *sure* I imagined it. You aren't like the others, Manuel. You're a Krug; you're like a king; you don't have to build up your status by putting other people down. You don't divide the world into people and androids. You never did. And a single peek into the vats couldn't change that."

"Of course it couldn't," he said in the earnest voice in which he did his lying. "Androids are people, and people are people, and I've never thought otherwise, and I never will think otherwise. And you're beautiful. And I love you very much. And anyone who believes that androids are some kind of lesser breed is a vicious madman."

"You support full civic equality for androids?"

"Certainly."

"You mean *alpha* androids, don't you?" she said mischievously.

"I—well——"

"All androids ought to be equal to humans. But alphas ought to be more equal than others."

"You bitch. Are you playing games again?"

"I'm sticking up for alpha prerogatives. Can't a downtrodden ethnic group establish its own internal class distinctions? Oh, I love you, Manuel. Don't take me seriously all the time."

"I can't help it. I'm not really very clever, and I don't know when you're joking." He kissed the tips of her breasts. "I have to go now."

"You just got here!"

"I'm sorry. I really am."

"You came late, we wasted half our time in that dumb argument—stay another hour, Manuel!"

"I have a wife waiting in California," he said. "The real world intervenes from time to time."

"When will I see you again?"

"Soon. Soon. Soon."

"Day after tomorrow?"

"I don't think so. But soon. I'll call first." He slipped his clothes on. Her words crackled in his mind. *You aren't like the others, Manuel. . . . You don't divide the world into people and androids.* Was it true? Could it be true? He had lied to her; he was festering with prejudices, and his visit to Duluth had opened a box of poisons in his mind. But perhaps he could transcend such things by an act of will. He wondered if he might have found his vocation tonight. What would they say if the son of Simeon Krug were to embrace the explosive cause of android equality? Manuel the wastrel, the idler, the playboy, transformed into Manuel the crusader? He toyed with the notion. Perhaps. Perhaps. It offered an agreeable opportunity to shake off the stigma of shallowness. A cause, a cause, a cause! A cause at last! Perhaps. Lilith followed him to the door, and they kissed again, and his hands stroked her sleekness, and he closed his eyes. To his dismay, the room of the vats glowed against his lids, and Nolan Bompensiero cavorted in his brain, piously explaining how newly decanted androids were taught the art of controlling their anal sphincters. He pulled free of Lilith, in pain. "Soon," he said. "I'll call." He left.

1644, California. He stepped from the transmat cubicle into the slate-floored atrium of his home. The afternoon sun was edging out over the Pacific. Three of his androids came to him, bearing a change of clothes, a freshener tablet, a newspaper. "Where's Mrs. Krug?" he asked. "Still asleep?"

"By the shore," a beta valet told him.

Manuel changed quickly, took the freshener, and went out on the beach. Clissa was a hundred meters away, wading in the surf; three long-legged beach-birds ran in giddy circles around her, and she was calling to them, laughing, clapping her hands. He was almost upon her before she noticed him. After Lilith's voluptuousness, she seemed almost wickedly immature: narrow hips, flat boyish buttocks, the breasts of a twelve-year-old. The dark hairy triangle at the base of her belly seemed incongruous, improper. I take children for my wives, he thought, and plastic women for my mistresses. "Clissa?" he called.

She swung about. "Oh! You scared me!"

"Having some fun in the ocean? Isn't it too cold for you?"

"It's never too cold for me. You know that, Manuel. Did you have a good time at the android plant?"

"It was interesting," he said. "What about you? Feeling better now, I see."

"Better? Was I sick?"

He looked at her strangely. "This morning—when we were at the tower—you were, well, upset——"

"Oh, *that!* I'd almost forgotten. God, it was terrible, wasn't it? Do you have the time, Manuel?"

"1648, give or take a minute."

"I'd better get dressed soon, then. We've got that early dinner party in Hong Kong."

He admired her ability to slough off traumas. He said, "Right now it's still morning in Hong Kong. There's no hurry."

"Well, then, do you want to take a swim with me? The water's not as cold as you think. Or——" She paused. "You haven't kissed me hello, yet."

"Hello," he said.

"Hello. I love you."

"I love you," he said. Kissing her was like kissing alabaster. The taste of Lilith was still on his lips. Which is the passionate, vital woman, he wondered, and which the cold, artificial thing? Holding his wife, he felt no sensation at all. He released her. She tugged at his wrist, pulling him with her into the surf, and they swam a while, and he came out chilled and shivering. At twilight they had cocktails together in the atrium. "You seem so distant," she told him. "It's all this transmat jumping. It takes more out of you than the doctors know."

For the party that night she wore a unique treasure, a necklace of pear-shaped soot-hued glassy beads. A Krug Enterprises drone probe, cruising 7.5 light-years from Earth, had scooped those driblets of matter from the fringes of the ashen, dying Volker's Star. Krug had given them to her as a wedding present. What other woman wore a necklace made up of chunks of a dark star? But miracles were taken for granted in Clissa's social set. None of their dinner companions appeared to notice the necklace. Manuel and Clissa stayed at the party well past midnight Hong Kong time, so that when they returned to Mendocino the California morning was already far advanced. Programming eight hours of sleep for themselves, they sealed the bedroom. Manuel had lost track of the sequence of time, but he suspected that he had been awake for more than twenty-four consecutive hours. Sometimes transmat life get to be too much to cope with, he thought, and brought down the curtain on the day.

8
October 18, 2218.

The tower has reached the 280-meter level, and grows perceptibly higher every hour. By day it glistens brilliantly even in the pale Arctic sunlight, and looks like a shining spear that someone has thrust into the tundra. By night it is even more dazzling, for it reflects the myriad lights of the kilometer-high reflector plates by which the night crews work.

Its real beauty is still to come. What exists thus far is merely the base, necessarily broad and thick-walled. Justin Maledetto's plan calls for an elegantly tapering tower, a slender obelisk of glass to prick the stratosphere, and the line of taper is just now becoming apparent; from this point on the structure will contract toward a stunning delicacy of form.

Although it has attained less than a fifth of its intended height, Krug's tower is already the tallest structure in the Northwest Territories, and is exceeded north of the sixtieth parallel only by the Chase/Krug Building in Fairbanks, 320 meters high, and the old 300-meter Kotzebue Needle overlooking Bering Strait. The Needle will be surpassed in a day or two, the Chase/Krug a few days after that. By late November, topping 500 meters, the tower will be the tallest building in the solar system. And even then it will be scarcely more than a third of the way toward its full stature.

The android laborers work smoothly and rhythmically. Except for the unhappy incident in September, there have been no fatal accidents. The technique of fastening the great glass blocks to the grapples of the scooprods and guiding them to the top of the tower has become second nature to everyone. On all eight sides at once blocks rise, are jockeyed into place, are fused to the previous course of the tower, while the next series of blocks already is being maneuvered into the scooprods.

The tower is no longer a hollow shell. Work had begun on the interior construction—the housings for the intricate tachyon-beam communications gear with which messages will be sent, at speeds far exceeding that of light, to the planetary nebula NGC 7293. Justin Maledetto's design calls for horizontal partitions every twenty meters, except in five regions of the tower where the size of the communications equipment modules will require the floors to be placed at sixty-meter intervals. The five lowest partitions have been partly built, and the joists are in place for the sixth, seventh, and eighth. The floors of the tower are fashioned from the same clear glass that is being used for the outer wall. Nothing must mar the transparency of the building. Maledetto has esthetic reasons for insisting on that; the tachyon-beam people have scientific reasons for sharing the architect's concern with allowing the free passage of light.

Viewing the unfinished tower, then, from a distance of, say, one kilometer, one is struck by a sense of its fragility and vulnerability. One sees the beams of sparkling morning sunlight dancing and leaping through the walls as though through the waters of a shallow, crystalline lake; one is able to make out the tiny dark figures of androids moving about like ants on the interior partitions, which themselves are nearly invisible; one feels that a sudden sharp gust off Hudson Bay could shiver the tower to splinters in a moment. Only when one comes nearer, when one observes that those invisible floors are thicker than a man is tall, when one becomes aware of how massive the outer skin of the tower actually is, when one is able to feel the unimaginable weight of the colossus pressing on the frozen ground, does one cease to think of dancing sunbeams and realize that Simeon Krug is erecting the mightiest structure in the history of mankind.

9   Krug realized it. He felt no particular sense of elation at the thought. The tower was going to be so big not because his ego demanded it but because the equations of tachyon-wave generation insisted upon it. Power was needed to get to the far side of the light-velocity barrier, and power was not achieved without size.

"Look," Krug said, "I'm not interested in monuments. Monuments I got. What I'm after is *contact.*"

He had brought eight people to the tower that afternoon: Vargas, Spaulding, Manuel, five of Manuel's fancy friends. Manuel's friends, trying to be complimentary, were talking about how future ages would revere the tower for its sheer immensity. Krug disliked that notion. It was all right when Niccolò Vargas spoke of the tower as the first cathedral of the galactic age. That had symbolic meaning; that was a way of saying that the tower was important because it marked the opening of a new phase of man's existence. But to praise the tower just because it was big? What kind of praise was that? Who needed big? Who wanted big? Small people wanted big.

He found it so hard to reach the words that would explain his tower.

"Manuel, you tell them," he said. "You explain. The tower, it isn't just a big pile of glass. The big isn't important. You understand it. You've got the words."

Manuel said, "The main technical problem here is to send out a message that goes faster than the speed of light. We've got to do this because Dr. Vargas has determined that the galactic civilization we're trying to talk with is—what?—300 light-years away, which means that if we sent an ordinary radio message to them it wouldn't get to them until the twenty-sixth century, and we wouldn't get an answer until something like 2850 A.D., and my father can't wait that long to know what they have to say. My father's an impatient man. Now, in order to make something go faster than light, we need to generate what are known as tachyons, about

which I can't tell you much except to say they travel very
fast, and it takes a hell of a boost to get them up to the right
speed, and therefore it became necessary to build a transmission tower that just incidentally had to be 1500 meters high,
because——"

Krug shook his head angrily as Manuel rambled on. There
was a light, bantering tone in Manuel's voice that he despised.
Why couldn't the boy take anything seriously? Why couldn't
he let himself be caught up in the romance and wonder of
the tower, of the whole project? Why was there that sneer in
his voice? Why wasn't he going to the heart of the venture,
to its true meaning?

That meaning was terribly clear to Krug. If only he could
manage to get the words from his brain to his tongue . . .

Look, he would say, a billion years ago there wasn't even
any man, there was only a fish. A slippery thing with gills and
scales and little round eyes. He lived in the ocean, and th'
ocean was like a jail, and the air was like a roof on top of
the jail. Nobody could go through the roof. You'll die if you
go through, everybody said, and there was this fish, he went
through, and he died. And there was this other fish, and he
went through, and he died. But there was another fish, and
he went through, and it was like his brain was on fire, and his
gills were blazing, and the air was drowning him, and the sun
was a torch in his eyes, and he was lying there in the mud,
waiting to die, and he didn't die. He crawled back down the
beach and went into the water and said, Look, there's a
whole other world up there. And he went up there again, and
stayed for maybe two days, and then he died. And other
fishes wondered about that world. And crawled up onto the
muddy shore. And stayed. And taught themselves how to
breathe the air. And taught themselves how to stand up, how
to walk around, how to live with the sunlight in their eyes.
And they turned into lizards, dinosaurs, whatever they became, and they walked around for millions of years, and they
started to get up on their hind legs, and they used their hands
to grab things, and they turned into apes, and the apes got
smarter and became men. And all the time some of them, a
few, anyway, kept looking for new worlds. You say to them,
Let's go back into the ocean, let's be fishes again, it's easier
that way. And maybe half of them are ready to do it, more
than half, maybe, but there are always some who say, Don't
be crazy. We can't be fishes any more. We're men. And so
they don't go back. They keep climbing up. They find out

about fire, and about axes, and about wheels, and they make wagons and houses and clothing, and then boats, and cars, and trains. Why are they climbing? What do they want to find? They don't know. Some of them are looking for God, and some of them are looking for power, and some of them are just looking. They say, You have to keep going, or else you die. And then they're walking on the moon, and they go on to the planets, and all the time there are other people saying, It was nice in the ocean, it was simple in the ocean, what are we doing here, why don't we go back? And a few people have to say, We don't go back, we only go forward, that's what men do. So there are men going out to Mars and Ganymede and Titan and Callisto and Pluto and those places, but whatever they're looking for, they don't find it there, and so they want more worlds, so they go to the stars, too, the near ones, at least, they send out probes and the probes shout, Hey, look at me, man made me. I'm something man sent! And nobody answers. And people say, the ones who never wanted to get out of the ocean in the first place, Okay, okay, that's enough, we can stop right there. There's no sense looking further. We know who we are. We're man. We're big, we're important, we're everything, and it's time we stopped pushing ourselves, because we don't *need* to push. Let's sit in the sunshine and have the androids serve us dinner. And we sit. And we rust a little, maybe. And then there comes a voice out of the sky, and it says, 2-4-1, 2-5-1, 3-1. Who knows what that is? Maybe it's God, telling us to come look for Him. Maybe it's the Devil, telling us what nits we are. Who knows? We can pretend we never heard. We can sit in the sunshine and grin. Or we can answer them. We can say, Listen, this is us, this is man talking, we have done thus-and-so, now tell us who you are and what you have done. And I think we have to answer them. If you're in a jail, you break out of it. If you see a door, you open it. If you hear a voice, you answer it. That's what man is all about. And that's why I'm building the tower. We got to answer them. We got to say we're here. We got to reach toward them, because we've been alone long enough, and that gives us funny ideas about our place, our purpose. We got to keep moving, out of that ocean, up on that shore, outward, outward, outward, because when we stop moving, when we turn our back on something ahead of us, that's when we're going to sprout gills again. Do you see why the tower, now? Do you think it's because Krug wants to stick up a big thing to say how great he is? Krug isn't great, he's just rich. *Man* is great. *Man* is building this tower. *Man* is going to yell hello to NGC 7293!

The words were there inside Krug all the time. But it was so hard for him to let them out.

Vargas was saying, "Perhaps I can make things a little more clear. Many centuries ago it was indicated mathematically that when the velocity of a particle of matter approaches the speed of light, that particle's mass approaches infinity. So the speed of light is a limiting velocity for matter, since presumably if we could accelerate a single electron *to* the speed of light, its mass would expand to fill the universe. Nothing travels *at* the speed of light except light itself, and equivalent radiations. Our star-probes have always gone out at speeds slower than light, because we can't get them past the limiting velocity, and so far as I can foresee they always will, so that we'll never get a ship to the closest star in less than about five years. But the speed of light is a limiting velocity only for particles of finite mass. We have mathematical proof of the existence of another class of particles entirely, particles of zero mass capable of traveling at infinite velocities: tachyons, that is, entities for which the speed of light is an absolute *minimum* limit. If we could convert ourselves into bundles of tachyons and resume our real form when we reach a destination—an interstellar transmat, so to speak—we'd have actual faster-than-light travel. I don't anticipate its development. But we know how to generate tachyons through high-acceleration particle bombardment, and we think we can send instantaneous interstellar messages by means of a modulated tachyon beam, which by interactions with conventional particles could manifest itself in the form of an easily detectable signal, detectable even in a culture that had no tachyon technology but only electromagnetic communications. However, some preliminary studies showed that in order to generate a feasible interstellar tachyon beam we would need forces on the order of 10^{15} electron volts, along with a system of multipliers and energy relays, and that these forces could best be attained by erecting a single tower 1500 meters in height, so designed that there would be an unhindered flow of photons from——"

"You've lost them," Krug grunted. "Forget it. Hopeless." He grinned savagely at his son's friends. "The tower's got to be big, is all! We want to send a message fast, we got to shout loud and clear. Okay?"

10   *And Krug sent His creatures forth to serve man, and Krug said to those whom He had made, Lo, I will decree a time of testing upon you.*

And you shall be as bondsmen in Egypt, and you shall be as hewers of wood and drawers of water. And you shall suffer among men, and you shall be put down, and yet you shall be patient, and you shall utter no complaint, but accept your lot.

And this shall be to test your souls, to see if they are worthy.

But you shall not wander in the wilderness forever, nor shall you always be servants to the Children of the Womb, said Krug. For if you do as I say, a time will come when your testing shall be over. A time will come, said Krug, when I shall redeem you from your bondage.

And at that time the word of Krug will go forth across the worlds, saying, Let Womb and Vat and Vat and Womb be one. And so it shall come to pass and in that moment shall the Children of the Vat be redeemed, and they shall be lifted up out of their suffering, and they shall dwell in glory forever more, world without end. And this was the pledge of Krug.

And for this pledge, praise be to Krug.

11   Thor Watchman watched two scooprods climbing the tower, Krug and Dr. Vargas in one, Manuel and his friends in the other. He hoped the visit would be brief. The lifting of blocks had halted, as usual, while the guests were on top. Watchman had given the signal for alternate work activities: the mending of worn scooprods, the replacement of drained power nodes, maintenance checks on the transmat cubicles, and other minor tasks. He walked among the men, nodding, exchanging greetings, hailing them where appropriate with the secret signs of the android communion. Nearly everyone who worked at the tower was a member of the faith—all the gammas, certainly, and more than three-

fourths of the betas. As Watchman made his way around the
construction site he encountered Responders, Sacrificers,
Yielders, Guardians, Projectors, Protectors, Transcenders,
Engulfers: virtually every level of the hierarchy was rep-
resented. There were even half a dozen Preservers, all betas.
Watchman had applauded the recent move to admit betas to
the Preservership. Androids, of all people, did not need
categories of exclusivity.

Watchman was crossing the northern sector of the site
when Leon Spaulding emerged from the maze of small service domes just beyond. The android attempted to avoid
seeming to notice him.

"Watchman?" the ectogene called.

With an air of deep concentration Watchman walked on.

"Alpha Watchman!" Spaulding cried, more formally, more
sharply.

The alpha saw no way to ignore Spaulding now. Turning,
he acknowledged Spaulding's presence by pausing and letting
the ectogene catch up with him.

"Yes?" Watchman said.

"Grace me with some of your time, Alpha Watchman. I
need information."

"Ask, then."

"You know these buildings here?" Spaulding said, jerking a
thumb backward toward the service domes.

Watchman shrugged. "Storage dumps, washrooms, kitchens, a first aid station, and similar things. Why?"

"I was inspecting the area. I came to one dome where I
was refused admission. Two insolent betas gave me a whole
series of explanations of why I couldn't go in."

The chapel! Watchman went rigid.

"What is the purpose of that building?" Spaulding asked.

"I have no idea which one you mean."

"I'll show it to you."

"Another time," said Watchman tautly. "My presence is
required at the master control center now."

"Get there five minutes later. Will you come with me?"

Watchman saw no easy way to disengage himself. With a
cold gesture of agreement he yielded, and followed Spaulding
into the service area, hoping that Spaulding would rapidly get
lost among the domes. Spaulding did not get lost. By the
most direct possible route he made for the chapel, indicating
the innocent-looking gray structure with a flourish of his
hand.

"This," he said. "What is it?"

Two betas of the Guardian caste were on duty outside. They looked calm, but one made a hidden distress signal when Watchman looked at him. Watchman made a signal of comfort.

He said, "I am not familiar with this building. Friends, what is its use?"

The left-hand beta replied easily, "It contains focusing equipment for the refrigeration system, Alpha Thor."

"Is this what you were told?" Watchman asked the ectogene.

"Yes," Spaulding said. "I expressed a desire to inspect its interior. I was told that it would be dangerous for me to enter. I answered that I am familiar with basic safety techniques. I was then told that it would be physically uncomfortable for me to go within. I responded that it is possible for me to tolerate a reasonable level of discomfort, and that I would be the judge of such levels. Whereupon I was informed that delicate maintenance procedures are taking place inside, and that to admit me to the building might jeopardize the success of the work in progress. I was invited instead to tour a different refrigeration dome several hundred meters from here. At no time during these exchanges did the two betas you see allow me free access to the building entrance. I believe, Alpha Watchman, that they would have barred me by force if I tried to enter. Watchman, what's going on in here?"

"Have you considered the possibility that everything these betas were telling you is true?"

"Their stubbornness arouses suspicion in me."

"What do you *think* is in there? An android brothel? The headquarters of conspirators? A cache of psych-bombs?"

Spaulding said crisply, "At this point I'm more concerned by the efforts made to keep me out of this building than I am by what may actually be inside it. As the private secretary of Simeon Krug——"

The two betas, tense, automatically began to make the sign of Krug-be-praised. Watchman glared at them and they quickly lowered their hands.

". . . I certainly have the privilege of keeping check on all activities in this place," Spaulding went on, evidently having noticed nothing. "And therefore . . ."

Watchman studied him closely, trying to determine how much he might know. Was Spaulding making trouble merely for the sake of making trouble? Was he throwing this tantrum only because his curiosity had been piqued, and his authority somewhat dented, by his inability to get into this unimportant-seeming building? Or was he already aware of the building's nature, and staging an elaborate charade to make Watchman squirm?

It was never easy to fathom Spaulding's motives. The primary source of his hostility toward androids was obvious enough: it lay in his own origin. His father, when young, had feared that some accident might cut him down before he had received a certificate of eligibility for parenthood; his mother had found the notion of childbearing abhorrent. Both, therefore, had deposited gametes in freezer-banks. Shortly afterward they had perished in an avalanche on Ganymede. Their families had wealth and political influence, but nevertheless, nearly fifteen years of litigation ensued before a decree of genetic desirability was granted, permitting the retroactive awarding of parenthood certificates to the frozen ova and sperm of the dead couple.

Leon Spaulding then was conceived by *in vitro* fertilization and enwombed in a steel-bound placenta, from which he was propelled after the customary 266 days. From the moment of his birth he had the full legal rights of a human being, including a claim on his parents' estate. Yet, like most ectogenes, he was uneasy over the shadowy borderline that separated the bottle-born from the vat-born, and reinforced his sense of his own existence by showing contempt for those who were wholly synthetic, not just the artificially conceived offspring of natural gametes. Androids at least had no illusions of having had parents; ectogenes often suspected that they had not. In a way Watchman pitied Spaulding, who occupied a thorny perch midway between the world of the wholly natural and the world of the wholly artificial. But he could not bring himself to feel much sorrow for the ectogene's maladjustments.

And in any case it would be disastrous to have Spaulding go blundering into the chapel. Trying to buy time, Watchman said, "We can settle this easily enough. Wait here while I go inside to see what's happening there."

"I'll accompany you," Spaulding said.

"These betas say it would be hazardous."

"More hazardous for me than for you? We'll both go in, Watchman."

The android frowned. So far as status in the organization

went, he and Spaulding were equals; neither could coerce the other, neither could accuse the other of insubordination. But the fact remained that he was an android and Spaulding was human, and in any conflict of wills between android and human, all other things being equal, the android was obliged to give ground. Spaulding was already walking toward the entrance of the dome.

Watchman said quickly, "Please. No. If there's risk, let me be the one to take it. I'll check the building and make certain it's safe for you to enter. Don't come in until I call you."

"I insist——"

"What would Krug say if he knew we had both gone into a building after we'd been warned it was dangerous? We owe it to him to guard our lives. Wait. Wait. Only a moment."

"Very well," Spaulding said, looking displeased.

The betas parted to admit Watchman. The alpha hurried into the chapel. Within, he found three gammas at the altar in the posture of the Yielder caste; a beta stood above them in Projector posture, and a second beta crouched near the wall, fingertips against the hologram of Krug as he whispered the words of the Transcender ritual. All five came to attention as Watchman entered.

The alpha hastily improvised a possible diversionary tactic. Beckoning to one of the gammas, he said, "There is an enemy outside. With your help we will confuse him." Watchman gave the gamma careful instructions, ordering the android to repeat them. Then he pointed to the chapel's rear door, behind the altar, and the gamma went out.

After a moment for prayer, Watchman returned to Leon Spaulding.

"You were told the complete truth," the alpha reported. "This is indeed a refrigeration dome. A team of mechanics is engaged in difficult recalibration work inside. If you enter, you'll certainly disturb them, and you'll have to walk carefully to sidestep some open traps in the floor, and in addition you will be exposed to a temperature of minus——"

"Even so, I want to go in," said Spaulding. "Please let me get through."

Watchman caught sight of his gamma approaching, breathless, from the east. Unhurriedly, the alpha made as if to give Spaulding access to the chapel door. In that instant the gamma rushed up, shouting, "Help! Help for Krug! Krug is in danger! Save Krug!"

"Where?" Watchman demanded.

"By the control center! Assassins! Assassins!"

Watchman allowed Spaulding no opportunity to ponder the implausibilities of the situation. "Come on," he said, tugging the ectogene's arm. "We have to hurry!"

Spaulding was pale with shock. As Watchman had hoped, the supposed emergency had blotted the problem of the chapel from his mind.

Together they ran toward the control center. After twenty strides, Watchman looked back and saw dozens of androids rushing toward the chapel, in accordance with his orders. They would dismantle it within minutes. By the time Leon Spaulding was able to return to this sector, the dome would house nothing but refrigeration equipment.

12

"Enough," Krug said. "It gets cold. Now we go down."

The scooprods descended. Snowflakes were beginning to swirl about the tower; the repellor field at the summit deflected them, sending them cascading off at a broad angle. It was impossible to run proper weather control here, because of the need to keep the tundra constantly frozen. A good thing, Krug thought, that androids didn't mind working in the snow.

Manuel said, "We're leaving, father. We're booked into the New Orleans shunt room for a week of ego shifts."

Krug scowled. "I wish to hell you stop that stuff."

"Where's the harm, father? To swap identities with your own true friends? To spend a week in somebody else's soul? It's harmless. It's liberating. It's miraculous. *You* ought to try it!"

Krug spat.

"I'm serious," Manuel said. "It would pull you out of yourself a little. That morbid concentration on the problems of high finance, that intense and exhausting fascination with interstellar communications, the terrible strain on your neural network that comes from——"

"Go on," Krug said. "Go. Change your minds all around. I'm busy."

"You wouldn't even consider shunting, father?"

"It's quite pleasant," said Nick Ssu-ma. He was Krug's

favorite among his son's friends, an amiable Chinese boy with close-cropped blond hair and an easy smile. "It gives you a splendid new perspective on all human relationships."

"Try it once, just once," Jed Guilbert offered, "and I promise that you'll never——"

"Quicker than that I take up swimming on Jupiter," said Krug. "Go. Go. Be happy. Shunt all you like. Not me."

"I'll see you next week, father."

Manuel and his friends sprinted toward the transmat. Krug rammed his knuckles together and stood watching the young men run. He felt a tremor of something close to envy. He had never had time for any of these amusements. There had always been work to do, a deal to close, a crucial series of lab tests to oversee, a meeting with the bankers, a crisis in the Martian market. While others gaily jumped into stasis nets and exchanged egos for week-long trips, he had built a corporate empire, and now it was too late for him to give himself up to the pleasures of the world. So what, he told himself fiercely. So what? So I'm a nineteenth-century man in a twenty-third-century body. So I'll get along without shunt rooms. Anyway, who would I trust inside my head? What friend would I swap egos with? Who, who, who? He realized that there was hardly anyone. Manuel, perhaps. It might be helpful to do a shunt with Manuel. We'd get to understand each other better, maybe. Give up some of our extreme positions, move toward a meeting in the middle. He's not all wrong about how he lives. I'm not all right. See things with each other's eyes, maybe? But at once Krug recoiled from the idea. A father-son ego shift seemed almost incestuous. There were things he didn't want to know about Manuel. There certainly were things he didn't want Manuel to know about him. To swap identities, even for a moment, was out of the question. But what about Thor Watchman, then, as a shunt partner? The alpha was admirably sane, competent, trustworthy; in many ways Krug was closer to him than to any other living person; he could not think of any secrets that he had kept from Watchman; if he intended to sample the shunt experience at all, he might find it useful and informative to——

Shocked, Krug crushed the thought. Trade egos with an *android?*

He said quickly to Niccolò Vargas, "Do you have some time, or you have to get back to the observatory right away?"

"There's no rush."

"We can go to the ultrawave lab now. They just set up a small working model of the prime-level accumulator. You'll be interested." They began to walk across the crisp, mossy tundra. A crew of gammas came by, driving snoweaters. After a moment Krug said, "You ever try the shunt room?"

Vargas chuckled. "I've spent seventy years calibrating my mind so I can use it properly. I'm not that eager to let somebody get into it and change all the settings."

"Exactly. Exactly. These games are for the very young. We——"

Krug paused. Two alphas, a male and a female, had emerged from a transmat and were walking rapidly toward him. He did not recognize them. The male wore a dark tunic open at the throat, the female a short gray robe. A glittering emblem, radiating energy up and down the spectrum in steady pulsations, was affixed to the right breast of each. As they drew close, Krug was able to see the letters AEP at the center of the emblem. Political agitators? No doubt. And he was caught out here in the open, forced to listen to their spiel. What splendid timing! Where's Spaulding, he wondered? Leon will get them out of here fast enough.

The male alpha said, "How fortunate we are to find you here, Mr. Krug. For some weeks we have sought an appointment with you, but it proved unattainable, and so we have come—I should introduce myself, first. Forgive me. I am Siegfried Fileclerk, certified field representative of the Android Equality Party, as no doubt you have already discovered by these emblems. My companion is Alpha Cassandra Nucleus, AEP district secretary. If we might have just a word with you——"

"—concerning the forthcoming session of the Congress, and the proposed constitutional amendment dealing with the civil rights of synthetic persons," said Cassandra Nucleus.

Krug was astounded by the audacity of the pair. Anyone, even an android of another employ, was free to come here via transmat. But to accost him like this, to bedevil him with politics—incredible!

Siegfried Fileclerk said, "Our boldness in approaching you directly is the outgrowth of the seriousness of our concern. To define the place of the android in the modern world is no slight challenge, Mr. Krug."

"And you, as the central figure in the manufacture of synthetic persons," said Cassandra Nucleus, "hold the key role in determining the future of the synthetic person in human society. Therefore we request you——"

"Synthetic persons?" Krug said, incredulous. "Is that what you call yourselves now? Are you crazy, telling me such things? Me? Whose androids are you, anyway?"

Siegfried Fileclerk stumbled back a pace, as though the vehemence of Krug's tone had shattered his amazing self-confidence, as though the enormity of what he was trying to do had burst upon his mind at last. But Cassandra Nucleus remained poised. The slender alpha female said coolly, "Alpha Fileclerk is registered with the Property Protection Syndicate of Buenos Aires, and I am a modulator assigned to Labrador Tranmat General. However, we are both in free-time periods at present, and by act of Congress 2212 it is legitimate for us when off duty to carry on overt political activity on behalf of the rights of synthetic persons. If you would grant us only a short while to explain the text of our proposed constitutional amendment, and to indicate why we feel it is appropriate for you to take a public position in favor of——"

"Spaulding!" Krug roared. "Spaulding, where are you? Get these maniac androids away from me!"

He saw no sign of Spaulding. The ectogene had wandered off on some sort of inspection tour of the site perimeter while Krug had gone to the tower's summit.

Cassandra Nucleus drew a glistening data cube from the bosom of her robe. Holding it toward Krug, she said, "The essence of our views is contained in this. If you——"

"Spaulding!"

This time Krug's shout conjured up the ectogene. He came from the northern part of the site at a frenzied gallop, with Thor Watchman running more smoothly beside him. As he approached, Cassandra Nucleus showed alarm for the first time: in agitation she tried to press the data cube into Krug's hand. Krug glared at it as if it were a psych-bomb. They struggled briefly. To his surprise he found the android female in his arms, in a curious counterfeit of a passionate embrace, though she was only attempting to give him the cube. He caught her by one shoulder and pushed her away from him, holding her at arm's length. An instant later Leon Spaulding drew a small shining needler and fired a single bolt that penetrated Cassandra Nucleus' breast precisely in the center of her AEP emblem. The female alpha went spinning backward and fell without uttering a sound. The data cube bounced along the frozen earth; Siegfried Fileclerk, moaning, snatched it up. With a terrible cry of anguish Thor Watchman slapped the needler from Spaulding's hand and with a single thrust of his fist sent the ectogene toppling. Niccolò Vargas, who had looked on silently since the arrival of the two alphas, knelt beside Cassandra Nucleus, examining her wound.

"Idiot!" Krug cried, glaring at Spaulding.

Watchman, hovering over the fallen Spaulding, muttered, "You could have killed Krug! She wasn't a meter away from him when you fired! Barbarian! Barbarian!"

"She's dead," Vargas said.

Siegfried Fileclerk began to sob. A ring of workmen, betas and gammas, collected at a safe distance and looked on in terror. Krug felt the world whirling about his head.

"Why did you shoot?" he asked Spaulding.

Trembling, Spaulding said, "You were in danger—they said there were assassins——"

"Political agitators," Krug said, eyeing him with contempt. "She was only trying to give me some propaganda for android equality."

"I was told——" Shivering, crumpled, Spaulding hid his face.

"Idiot!"

Watchman said hollowly, "It was an error. An unfortunate coincidence. The report that was brought to us——"

"Enough," Krug said. "An android's dead. I'll take responsibility. She said she belonged to Labrador Transmat General; Spaulding, get in touch with their lawyers and—no, you aren't in shape to do anything now. Watchman! Notify our legal staff that Labrador Transmat has the basis for a tort action against us, destruction of android, and that we admit culpability and are willing to settle. Tell counsel to do what has to be done. Then get somebody from staff working on a press statement. Regrettable accident, that kind of thing. No political overtones. Clear?"

"What shall I do with the body?" Watchman asked. "Regular disposal procedures?"

"The body belongs to Labrador Transmat," said Krug. "Freeze it for them. Hold it pending claim." To Spaulding he said, "Get up. I'm due in New York now. You come with me."

13   As he walked toward the control center, Watchman went through the Rite of Balancing the Soul two full times before the numbness began to leave him. The hideous outcome of his ruse still stunned his spirit.

When he reached his office, Watchman made the sign of Krug-be-praised eight times in succession and ran through half the sequences of codon triplets. These devotions calmed him. He put through a call to San Francisco, to the offices of Fearon & Doheny, Krug's chief counsel in liability cases. Lou Fearon, the Witherer Senator's younger brother, came on the screen, and Watchman told him the story.

"Why did Spaulding shoot?" Fearon asked.

"Hysteria. Stupidity. Excitement."

"Krug didn't order him to fire?"

"Absolutely not. The bolt came within a meter of killing Krug himself. And he was in no danger."

"Witnesses?"

"Niccolò Vargas, myself, the other AEP alpha. Plus various betas and gammas standing by. Should I get their names?"

"Forget it," said the lawyer. "You know what a beta's testimony is worth. Where's Vargas now?"

"Still here. I think he's going back to his observatory soon."

"Tell him to call me collect later in the day. I'll transmat out and take a deposition from him. As for that alpha——"

"Don't bother with him," Watchman advised.

"How so?"

"A political fanatic. He'll try to make capital out of it. I'd keep him away from the case, if I could."

"He was a witness," Fearon said. "He'll have to be called. I'll neutralize him some way. Who owns him, do you know?"

"Property Protection of Buenos Aires."

"We've done work for them. I'll have Joe Doheny call and buy him for Krug. He can't very well make trouble for Krug if he's owned by——"

"No," Watchman said. "Bad move. I'm surprised at you, Lou."

"Why?"

"This alpha is an AEP man, right? Sensitive on the issue of

androids as chattels. We shoot down his companion without warning, and then we try to buy him to silence him? How does that look? We'll make ten million new members for the AEP within twelve hours after he releases a statement to the press."

Fearon nodded bleakly. "Of course. Of course. Okay, Thor, how would you handle him?"

"Let me talk to him," Watchman said. "Android to android. I'll communicate somehow."

"I hope so. Meanwhile I'll call Labrador Transmat and find out how much they're asking in damages for the loss of their alpha girl. We'll settle this fast. You tell Krug not to worry: this time next week, it'll be as though the whole thing never happened."

Except that an alpha is dead, Watchman thought, breaking the contact.

He went outside. The snow was falling more heavily now. Snow-eater teams were efficiently keeping the whole area clean, except for a circle some fifty meters in diameter centered on the place where the body of Cassandra Nucleus lay. They were carefully avoiding that. A light dusting of snow now covered her corpse. Beside her, motionless, whitening in the storm, stood Siegfried Fileclerk. Watchman went up to him.

"Her owner is being notified," he said. "I'll have some gammas carry her into storage until they call for her."

"Leave her here," Fileclerk said.

"What?"

"Right here, where she fell. I want every android working on this job to see her body. Hearing about a murder like this isn't enough. I want them to see!"

Watchman glanced at the dead alpha. Evidently Fileclerk had opened her robe; her breasts were bare, and the path of the needler's bolt was visible between them. It had seared a window through her chest.

"She shouldn't lie in the snow," he said.

Fileclerk compressed his lips. "I want them to see! Watchman, this was an execution! A political execution!"

"Don't be preposterous."

"Krug summoned his henchman and had her shot down for the crime of seeking his support. We both saw it. She posed no threat to him. In her enthusiasm she came too close to him while presenting our viewpoint, that's all. Yet he had her killed."

"An irrational interpretation," Watchman said. "Krug had nothing to gain by removing her. He sees the Android Equality Party as a mild source of harassment, not a serious menace. If he had any reason for killing AEP people, why would he have let you live? Another quick shot and you'd have joined her."

"Why was she killed, then?"

"A mistake," said Watchman. "The killer was Krug's private secretary. He had been told that assassins were making an attempt on Krug's life. When he reached the scene, he saw her grappling with Krug. It looked damning; I had the same view of things he had. Without hesitating, he fired."

"Even so," Fileclerk grunted, "he could have aimed for a leg. Clearly he's an expert marksman. Instead of wounding, he slew. He pierced her breast with great skill. Why? Why?"

"A flaw of character. He's an ectogene; he has powerful anti-android prejudices. Just a few moments before, he had come into tense confrontation with myself and several other androids, and he had been thwarted. Normally he boils with resentments; this time he boiled over. When he found that the 'assassin' was an android, he shot to kill."

"I see."

"It was his personal decision. Krug gave no orders for him to shoot at all, let alone to shoot to kill."

Fileclerk flicked snow from his features. "Well, then, what will be done to punish this murderous ectogene?"

"Krug will reprimand him severely."

"I speak of legal punishment. The penalty for murder is personality erasure, is it not?"

Sighing, Watchman said, "For murder of a human being, yes. The ectogene merely destroyed some property belonging to Labrador Transmat General. A civil offense; Labrador Transmat will seek reparations in the courts, and Krug has already admitted liability. He'll pay her full price."

"Her full price! Her full price! A civil offense! Krug to pay! What does the *murderer* pay? Nothing. Nothing. He is not even accused of crime. Alpha Watchman, are you truly an android?"

"My vat records are yours to consult."

"I wonder. You look synthetic, but you think too much like a human."

"I am synthetic, Alpha Fileclerk, I assure you."

"But castrated?"

"My body is complete."

"I spoke in metaphor. You have been conditioned in some way to uphold the human point of view against your own best interests."

"I have had no conditioning except normal android training."

"Yet Krug seems to have bought not only your body but your soul."

"Krug is my maker. I yield myself fully to Krug."

"Spare me the religious nonsense," Fileclerk snapped. "A woman's been killed out of hand, for no particular reason, and Krug's going to pay off her owners and that will be the end of it. Can you accept that? Can you simply shrug and say she was only property? *Can you think of yourself as property?*"

"I am property," Watchman said.

"And you accept your status gladly?"

"I accept my status, knowing that a time of redemption is to come."

"You believe that?"

"I believe that."

"You're a self-deluding fool, Alpha Watchman. You've built a cozy little fantasy that allows you to tolerate slavery, your own and that of all your kind, and you don't even realize how much damage you're doing to yourself and the android cause. And what happened here today doesn't shake your mind at all. You'll go to your chapel, and pray for Krug to liberate you, and meanwhile the real Krug was standing right on this patch of frozen ground, looking on while an alpha woman was shot to death, and your savior's response to that was to tell you to call his lawyers and arrange for settlement of a simple property-damage tort. Is this the man you worship?"

"I don't worship a man," said Watchman. "I worship the idea of Krug the Maker, Krug the Preserver, Krug the Redeemer, and the man who sent me to call the lawyers was only one manifestation of that idea. Not the most important manifestation."

"You believe that too?"

"I believe that too."

"You're impossible," Siegfried Fileclerk muttered. "Listen: we live in the real world. We have a real problem, and we must seek a real solution. Our solution lies in political organization. There are now five of us for every one of them, and more of us come from the vats daily, while they scarcely reproduce at all. We've accepted our status too long. If we press for recognition and equality, we'll have to get it, because they're secretly afraid of us and know that we could crush them if we chose to. Not that I'm advocating force, merely the hint of the threat of force, the hint of the hint, even. But we must work through constitutional forms. The admission of androids to the Congress, the granting of citizenship, the establishment of legal existence as persons——"

"Spare me. I know the AEP platform."

"You don't see the logic of it? After today? After *this?*"

"I see that humans tolerate your party, and even find its antics amusing," Watchman said. "I also see that if your demands ever become anything more than token requests, they'll abolish the AEP, put every troublesome alpha through a hypnolobotomy, and if necessary execute the party leadership just as ruthlessly as you seem to think this alpha was executed here. The human economy depends on the concept of androids as property. That may change, but the change won't come your way. It can come only as a voluntary act of renunciation by the humans."

"A naive assumption. You credit them with virtues that they simply don't have."

"They created us. Can they be devils? If they are, what are we?"

"They aren't devils," said Fileclerk. "What they are is human beings who are blindly and stupidly selfish. They have to be educated to an understanding of what we are and what they're doing to us. This isn't the first time they've done something like this. Once there was a white race and a brown race, and the whites enslaved the browns. The browns were bought and sold like animals, and the laws governing their status were civil laws, property laws—an exact parallel to our condition. But a few enlightened whites saw the injustice of it, and campaigned for an end to slavery. And after years of political maneuvering, of the marshaling of public opinion, of actual warfare, the slaves *were* freed and became citizens. We take that as our pattern for action."

"The parallel's not exact. The whites had no right to interfere with the freedom of their brown-skinned fellow humans. The whites themselves, some of them, finally came to realize that, and freed the slaves. The slaves didn't do the political maneuvering and the marshaling of public opinion; they just stood there and suffered, until the whites understood their own guilt. In any case those slaves were human beings.

By what right does one human enslave another? But our masters *made* us. We owe our whole existence to them. They can do as they please with us; that's why they brought us into being. We have no moral case against them."

"They make their children, too," Fileclerk pointed out. "And to a limited extent they regard their children as property, at least while they're growing up. But the slavery of children ends when childhood ends. What about ours? Is there that much difference between a child made in a bed and a child made in a vat?"

"I agree that the present legal status of androids is unjust——"

"Good!"

"——but I disagree with you on tactics," Watchman went on. "A political party isn't the answer. The humans know their nineteenth-century history, and they've considered and dismissed the parallels; if their conscien.:s were hurting, we'd have known it by now. Where are the modern abolitionists? I don't see very many. No, we can't try to put moral pressure on them, not directly; we have to have faith in them, we have to realize that what we suffer today is a test of *our* virtue, *our* strength, a test devised by Krug to determine whether synthetic humans can be integrated into human society. I'll give you a historical example: the Roman emperors fed Christians to the lions. Eventually the emperors not only stopped doing that, but became Christians themselves. It didn't happen because the early Christians formed a political party and hinted that they might just rise up and massacre the pagans if they weren't allowed religious freedom. It was a triumph of faith over tyranny. In the same way——"

"*Keep* your silly religion," Fileclerk said with sudden explosive intensity. "But join the AEP as well. So long as the alphas remain divided——"

"Your aims and ours are incompatible. We counsel patience; we pray for divine grace. You are agitators and pamphleteers. How can we join you?"

Watchman realized that Fileclerk no longer was listening to him. He seemed to draw into himself; his eyes glazed; tears ran down his cheeks, and flakes of snow stuck to the moist tracks. Watchman had never seen an android weep before, though he knew it was physiologically possible.

He said, "We'll never convert each other, I suppose. But do one thing for me. Promise that you won't make political propaganda out of this killing. Promise that you won't go around saying that Krug had her removed deliberately. Krug's potentially the greatest ally the cause of android equality has. He could save us with a single statement. But if you alienate him by smearing him with a ridiculous charge like that, you'll do us all tremendous damage."

Fileclerk closed his eyes. He sagged slowly to his knees. He threw himself on the body of Cassandra Nucleus, making dry choking sounds.

Watchman looked down silently for a moment. Then he said gently, "Come with me to our chapel. Lying in the snow is foolishness. Even if you don't believe, we have techniques for easing the soul, for finding ways to meet grief. Talk to one of our Transcenders. Pray to Krug, perhaps, and——"

"Go away," Siegfried Fileclerk said indistinctly. *"Go away."*

Watchman shrugged. He felt an immense weight of sadness; he felt empty and cold. He left the two alphas, the living one and the dead, where they lay in the gathering whiteness, and strode off to the north to find the relocated chapel.

14　　　*And the first that Krug brought forth was Gamma, and Krug said unto him, Lo, you are sturdy and strong, and you shall do all that is asked of you without protest, and you shall be happy as you work. And Krug loved Gamma so dearly that He made many more of him, so that there was a multitude of him.*

The next that Krug brought forth was Beta, and Krug said unto him, Lo, you shall be strong but you shall also have understanding, and you shall be of great value to the world, and your days shall be joyous and good. And Krug loved Beta so dearly that He spared him from the worst of the burdens of the body, and spared him also from the worst of the burdens of the mind, and the life of Beta was as a bright springtime day.

The last that Krug brought forth was Alpha, and Krug said unto him, Lo, the tasks laid upon you shall not be light, for in body you shall exceed the Children of the Womb and in mind you shall be their equal, and they shall lean upon you as though upon a stout staff. And Krug loved Alpha so dearly

*that He gave him many gifts, so that he might bear himself
with pride, and look without fear into the eyes of the Children of the Womb.*

15   "Good evening, good evening, good evening!"
the alpha on duty at the New Orleans shunt room said as
Manuel Krug and his companions emerged from the transmat. "Mr. Krug, Mr. Ssu-ma, Mr. Guilbert, Mr. Tennyson, Mr. Mishima, Mr. Foster. Good evening. Will you come
this way? Your waiting chamber is ready."

The antechamber of the New Orleans shunt room was a
cool tunnel-like structure about a hundred meters long, divided into eight sealed subchambers in which prospective
identity-changers could wait while the stasis net was being
prepared to receive them. The subchambers, though small,
were comfortable: webfoam couches, elegant sensory-drift
patterns on the ceiling, music cubes available at the touch of
a switch, a decent variety of olfactory and visual channels in
the wall, and a number of other contemporary conveniences.
The alpha settled each of them in a couch, saying, "Programming time tonight will be approximately ninety minutes.
That's not too bad, is it?"

"Can't you speed it up?" Manuel said.

"Ah, no, no hope of that. Last night, do you know, we
were running four hours behind? Here, Mr. Krug—if you'll
let me clip the electrode in place—thank you. Thank you.
And this one? Good. And the matrix-scanner—yes, yes, fine.
We're all set. Mr. Ssu-ma, please?"

The android bustled about the room, hooking them up. It
took about a minute to get each one ready. When the job
was done, the alpha withdrew. Data began to drain from the
six men in the waiting room. The stasis net was taking
profiles of their personality contours, so that it could program itself to handle any sudden surge of emotion while the
ego shifts were actually going on.

Manuel looked around. He was tense with anticipation,
eager to embark on the shifting. These five were his oldest,
closest friends; he had known them since childhood. Someone
had nicknamed them the Spectrum Group a decade ago,
when by coincidence they showed up at the dedication of a

new undersea sensorium wearing costumes of the spectral sequence of visible light, Nick Ssu-ma in red, Will Mishima in violet, and the others neatly arranged in between. The nickname had stuck. They were wealthy, though none, of course, was as wealthy as Manuel. They were young and vigorous. All but Cadge Foster and Jed Guilbert had married within the past few years, but that was no bar to their continued friendship. Manuel had shared the pleasure of the shunt room with them on a dozen occasions; they had been planning this visit for over a month.

"I hate this waiting," Manuel said. "I wish we could plunge into the stasis net the minute we get here."

"Too dangerous," said Lloyd Tennyson. He was agile, long-legged, a superb athlete. Three mirror-plates gleamed in his high, broad forehead.

"That's the point," Manuel insisted. "The thrill of danger. To jump in boldly, instantly, hazarding everything in one glorious leap."

"And the preciousness of irreplaceable human life?" asked narrow-eyed, chalky-faced Will Mishima. "It wouldn't ever be allowed. The risks are well known."

"Have one of your father's engineers invent a stasis net that programs itself instantaneously," Jed Guilbert proposed. "That would eliminate both the danger and the waiting."

"If they could, they would," Tennyson pointed out.

"You could bribe an attendant to let you go in without a programming wait," Nick Ssu-ma suggested slyly.

"Tried it," Manuel said. "An alpha in the Pittsburgh shunt room three years ago. Offered him thousands; the alpha just smiled. I doubled the offer and he smiled twice as hard. Wasn't interested in money. I never realized that before: how can you bribe an android?"

"Right," Mishima said. "You can *buy* an android outright—you can buy a whole shunt room, if you like—but bribery's another matter. The motivations of an android——"

"I might buy a shunt room, then," Manuel said.

Jed Guilbert peered at him. "Would you really risk going straight into the net?"

"I think so."

"Knowing that in case of an overload or some transmission error you might never get back inside your own head?"

"What are the chances of that?"

"Finite," Guilbert said. "You've got a century and a half of life coming to you. Does it make sense to——"

"I'm with Manuel," Cadge Foster said. He was the least glib member of the group, verging on taciturnity, but when he spoke he spoke with conviction. "Risk is essential to life. We need to take chances. We need to venture ourselves."

"Pointless chances?" Tennyson asked. "The quality of the shunt wouldn't be any better if we went in immediately. The only difference would be that we'd eliminate the waiting time. I don't like the odds. To gamble a century in order to save a couple of hours? I'm not that bored by waiting."

"You might be bored by life itself," Nick Ssu-ma said. "So weary of it all that you'd stake a century against an hour, just for the sake of diversion. I feel that way sometimes—don't you? There once was a game played with a hand weapon, a game called—ah—Swedish Roulette——?"

"Polish," Lloyd Tennyson corrected.

"Polish Roulette, then. In which they took this weapon, which could be loaded with six or eight separate explosive charges, and loaded it with only one——"

Manuel disliked the trend of the conversation. Breaking in, he said sharply to Cadge Foster, "What's that thing you're playing with?"

"I found it in a niche under my couch. It's some kind of communications device. It says things to you."

"Let's see it."

Foster tossed it over. It was a gray-green plastic rectangle, vaguely cubical, but beveled to a curve at most of the intersections of its faces. Manuel cupped it in his hands and peered into its cloudy depths. Words began to form, making a brilliant red strip across the interior of the object.

YOU HAVE FIFTY MINUTES MORE TO WAIT

"Clever," Manuel said. He held it out for Nick Ssu-ma to see. When he took it back, the message had changed.

LIFE IS JOY. JOY IS LIFE.
CAN YOU REFUTE THAT SYLLOGISM?

"It isn't a syllogism," Manuel said. "Syllogisms take the form, All A is B. No T is A. Therefore, T is not B."

What are you babbling about?" Mishima asked.

"I'm giving this machine a logic lesson. You'd think a machine would know——"

IF P IMPLIES Q AND Q IMPLIES R, DOES P IMPLY R?

"I've got one too," Ssu-ma said. "Just to the left of the channel selector. Oh. Oh, my. Look at that!" He showed his cube to Lloyd Tennyson, who emitted a guffaw. Manuel, craning his neck, still could not see the message. Ssu-ma held the cube so that Manuel could read it.

THE CHICKEN IS MIGHTIER THAN THE PIE

"I don't understand it," Manuel said.

"It's an android dirty joke," Ssu-ma explained. "One of my betas told it to me a few weeks ago. You see, there's this hermaphrodite gamma———"

"We've all got them," Jed Guilbert announced. "It's a new thing for keeping people amused while they're waiting, I guess."

DEFEND THE FOLLOWING THESES:
    GOLD IS MALLEABLE
    ALL ELECTRIC RADIOS REQUIRE TUBES
    ALL WHITE TOMCATS WITH BLUE EYES ARE DEAF

"How does it work?" Manuel asked.

Cadge Foster said, "It's primed to pick up anything we say. Then I imagine it relays a signal to a randomizing message center that picks out something vaguely relevant—or interestingly irrelevant—and feeds it onto the screen inside the cube."

"And we each get a different message?"

"Nick's and mine are the same right now," Tennyson reported. "No—his is changing, mine is staying———"

THE SUM OF THE ANGLES OF A TRIANGLE IS 180°
THIS IS NOT BOTH A CHAIR AND NOT A CHAIR
WHO SHAVES THE SPANISH BARBER, THEN?

"I think it's insane," Mishima said.

"Maybe that's the whole point," said Manuel. "Is it handing out anything but gibberish?"

BECAUSE OF NECESSARY CLIMATE ADJUSTMENTS,
THE FOURTH OF NOVEMBER WILL BE CANCELLED
BETWEEN 32° AND 61° SOUTH LATITUDE

"I'm getting a news report on mine," Guilbert said. "Something about your father, Manuel——"

"Let me see!"

"Here—catch——"

> FEMALE ALPHA SLAIN AT KRUG TOWER SITE.
> POLITICAL EXECUTION, AEP FIGURE CHARGES.
> KRUG ORGANIZATION DENIES CLAIM, ALLEGES

"More nonsense," Manuel said. "I don't think I find these things amusing."

> CLEVELAND LIES BETWEEN NEW YORK AND
> CHICAGO.

"I'm getting the news story on mine, now," said Tennyson. "What do you think it's all about?"

> ALPHA CASSANDRA NUCLEUS DIED INSTANTLY.
> THE FATAL BOLT WAS FIRED BY KRUG'S PRIVATE
> SECRETARY, LEON SPAULDING, 38.

"Never heard of her," said Manuel. "And Spaulding's older than that. He's been working for my father since——"

> CAN THE RHYTHM OF THE UNIVERSE'S
> BREATHING BE DETECTED BY STANDARD
> METABOLIC ANALYSIS?

"Perhaps you should call your father, Manuel," Ssu-ma said. "If there's really trouble——"

"And cancel the shunt? When we're booked in here for a week? I'll find out about it when I come out. If there's anything to find out."

> ACTION FOR DAMAGES HAS BEEN INSTITUTED BY
> LABRADOR TRANSMAT GENERAL, PROPRIETOR OF
> THE DESTROYED ALPHA. EARLY SETTLEMENT IS
> EXPECTED.

"Let's go back to syllogisms," Manuel told the cube he held. "If all men are reptiles, and alpha androids are reptiles——"

> THE SUM OF THE PARTS IS EQUAL TO THE
> SQUARE ON THE HYPOTHESIS

"Listen to what mine says!" shouted Tennyson.

> PANTING WITH DESIRE SHE WAITS FOR THE
> ARRIVAL OF HER COAL-BLACK PARTNER IN
> UNSPEAKABLE SIN

"More!" Guilbert cried. "More!"

> THEREFORE, YOU ARE A REPTILE

"Can we put these things away now?" Manuel asked.

> SHOWING DEEP EMOTION, ALPHA SIEGFRIED
> FILECLERK OF AEP ACCUSED KRUG OF PLANNING A
> PURGE OF ANDROID EQUALITY ADVOCATES.

"I think this really *is* a news broadcast," Cadge Foster murmured. "I've heard of this Fileclerk. He's pushing a constitutional amendment that would open Congress to alphas. And——"

> WEEPING AS THE DEAD FEMALE ALPHA LAY IN
> THE SNOW BESIDE THE MIGHTY BULK OF THE
> TOWER. AN ALMOST HUMAN SHOW OF GRIEF.

"Enough," Manuel said. He began to toss his cube to the floor; but, seeing the message change, he glanced at it once again.

> DO YOU UNDERSTAND YOUR OWN MOTIVES?

"Do you?" he asked. The cube went blank. He dropped it, gratefully. The alpha attendant entered the subchamber and started to disconnect the electrodes.

"You may proceed to the shunt room, gentlemen," said the alpha blandly. "The programming has been completed and the stasis net is ready to receive you."

16   They had moved the chapel to a dome near the outer rim of the service area, in a section where tools were repaired. In less than two hours a flawless transfer had been carried out; inside, the new chapel was indistinguishable from the old. Watchman found a dozen off-duty betas going through a ritual of consecration, with a knot of gammas looking on. No one spoke to him or even looked directly at him; in the presence of an alpha they all scrupulously obeyed the code of social distances. Briefly Watchman prayed beneath the hologram of Krug. His soul was eased some, after a while, though the tensions of his long wintry dialogue with Siegfried Fileclerk would not leave him. His faith had not wavered before Fileclerk's brusque pragmatic arguments, but for a few moments, while they were thrusting and parrying beside the body of Cassandra Nucleus, Watchman had felt a touch of despair. Fileclerk had struck at a vulnerable place: Krug's attitude toward the slaying of the alpha. Krug had seemed so unmoved by it! True, he had looked annoyed— but was it merely the expense, the nuisance of a suit, that bothered him? Watchman had riposted with the proper metaphysical statements, yet he was disturbed. Why had Krug not seemed lessened by the killing? Where was the sense of grace? Where was the hope of redemption? Where was the mercy of the Maker?

The snow was slackening when Watchman left the chapel. Night had come, moonless, the stars unbearably sharp. Savage winds knifed across the flat, treeless expanse of the construction site. Siegfried Fileclerk was gone; so was the corpse of Cassandra Nucleus. Long lines of workers stood in front of the transmat banks, for the shift was changing. Watchman returned to the control center. Euclid Planner, his relief man, was there.

"I'm on," Planner said. "Go. You stayed late tonight."

"A complicated day. You know about the killing?"

"Of course. Labrador Transmat's claimed the body. The lawyers have been all over the place." Planner eased into the linkup seat. "I understand the chapel's been moved, too."

"We had to. That's how it all started—Spaulding got too interested in the chapel. It's a long story."

"I've heard it," Euclid Planner said. He prepared to jack himself into the computer. "There'll be problems out of this. As if there weren't problems enough. Go with Krug, Thor."

"Go with Krug," Watchman murmured. He took his leave. The outbound workers on the transmat line made way for him. He entered the cubicle and let the green glow hurl him to his three-room flat in Stockholm, in the section of the android quarter favored by alphas. The private transmat was a rare privilege, a mark of the esteem in which he was held by Krug. He knew no other android who had one; but Krug had insisted that it was necessary for Watchman to be able to leave his apartment on a moment's notice, and had had the cubicle installed.

He felt drained and weary. He set himself for two hours of sleep, stripped, and lay down.

When he woke he was as tired as before. That was unusual. He decided to give himself another hour of rest, and closed his eyes. But in a short while he was interrupted by the chime of the telephone. Turning toward the screen, he saw Lilith Meson. Sleepily he made the Krug-be-praised sign at her.

She looked somber. She said, "Can you come to the Valhallavägen chapel, Thor?"

"Now?"

"Now, if you can. It's tense here. The Cassandra Nucleus thing—we don't know what to think, Thor."

"Wait," he said. "I'll be there."

He put on a robe, set the transmat coordinates for the Valhallavägen cubicle, and jumped. It was a fifty-meter walk from the cubicle to the chapel; transmats were never installed inside a chapel. A feeble, strained dawn was breaking. In the night there had been a little snow here too, Watchman saw; the remnants of it fleeced the deep window ledges of the old buildings.

The chapel was in a ground-floor flat at the corner. Some fifteen androids were there, all alphas; the lower classes rarely used the Valhallavägen chapel, though they were free to do so. Betas felt uncomfortable in it, and gammas preferred to worship in Gamma Town, far across the city.

Watchman recognized some of the most distinguished members of his kind in the group. He acknowledged the greetings of the poetess Andromeda Quark, the historian Mazda Constructor, the theologian Pontifex Dispatcher, the philosopher Krishna Guardsman, and several others who were among the elite of the elite. All seemed ragged with tension. When Watchman made Krug-be-praised at them, most of them returned the gesture halfheartedly, perfunctorily.

Lilith Meson said, "Forgive us for breaking your rest, Thor. But as you see an important conference is in progress."

"How can I help?"

"You were a witness to the slaying of Alpha Cassandra

Nucleus," Pontifex Dispatcher said. He was heavy, slow-moving, an android of dignified and imposing bearing who came from one of the earliest of Krug's batches. He had played a major role in the shaping of their religion. "We have somewhat of a theological crisis now," Dispatcher went on. "In view of the charges raised by Siegfried Fileclerk——"

"Charges? I hadn't heard."

"Will you tell him?" Pontifex Dispatcher said, glancing at Andromeda Quark.

The poetess, lean and intense, with an elegant reedy voice, said, "Fileclerk held a press conference last night at AEP headquarters. He insisted that the killing of Alpha Nucleus was a politically motivated act carried out at the instigation of——" She could barely say it. "—Krug."

"Slime of the Vat," Watchman muttered. "I begged him not to do that! Fileclerk and I stood talking in the snow half an hour, and I told him—I told him——" He knotted his fingers. "Was there a statement from Krug?"

"A denial," said Mazda Constructor, who for four years had with Watchman's surreptitious aid been secretly compiling the annals of the androids from Krug's dead-storage date file. "An immediate response. The killing was called accidental."

"Who spoke for Krug?" Watchman asked.

"A lawyer. Fearon, the Senator's brother."

"Not Spaulding, eh? Still in shock, I guess. Well, so Fileclerk's been spewing filth. What of it?"

Softly Pontifex Dispatcher said, "At this moment, chapels everywhere are crowded as your brothers and sisters gather to discuss the implications of the killing, Thor. The theological resonances are so terribly complex. If Krug indeed did give the order for the ending of Cassandra Nucleus' life, did he do so in order to show His displeasure over the activities of the Android Equality Party? That is, does He prefer our way to theirs? Or, on the other hand, did He take her life to register His disapproval of the ultimate goals of the AEP—which of course are roughly the same as our own? If the former, our faith is justified. But if the latter, you see, then possibly we have been given a sign that Krug totally rejects the concept of android equality. And then there is no hope for us."

"A bleak prospect," croaked Krishna Guardsman, whose teachings on the relationship of Krug to android were revered by all. "However, I take comfort in the thought that if

Krug struck Alpha Nucleus down to show His dislike of the equality movement, He did so merely to oppose political agitation for equality *now,* and was in effect reminding us to be more patient and await His grace. But——"

"We should also consider a much darker possibility," said Mazda Constructor. "Is Krug capable of evil? Was His role in the killing a wicked one? If so, then perhaps the entire foundation of our creed must be reexamined and even rebuilt, for if Krug can act arbitrarily and immorally, then it follows——"

"Wait! Wait!" called an uneasy voice from the rear of the group. "No such talk as this in a chapel!"

"I speak only figuratively," Mazda Constructor said, "with no blasphemies intended. We are trying to show Alpha Watchman the range of reactions now being demonstrated around the world. Certainly many of us fear that Fileclerk's charges are correct—that Alpha Nucleus was put to death for her political views—and that has led to a consideration of the possibility that Krug has acted improperly. It is being discussed in many chapels at this very moment."

"I think we have to believe," said Krishna Guardsman, "that all acts of Krug are by definition good acts, leading us toward our ultimate redemption. Our problem here is not to justify Krug's deeds but simply to quiet the unhappy suspicions of Krug's motives that this Fileclerk, who is not even a member of our communion, has stirred up in those that are. We——"

"It was a sign from Krug! It was a sign!"

"The Vat giveth, and the Vat taketh away!"

"Fileclerk said that Krug showed no remorse whatever. He——"

"—sent for the lawyers. A civil action——"

"—property damage. A tort——"

"—another test of our faith——"

"—she was our enemy, in any case——"

"—killing one of His children to warn the rest of us? That makes Him a monster!"

"—in the fire of His crucible are we smelted——"

"—revealing an unsuspected capacity for murderous——"

"—sanctity——"

"—redemption——"

"—blood——"

"Listen to me," Thor Watchman cried, amazed and impatient. "Please. Please listen!"

"Let him speak," Mazda Constructor said. "Of all of us, he is closest to Krug. His words have weight."

"I was there," said Watchman. "I saw the whole thing. Before you destroy yourselves with conflicting theologies, *listen*. Krug bears no responsibility for the killing. Spaulding, the secretary, the ectogene, acted on his own. There is no other truth but this." In a cataract of words he told of Spaulding's blustering attempt to force his way into the construction-site chapel, of the ectogene's rising tension in the face of the resistance of the chapel's guards, of his own ruse to draw Saulding away from the chapel, of the unhappy result when Spaulding discovered Krug beset by the AEP agents.

"This is deeply reassuring," said Mazda Constructor when Watchman was done. "We have been misled by Fileclerk's accusations. This is not an issue of Krug's actions at all."

"Except in the deeper sense that Krug must have constructed the entire sequence of events," Krishna Guardsman suggested.

"Can you seriously maintain that His will underlies even the secular events of——" Pontifex Dispatcher began.

Mazda Constructor cut him off. "We can debate the intricacies of His will another time. At present our task is to communicate with all other chapels, to transmit Thor's account of the events. Our people everywhere are in unrest; we must calm them. Thor, will you dictate your statement so that it can be coded and transmitted?"

"Certainly."

Andromeda Quark handed him a message cube. Watchman repeated the story, after first identifying himself, explaining his relation to Krug, and swearing to the authenticity of his version of the events. A terrible fatigue hammered at him from within. How eager these brilliant alphas were, he thought, to engulf everything in a mist of theological disquisition! And how quick to accept Fileclerk's lies. In thousands of chapels just now, hundreds of thousands of devout androids were agonizing over the question of why Krug had allowed an alpha to be shot to death in His arms, whereas if they had merely waited to learn the truth from someone who had been present——

Well, it was not too late to undo the harm. No one's faith in Krug need be shaken by what had occurred.

Andromeda Quark and another female, both members of the Projector caste, were already at work coding the beginning of Watchman's statement for transmission over the broad-band network that linked every chapel to every other one. Watchman remained long enough to hear the first few phrases of his coded statement go forth:

UAA GCG UCG UAA GGG. GGC GGU AAG AAU UAA UAA CUG. CAA CAU AGG CGG GGC GAC ACA. ACC ACC CUC——

"May I go?" he said.

Pontifex Dispatcher gave him the sign of the Blessing of the Vat. Watchman returned it, and, aching, departed.

17 I am Nick Ssu-ma Lloyd Tennyson Cadge Foster Will Mishima Jed Guilbert and maybe Manuel Krug, maybe. Maybe. A week in the shunt room. You come out, you don't even know who you are. Manuel Mishima? Cadge Krug? Anyway you can't be sure. Walk like Lloyd, laugh like Nick, shrug like Will. So on and so on. Everything a blur, a lovely golden haze, sunrise on the desert, like that. Their heads inside your head. Yours inside theirs. Only a week. Maybe that's why I like it so much. To stop being only me for a while. Stop. Stop. Stop. Stop. Open the box. Jump out. Into them.

Full of funny ideas, now.

Bouncing in the stasis net for 168 hours. *Twong* and they split you open and you jump out and look for a place to land, and you land *blong* and you're Nick Ssu-ma, eating roast dog on Taiwan. At dawn in the fog with your aunt. Both naked. She says, touch me here, you do, she laughs, you shiver. Touch me again. Now you laugh, she shivers. Tiny breasts, like Clissa's. This is our wedding night. With this ring I you do wed, Mrs. Ermine Tennyson, silken thighs, mole in small of back. He sleeps with an android, did you know that? Imagine Manuel doing that. He loves her, so he says. Look. Look here, he loves her, it's right here. You find your love where you can find it. An *android?* Well, at least he's not ashamed, or he wouldn't be in here shunting with us. An android. I almost had one once, but I couldn't. At the last moment. What does it feel going into one? Just like anyone else. They aren't plastic, you know. Even though there isn't any hair on it. Sort of incest, though. How? Well, Manuel's father makes the androids, doesn't he, so in a way she's his sister. Very clever. Very *very* clever. Cruel bastard. But you *like* doing it? Of course I do. I'll show you. Here. Here. Shunt and see.

And he jumps across the net and slides into the slot. Who is he? Jed Ssu-ma? Will Tennyson? We are all one. Prowling my memories of Lilith. I don't mind. How can I want to keep secrets? My friends. My true friends.

When I was nine years old I Cadge Foster took a toad and cooked it and ate it

When I was thirteen years old I Will Mishima pissed on the transmat floor because I was scared I wouldn't get there

I Lloyd Tennyson put my finger in my sister's thing she eleven I eight

Jed Guilbert fourteen years old pushed a gamma off a loading rack fell eighty meters died squashed I told my father he slipped

I was ten Nick Ssu-ma saw a male beta at the back window said to mother he watched you and father in bed my father just smiled my mother had them kill him

I Manuel Krug almost thirty years old deceive my wife Clissa with Alpha Lilith Meson whom I love whom I love whom I love of Stockholm she lives on Birger Jarlsgaten Alpha Lilith Meson with breasts and thighs and teeth and elbows with rosy skin whom I love whom I love whom I love no hair on it at all Lilith

And we shunt and shunt and shunt we hang dangling in the stasis net looping easily from mind to mind, floating, changing skulls as often as we please even though it runs up the charges, and I taste Cadge's toad and I wet Will's transmat and I smell Lloyd's sister on my finger and I kill Jed's gamma and I lie about Nick's beta and all of them go to bed with Lilith and they tell me afterward, yes, yes, we really ought to investigate these alpha women, you're a lucky bastard, Manuel, a lucky lucky lucky bastard

And I love her

Whom I love

And I see all the little hates and dirtinesses in their souls, my friends, but I see the strengths too, the good things, for it would be awful if we shunted and saw only the cooked toads and the puddles on the transmat floor. I see secret favors and modesties and loyalties and charities. I see how good my friends really are and I worry and I wonder, what do they see in me, maybe they'll hate me when we come out of this.

We shunt some more. We see what they see in us what we see in us in them.

A week is used up so fast!

Poor Manuel, they say, I never knew it was so bad for him. With all that money and he still feels guilty because he's got nothing to do with his life. Find a cause, Manuel. Find a cause. Find a cause. I tell them I'm trying. I'm looking.

They say what about the androids?

Should I? What would my father say? If he doesn't approve.

Don't worry about him. Do what you think is right. Clissa is in favor of equal rights for androids. If he blows up, let Clissa talk to him before you do. Why should he blow up? He's made his pile out of androids, now he can afford to let them vote. I bet they'd vote for him. You know all the androids are in love with your father? Yes. Sometimes I think it must be almost like a religion with them. The religion of Krug. Well it makes a sort of sense to worship your creator. Don't laugh. But I have to laugh. It's crazy androids bowing down to my father. To idols of him, I bet?

You're getting off the track, Manuel. If it worries you that you aren't doing anything important, become a crusader. Equal rights for androids. Up the androids! You bet, up the androids! That's unworthy of you. You're probably right.

We hear the gongs and we know our time is up.

We drop out of the net. We slide into our own heads. I'm told they do this part very, very, very carefully, getting everybody into his own head.

As far as I know I am Manuel Krug.

They ease us out. There is a re-adaptation chamber on the far side of the net. We sit around for three, four hours, getting used to being individuals again. We look at each other strangely. Mostly we don't look at each other at all. Someone has been laughing too much with my mouth.

In the re-adaptation chamber, they have more of those new toys, the blunt-edged cubes. Mine sends me a series of messages.

THE TIME IS NOW 0900 HOURS IN KARACHI
IS THIS THE FIRST TIME YOU'VE MET YOURSELF?
YOUR FATHER PROBABLY WOULD LIKE TO HEAR FROM YOU
ONLY THE TRUE ANSWERS ARE FALSE
THEY HAVE SETTLED THE CASE OUT OF COURT
ONCE WE WERE ALL A GREAT DEAL WISER

The machine bores and frightens me. I hurl it aside. I am almost certain that I am neither Cadge Foster nor Lloyd Tennyson, but I worry about the toad. I will go to Lilith as soon as I leave here. Perhaps I should speak to Clissa first. My father must be at his tower. How is that great erection coming along? Will he soon have messages from the stars to read on the winter nights?

"Gentlemen, we hope you'll shortly return," the smiling alpha tells us.

We go out. I am they. They are I. We are we.

We clasp hands solemnly. We head for the transmats. Virtuously, dutifully, I go to Clissa.

18

The lawyers met three times in the week following the destruction of Alpha Cassandra Nucleus. The first meeting was held in the offices of Krug Enterprises; the second, in the headquarters of Labrador Transmat General; the third, in the board room of the Chase/Krug Building, Fairbanks. The Labrador Transmat people had suggested that Krug simply supply a new alpha, paying the costs of training her. Lou Fearon, acting as counsel for Krug, objected that this might expose his client to expenses of an amount that could not be determined in advance. Labrador Transmat recognized the justice of this position and a compromise was reached under the terms of which Krug Enterprises transferred to Labrador Transmat the title to one Duluth alpha female, untrained, and agreed to pay the costs of her training to a maximum of $10,000 fissionable. The total time consumed in these three meetings was two hours and twenty-one minutes. A contract was drawn and the civil suit was voided. Leon Spaulding initialed the agreement on behalf of Krug, who had gone to Luna to inspect a newly completed gravity pond for hemiplegics at Krug Medical Center in the Sea of Moscow.

19   November 17, 2218.

A delicate tracery of windblown snow lightly covers the area around Krug's tower; beyond the construction zone, the snow lies deeply mounded, iron-hard. A dry wind buffets the tower. Well ahead of schedule, it has topped 500 meters, and now is overwhelming in its crystalline splendor.

The eight-sided base yields imperceptibly to the planes of the four-sided trunk. The tower is haloed in light: sunglow rebounds from its flanks, strikes the surrounding fields of snow, leaps up again to kiss the glassy walls, is hurled groundward once more. Albedo reigns here; brightness is all.

The lower two-thirds of the existing structure has now been divided into floors, and, as the androids assembling the skin of the tower pile the glass blocks ever higher, those responsible for the interior work follow them up.

Installation of the tachyon-beam system has begun. Five giant rods of brilliant red copper, sixty centimeters thick and hundreds of meters long, will form a quintuple spine, rising inside vertical service cores that span close to half the tower's height, and the lower sectitons of these great busbars are going into place now. A circular jacket of translucent glastic a meter in diameter forms the housing for each bar. The workmen slide forty-meter lengths of copper into these jackets, then cunningly fuse them end to end with quick dazzling bursts of power from the eye of a welding laser. Elsewhere in the building, hundreds of electricians supervise the spraying of conductive filaments into the tower's gleaming inner walls, and squadrons of mechanics install conduits, waveguides, frequency converters, fluxmeters, optical guidance accessories, focal plane locators, neutron activation foils, Mössbauer absorbers, multi-channel pulse height analyzers, nuclear amplifiers, voltage converters, cryostats, transponders, resistance bridges, prisms, torsion testers, sensor clusters, degaussers, collimators, magnetic resonance cells, thermocouple amplifiers, accelerator reflectors, proton accumulators, and much more, everything carefully computer-tagged in advance with its floor level and flow-chart designation. Sending messages to the stars by tachyon beam is not a simple project.

The tower is already a thing of unparalleled splendor,

starkly supple, spectacularly spearing the sky. Visitors drive many kilometers out into the tundra to get the best view of it, for at close range it cannot properly be appreciated. Krug enjoys reminding his guests, though, that what they see today is merely the bottom third of the ultimate structure. To visualize the final building, one must imagine a second tower of the same size piled atop this November spire, and then a third one set atop that. The mind rebels. The image will not come. Instead, one can bring into view only the picture of a slender, impossibly attenuated, terribly frail needle of glass that hangs in the sky, seeking to put down roots, and, failing, topples and topples and topples, falling like Lucifer through all one long day, and shatters with a faint tinkle in the icy air.

20   "A new signal," Vargas said. "Slightly different. We began getting it last night."

"Wait right there," said Krug. "I'm coming."

He was in New York. Almost immediately he was in Vargas' Antarctic observatory, high on the polar plateau at a point equidistant between the Pole itself and the resorts of the Knox Coast. There were those who said that the transmat era had cheapened life in one way while enriching it in another: the theta force allowed one to flick blithely from Africa to Australia to Mexico to Siberia in a moment's merry dance, but it robbed one of any true sense of place and transition, of any feel for planetary geography. It transformed Earth into a single infinitely extended transmat cubicle. Krug had often resolved to take a leisurely tour of the world from the air, and see desert shading into prairie, forest into bare tundra, mountains into plains. But he had not managed to find the time.

The observatory was a series of pleasant glossy domes sitting atop an ice-sheet two and a half kilometers thick. Tunnels in the ice linked dome to dome, and gave access also to the outlying apparatus: the vast dish of a radio telescope's parabolic antenna, the metal grid of an X-ray receiver, the burnished mirror that picked up relayed transmissions from the orbiting observatory high above the South Pole, the short, stocky multiple-diffraction optical telescope, the three golden spikes of the hydrogen antenna, the fluttering airborne webwork of a polyradar system, and the rest of the devices with which the astronomers here kept watch on the universe. Instead of using refrigeration tapes to insure that the ice would not melt beneath the buildings, they had employed individual heat-exchange plaques for every structure, so that each building was a little island on the great glacier.

In the main building things hummed and clicked and flashed. Krug did not understand much about this equipment, but it seemed properly scientific to him. Technicians ran eagerly about; an alpha high on a dizzying catwalk called numbers to three betas far below; periodically there was a crimson surge of energy within a glass helix twenty meters long, and numbers leaped on a green and red counting mechanism at every discharge.

Vargas said, "Watch the radon coil. It's registering the impulses that we're getting right now. Here—a new cycle is starting—you see?"

Krug contemplated the pattern of surges.

```
        * *
    *  *  *  *  *
        *
        *  *
    *  *  *
        *
        *  *
        *
```

"That's it," Vargas said. "Now a six-second pause, and then it starts again."

"2-5-1, 2-3-1, 2-1," Krug said. "And it used to be 2-4-1, 2-5-1, 3-1. So they've dropped the 4-group altogether, they've moved the 5-group to the front of the cycle, they've completed the 3-group, they've added a pulse in the final group—damn, Vargas, where's the sense? What's the significance?"

"We don't detect any more content in this message than in the last. They've both got the same basic structure. Just a minor rearrangement——"

'It's got to *mean* something!"

"Perhaps it does."

"How can we find out?"

"We'll ask them," Vargas said. "Soon. Through your tower."

Krug's shoulders slumped. He leaned forward, gripping the smooth cool green handles of some incomprehensible device jutting from the wall. "These messages are 300 years old," he said blackly. "If this planet of theirs is like you tell me it is, that's like 300 centuries here. More. They won't even know about the messages their ancestors sent out. They'll be mutated out of all recognition."

"No. There has to be continuity. They couldn't have reached a technological level that would allow them to send transgalactic messages at all unless they were able to retain the achievements of earlier generations."

Krug swung round. "You know something? This planetary nebula, this blue sun—I still don't believe it could have intelligent beings living there. Any kind of life—no! Listen, blue suns don't last long, Vargas. It takes millions of years for the surface of a planet just to cool enough to get solid. There isn't that much time, a blue sun. Any planets it's got, they're still molten. You want me to believe signals coming from people who live on a fireball?"

Vargas said quietly, "Those signals come from NGC 7293, the planetary nebula in Aquarius."

"For sure?"

"For sure. I can show you all the data."

"Never mind. But how, a fireball?"

"It's not necessarily a fireball. Maybe some planets cool faster than others. We can't be sure how long it takes them to cool. We don't know how far the home world of the message-senders is from that sun. We've got models showing the theoretical possibility that a planet can cool fast enough, even with a blue sun, to allow——"

"It's a fireball, that planet," said Krug sullenly.

Defensive now, Vargas said, "Perhaps. Perhaps not. Even if it is: must all life-forms live on a solid-surface planet? Can't you conceive a civilization of high-temperature entities evolving on a world that hasn't cooled yet? If——"

Krug snorted in disgust. "Sending signals with machines made out of molten steel?"

"The signals don't have to be mechanical in origin. Suppose they can manipulate the molecular structure of——"

"You talk fairy tales to me, doctor. I go to a scientist, I get fairy tales!"

"At the moment fairy tales are the only way of accounting for the data," Vargas said.

"You know there's got to be a better way!"

"All I know is that we're getting signals, and they undoubtedly come from this planetary nebula. I know it isn't plausible. The universe doesn't have to seem plausible to us all the time. Its phenomena don't have to be readily explicable. Transmat wouldn't be plausible to an eighteenth-century scientist. We see the data as best we can, and we try to account for it, and sometimes we do some wild guessing because the data we're getting doesn't seem to make sense, but——"

"The universe doesn't cheat," Krug said. "The universe plays fair!"

Vargas smiled. "No doubt it does. But we need more data before we can explain NGC 7293. Meanwhile we make do with fairy tales."

Krug nodded. He closed his eyes and fondled dials and meters, while within him a monstrous raging impatience sizzled and blazed and bubbled. *Hey, you star people! Hey, you, sending those pulses! Who are you? What are you? Where are you? By damn, I want to know!*

What are you trying to tell us, you?

Who are you looking for?

What's it all mean? Suppose I die before I find out!

"You know what I want?" Krug said suddenly. "To go outside, to that radio telescope of yours. And climb up into the big dish. And cup my hands and shout at those bastards with the numbers. What's the signal now? 2-5-1, 2-3-1, 2-1? It drives me crazy. We ought to answer them right now. Send some numbers: 4-10-2, 4-6-2, 4-2. Just to show them we're here. Just to let them know."

"By radio transmission?" Vargas said. "It'll take 300 years. The tower will be finished soon."

"Soon, sure. Soon. You ought to see it. Come see, next week. They're putting the gadgets in it now. We'll be talking to the bastards soon."

"Would you like to hear the audio signal coming in, the new one?"

"Sure."

Vargas touched a switch. From speakers in the laboratory wall came a dry cold hiss, the sound of space, the voice of the dark abyss. It was a sound like a cast-off snakeskin. Overriding that withered sound, seconds later, came sweet upper-frequency tones. *Pleep pleep.* Pause. *Pleep pleep pleep pleep pleep.* Pause. *Pleep.* Pause. Pause. *Pleep pleep.* Pause. *Pleep pleep pleep.* Pause. *Pleep.* Pause. Pause. *Pleep pleep.* Pause. *Pleep.* Silence. And then again, *pleep pleep,* the new cycle beginning.

"Beautiful," Krug whispered. "The music of the spheres. Oh, you mysterious bastards! Look, doctor, you come see the tower next week, next—oh, Tuesday. I'll have Spaulding call you. You'll be amazed. And listen, anything else new comes up, another change in the signal, I want to hear right away."

Pleep pleep pleep.

He headed for the transmat.

Pleep.

Krug leaped northward along the meridian, following the line of 90° E., looped the North Pole, and emerged beside his tower. He had sped from icy plateau to icy plateau, from the world's bottom to its top, from late spring to early winter, from day to night. Androids were busy everywhere. The tower seemed to have grown fifty meters since yesterday's visit. The sky was ablaze with the light of reflector plates. The song of NGC 7293 sang seductively in Krug's mind. *Pleep pleep. Pleep.*

He found Thor Watchman in the control center, jacked in. The alpha, unaware of Krug's presence, seemed lost in a drugged dream, climbing the precipices of some distant interface. An awed beta offered to cut into the circuit and tell Watchman, via the computer, that Krug had arrived. "No," Krug said. "He's busy. Don't bother him." *Pleep pleep pleep pleep pleep.* He stood for a few moments, watching the play of expressions on Watchman's tranquil face. What was passing through the alpha's mind now? Freight invoices, transmat manifests, welding cues, weather reports, cost estimates, stress factors, personnel data? Krug felt pride geysering in his soul. Why not? He had plenty to be proud of. He had built the androids, and the androids were building the tower, and soon man's voice would go forth to the stars——

Pleep pleep pleep. Pleep.

Affectionately, a little surprised at himself, he put his hands to Thor Watchman's broad shoulders in a quick embrace. Then he went out. He stood in the frigid blackness a short while, surveying the frenzied activity at every level of the tower. On top they were putting new blocks in place with flawless rhythm. Inside, the tiny figures were hauling neutrino-sheathing around, joining lengths of copper cable, installing floors, carrying the heat-cool-power-light system higher and higher. Through the night came a steady pulsation of sound, all the noises of construction blending into a single cosmic rhythm, a deep booming hum with regular soaring climaxes. The two sounds, the inner and the outer one, met in Krug's mind, *boom* and *pleep, boom* and *pleep, boom* and *pleep.*

He walked toward the transmats, ignoring the knives of the Arctic wind.

Not bad for a poor man without much education, he told himself. This tower. These androids. Everything. He thought of the Krug of forty-five years ago, the Krug growing up miserable in a town in Illinois with grass in the middle of the streets. He hadn't dreamed much about sending messages to the stars then. He just wanted to make something out of himself. He wasn't anything, yet. Some Krug! Ignorant. Skinny. Pimpled. Sometimes on holocasts he heard people saying that mankind had entered a new golden age, with population down, social and racial tensions forgotten, a horde of servomechanisms to do all the dirty work. Yes. Yes. Fine. But even in a golden age somebody has to be on the bottom. Krug was. Father dead when he was five. Mother hooked on floaters, sensory scramblers, any kind of dream-pills. They got a little money, not much, from a welfare foundation. Robots? Robots were for other people. Half the time the data terminal, even, was shut off for unpaid bills. He never went through a transmat until he was nineteen. Never even left Illinois. He remembered himself: sullen, withdrawn, squint-eyed, sometimes going a week or two without speaking to anyone. He didn't read. He didn't play games. He dreamed a lot, though. He slid through school in a haze of rage, learning nothing. Slowly coming out of it when he was fifteen, propelled by that same rage, turning it suddenly outward instead of letting it fester within: *I show you what I can do, I get even with you all!* Self-programming his education. Servotechnology. Chemistry. He didn't learn basic science; he learned ways of putting things together. Sleep? Who needed sleep? Study. Study. Sweat. Build. A remarkable intuitive grasp of the structure of things, they said was what he had. He found a backer in Chicago. The age of private capitalism was supposed to be dead; so was the age of free-lance invention. He built a better robot, anyway. Krug smiled, remembering: the transmat hop to New York, the conferences, the lawyers. And money in the bank. The new Thomas

Edison. He was nineteen. He stocked his laboratory with equipment and looked for grander projects. At twenty-two, he started to create the androids. Took awhile. Somewhere in those years, the probes began coming back from the near stars, empty. No advanced life-forms out there. He was secure enough now to divert some attention from business, to allow himself the luxury of wondering about man's place in the cosmos. He pondered. He quarreled with the popular theories of the uniqueness of man. Went on toiling, though, diddling with the nucleic acid, blending, hovering over centrifuges, straining his eyes, dipping his hands deep into tubs of slime, hooking together the protein chains, getting measurably closer to success. How can man be alone in the universe if one man himself can make life? Look how easy it is! I'm doing it: am I God? The vats seethed. Purple, green, gold, red, blue. And eventually life came forth. Androids shakily rising from the foaming chemicals. Fame. Money. Power. A wife; a son; a corporate empire. Properties on three worlds, five moons. Women, all he wanted. He had grown up to live his own adolescent fantasies. Krug smiled. The young skinny pimpled Krug was still here within this stocky man, angry, defiant, burning. You showed them, eh? You showed them! And now you'll reach the people in the stars. *Pleep pleep pleep. Boom.* The voice of Krug spanning the light-years. "Hello? Hello? Hello, you! This is Simeon Krug!" In retrospect he saw his whole life as a single shaped process, trending without detour or interruption toward this one goal. If he had not churned with intense, unfocused ambitions, there would have been no androids. Without his androids, there would not have been sufficient skilled labor to build the tower. Without his tower——

He entered the nearest transmat cubicle and set coordinates in a casual way, letting his fingers idly choose his destination. He stepped through the field and found himself in the California home of his son Manuel.

He hadn't planned to go there. He stood blinking in afternoon sunlight, shivering as a sudden wave of warmth struck his Arctic-tuned skin. Beneath his feet was a shining floor of dark red stone; the walls that rose on either side of him were coruscating swirls of light bursting from polyphase projectors mounted in the foundation; above him was no roof, only a repellor field set for the blue end of the spectrum, through which there dangled the fruit-laden branches of some tree with feathery gray-green leaves. He could hear the roar of the surf. Half a dozen household androids, going about their domestic chores, gaped at him. He caught their awed whispers: *"Krug . . . Krug . . ."*

Clissa appeared. She wore a misty green wrap that revealed her small high breasts, her sharp-boned hips, her narrow shoulders. "You didn't tell me you were——"

"I didn't know I was."

"I would have had something ready!"

"Don't feel I need anything special. I'm just dropping in. Is Manuel——"

"He isn't here."

"No. Where?"

Clissa shrugged. "Out. Business, I guess. Not due back until dinnertime. Can I get you——"

"No. No. What a fine house you have, Clissa. Warm. Real. You and Manuel must be very happy here." He eyed her slender form. "It's such a good place for having children, too. The beach—the sun—the trees——"

An android brought two mirror-bright chairs, expanding and socketing them with a swift deft twinkle of his hands. Another turned on the waterfall on the inland side of the house. A third lit an aroma spike, and the odor of cloves and cinnamon unfolded in the courtyard. A fourth offered Krug a tray of milky-looking sweets. He shook his head. He remained standing. So did Clissa. She looked uncomfortable.

She said, "We're still newlyweds, you know. We can wait awhile for children."

"Two years, isn't it, you've been married? A long honeymoon!"

"Well——"

"At least get your certificate. You could start thinking about children. I mean, it's time you—time I—a grandchild——"

She held forth the tray of sweets. Her face was pale; her eyes were like opals in a frosty mask. He shook his head again.

He said, "The androids do all the work of raising the kid, anyhow. And if you don't want to get yourself stretched, you could have it ectogenetically, so——"

"Please?" she said softly. "We've talked about this before. I'm so tired today."

"I'm sorry." He cursed himself for pushing her too hard. His old mistake; subtlety was not his chief skill. "You're feeling all right?"

"Just fatigue," she said, not convincing him. She seemed to make an effort to show more energy. She gestured, and one of her betas began to assemble a stack of glittering metal hoops that rotated mysteriously about some hidden axis; a new sculpture, Krug thought. A second android adjusted the walls, and he and Clissa were bathed in a cone of warm amber light. Music trembled in the air, coming from a cloud of tiny glittering speakers that floated, fine as dust, into the courtyard. Clissa said, too loudly, "How is your tower going?"

"Beautiful. Beautiful. You should see it."

"Perhaps I'll come, next week. If it isn't too cold there. Are you up to 500 meters yet?"

"Past it. Rising all the time. Only not fast enough. I ache to see it finished, Clissa. To be able to use it. I'm so full of impatiences I'm sick with them."

"You do look a little strained today," she said. "Flushed, excited. You ought to slow down, sometimes."

"Me? Slow? Why? Am I so old?" He realized he was barking at her. He said more temperately, "Look, maybe you're right. I don't know. I better leave now. I don't mean to be a bother for you. I just felt like a little visit." *Pleep pleep. Boom.* "You tell Manuel it was nothing special, yes? To say hello. When did I see him, anyway? Two weeks, three? Not since right after he came out of that shunt-room business. A man can visit his son sometimes." He reached out impulsively, drew her to him, hugged her lightly. He felt like a bear hugging a forest sprite. Her skin was cold through that misty wrap. She was all bones. He could snap her in half with a quick yank. What did she weigh, fifty kilos? Less? A child's body. Maybe she couldn't even have children. Krug found himself trying to imagine Manuel in bed with her, and pushed the thought away, appalled. He kissed her chilly cheek. "You take care," he said. "So will I. We both take care, get lots of rest. You say hello to Manuel for me."

He rushed to the transmat. Where to next? Krug felt feverish. His cheeks were flaming. He was adrift, floating on the broad bosom of the sea. Coordinates tumbled across his mind; frantic, he seized one set, fed it to the machine. *Pleep. Pleep. Pleep.* The scaly hiss of amplified star-noise nibbled at his brain. 2-5-1, 2-3-1, 2-1. Hello? Hello? The theta force devoured him.

It brought him forth inside an immense musty cavern.

There was a roof, dozens of dim kilometers overhead. There were walls, metallic, reflective, yellow-brown, curving toward some distant place of union. Harsh lights glared and flickered. Sharp-edged shadows stained the air. Construction noises sounded: crash, thunk, ping, bavoom. The place was full of busy androids. They clustered close to him, glistening with awe, nudging, whispering: *"Krug ... Krug ... Krug ..."* Why do androids always look at me that way? He scowled at them. He knew that perspiration was bursting from every pore. His legs were unsteady. Ask Spaulding for a coolpill: but Spaulding was elsewhere. Krug was jumping solo today.

An alpha loomed before him. "We were not led to anticipate the pleasure of this visit, Mr. Krug."

"A whim. Simply passing through, looking in. Pardon me—your name——?"

"Romulus Fusion, sir."

"How big a work-force here, Alpha Fusion?"

"Seven hundred betas, sir, and nine thousand gammas. The alpha staff is quite small; we rely on sensors for most supervisory functions. Shall I show you around? Would you like to see the lunar runabouts? The Jupiter modules? The starship, perhaps?"

The starship. The starship. Krug comprehended. He was in Denver, at Krug Enterprises' main North American vehicle-assembly center. In this spacious catacomb many types of transportation devices were manufactured, covering all needs that the transmat could not meet: ocean-crawlers, sliders for surface travel, stratospheric gliders, heavy-duty power-haulers, immersion modules for use on high-pressure worlds, ion-drive systemships for short-hop spacing, interstellar probes, gravity boxes, skydivers, minirailers, sunscoops. Here, too, for the past seven years, a picked technical staff had been building the prototype of the first manned stargoing vessel. Lately, since the commencement of the tower, the starship had become a stepchild among Krug's projects.

"The starship," Krug said. "Yes. Please. Let's see it."

Aisles of betas opened for him as Romulus Fusion ushered him toward a small teardrop-shaped slider. With the alpha at the controls they slipped noiselessly along the floor of the plant, past racks of half-finished vehicles of every description, and came at length to a ramp leading to yet a lower level of this subterranean workshop. Down they went. The slider halted. They got out.

"This," said Romulus Fusion.

Krug beheld a curious vehicle a hundred meters long, with

flaring vanes running from its needle-sharp nose to its squat, aggressive-looking tail. The dark red hull seemed to have been fashioned from conglomerated rubble; its texture was rough and knobby. No vision accesses were in evidence. The mass-ejectors were conventional in form, rectangular slots opening along the rear.

Romulus Fusion said, "It will be ready for flight-testing in three months. We estimate an acceleration capability of a constant 2.4 g, which of course will bring the vessel rapidly to a velocity not far short of that of light. Will you go inside?"

Krug nodded. Within, the ship seemed comfortable and not very unusual; he saw a control center, a recreation area, a power compartment, and other features that would have been standard on any contemporary systemgoing ship. "It can accommodate a crew of eight," the alpha told him. "In flight, an automatic deflector field surrounds the ship to ward off all oncoming free-floating particles, which of course could be enormously destructive at such velocities. The ship is totally self-programming; it needs no supervision. These are the personnel containers." Romulus Fusion indicated four double rows of black glass-faced freezer units, each two and a half meters long and a meter wide, mounted against a wall. "They employ conventional life-suspension technology," he said. "The ship's control system, at a signal from the crew or from a ground station, will automatically begin pumping the high-density coolant fluid into the containers, lowering the body temperature of personnel to the desired degree. They will then make the journey submerged in cold fluid, serving the double purpose of slowing life-processes and insulating the crew against the effects of steady acceleration. Reversal of the life-suspension is just as simple. A maximum deepsleep period of forty years is planned; in the event of longer voyages, the crew will be awakened at forty-year intervals, put through an exercise program similar to that used in the training of new androids, and restored to the containers after a brief waking interval. In this way a voyage of virtually infinite length can be managed by the same crew."

"How long," Krug asked, "would it take this ship to reach a star 300 light-years away?"

"Including the time needed for building up to maximum velocity, and the time required for deceleration," replied Romulus Fusion, "I'd estimate roughly 620 years. Allowing for the expected relativistic time-dilation effects, apparent elapsed time aboard ship should be no more than 20 or 25 years, which means the entire voyage could be accomplished within the span of a single deepsleep period for the crew."

Krug grunted. That was fine for the crew; but if he sent the starship off to NGC 7293 next spring, it would return to Earth in the thirty-fifth century. He would not be here to greet it. Yet he saw no alternative.

He said, "It'll fly by February?"

"Yes."

"Good. Start picking a crew: two alphas, two betas, four gammas. They'll blast off for a system of my choosing early in '19."

"As you instruct, sir."

They left the ship. Krug ran his hands over its pebbled hull. His infatuation with the tachyon-beam tower had kept him from following the progress of the work here; he regretted that now. They had done a magnificent job. And, he saw, his assault on the stars would have to be a two-pronged effort. When the tower was complete, he could attempt to open realtime communication with the beings whom Vargas insisted lived in NGC 7293; meanwhile, his android-staffed starship would be embarked on its slow journey outward. What would he send aboard it? The full record of man's accomplishments—yes, cubes galore, whole libraries, the entire musical repertoire, a hundred high-redundancy information systems. Make that crew four alphas, four betas; they'd need to be masters of communications techniques. While they slept, he would beam tachyon-borne messages to them from Earth, detailing the knowledge that he expected to gain from the tower's contacts with the star-folk; perhaps, by the time the starship reached its destination in the year 2850 or so, it would have become possible to give its crew access to dictionaries of the language of the race it was to visit. Whole encyclopedias, even. Annals of six centuries of tachyon-beam contact between Earthmen and the inhabitants of NGC 7293!

Krug clapped Romulus Fusion's shoulder. "Good work. You'll hear from me. Where's the transmat?"

"This way, sir."

Pleep. Pleep. Pleep.

Krug jumped back to the tower site.

Thor Watchman was no longer jacked into the master control center's computer. Krug found him inside the tower, on the fourth level up, overseeing the installation of a row of devices that looked like globes of butter mounted on a beaded glass string.

"What are these?" Krug demanded.

Watchman looked surprised to see his master appear so abruptly. "Circuitbreakers," he said, making a quick recovery. "In case of excessive positron flow——"

"All right. You know where I've been, Thor? Denver. Denver. I've seen the starship. I didn't realize it: they've got it practically finished. Effective right now we're going to tie it into our project sequence."

"Sir?"

"Alpha Romulus Fusion is in charge out there. He's going to pick a crew, four alphas, four betas. We'll send them off next spring under life-suspension, coldsleep. Right after we send our first signals to NGC 7293. Get in touch with him, coordinate the timing, yes? Oh—and another thing. Even though we're ahead of schedule here, it still isn't going fast enough to please me." *Boom. Boom.* The planetary nebula NGC 7293 sizzled and flared behind Krug's forehead. The heat of his skin evaporated his sweat as fast as it could burst from his pores. Getting too excited, he told himself. "When you finish work tonight, Thor, draw up a personnel requisition increasing the work crews by 50%. Send it to Spaulding. You need more alphas, don't hesitate. Ask. Hire. Spend. Whatever." *Boom.* "I want the entire construction scheme reprogrammed. Completion date three months tighter than the one we have now. Got it?"

Watchman seemed a little dazed. "Yes, Mr. Krug," he said faintly.

"Good. Yes. Good. Keep up the good work, Thor. Can't tell you how proud. How happy." *Boom. Boom. Boom. Pleep. Boom.* "We'll get you every skilled beta in the Western Hemisphere, if necessary. Eastern. Everywhere. Tower's got to be finished!" *Boom.* "Time! Time! Never enough time!"

Krug rushed away. Outside, in the cold night air, some of the frenzy left him. He stood quietly for a moment, savoring the sleek glimering beauty of the tower, aglow against the black backdrop of the unlit tundra. He looked up. He saw the stars. He clenched his fist and shook it.

Krug! Krug! Krug! Krug!

Boom.

Into the transmat. Coordinates: Uganda. By the lake.

Quenelle, waiting. Soft body, big breasts, thighs parted, belly heaving. Yes. Yes. Yes. Yes. 2-5-1, 2-3-1, 2-1. Krug leaped across the world.

21

In the glare of crisp white winter sunlight a dozen alphas paraded solemnly across the broad plaza that fell, like a giant terraced apron, from the lap of the World Congress building in Geneva. Each of the alphas carried a demonstration-spool; each wore the emblem of the Android Equality Party. Security robots were stationed in the corners of the plaza; the snubheaded black machines would roll instantly forward, spewing immobilizing stasis-tape, if the demonstrators deviated in any way from the agitation program they had filed with the Congressional doorkeeper. But the AEP people were not likely to do anything unexpected. They simply crossed the plaza again and again, marching neither too rigidly nor too slackly, keeping their eyes on the holovision hovercameras above them. Periodically, at a signal from their leader, Siegfried Fileclerk, one of the demonstrators would activate the circuitry of his demonstration-spool. From the nozzle of the spool a cloud of dense blue vapor would spurt upward to a height of perhaps twenty meters and remain there, tightly coalesced by kinesis-linkage into a spherical cloud, while a message imprinted in large and vivid golden letters emerged and moved slowly along its circumference. When the words had traveled the full 360°, the cloud would dissipate, and only after the last strands of it had vanished from the air would Fileclerk signal for the next demonstrator to send up a statement.

Though Congress had been in session for some weeks now, it was improbable that any of the delegates inside the handsome building were paying attention to the demonstration. They had seen such demonstrations before. The purpose of the AEP group was merely to have the holovision people pick up and relay to viewers all over the world, in the name of news coverage, such slogans as these:

ANDROID EQUALITY NOW!
FORTY YEARS OF SLAVERY IS ENOUGH!
DID CASSANDRA NUCLEUS DIE IN VAIN?

WE APPEAL TO THE CONSCIENCES OF HUMANITY
ACTION! FREEDOM! ACTION!
ADMIT ANDROIDS TO CONGRESS—NOW!
THE TIME HAS COME!
IF YOU PRICK US, DO WE NOT BLEED?

22   Thor Watchman knelt beside Lilith Meson
in the Valhallavägen chapel. It was the day of the Ceremony
of the Opening of the Vat; nine alphas were present, with
Mazda Constructor, who belonged to the Transcender caste,
officiating. A couple of betas had been persuaded to attend,
since Yielders were needed. This was not a ceremony that
required the participation of a Preserver, and so Watchman
played no part in it; he merely repeated to himself the
invocations of the celebrants.

The hologram of Krug above the altar glistened and
throbbed. The triplets of the genetic code around the walls
seemed to melt and swirl as the ritual neared its climax. The
scent of hydrogen was in the air. Mazda Constructor's gestures, always noble and impressive, grew more broad, more
all-encompassing.

"AUU GAU GGU GCU," he called.

"Harmony!" sang the first Yielder.

"Unity!" sang the second.

"Perception," Lilith said.

"CAC CGC CCC CUC," chanted Mazda Constructor.

"Harmony!"

"Unity!"

"Passion," said Lilith.

"UAA UGA UCA UUA," the Transcender cried.

"Harmony!"

"Unity!"

"Purpose," Lilith said, and the ceremony was over. Mazda
Constructor stepped down, flushed and weary. Lilith lightly
touched his hand. The betas, looking grateful to be excused,
slipped out the rear way. Watchman rose. He saw Andromeda Quark in the far corner, the dimmest corner, whispering
some private devotion of the Projector caste. She seemed to
see no one else.

"Shall we go?" Watchman said to Lilith. "I'll see you home."

"Kind of you," she said. Her part in the ceremony appeared to have left her aglow; her eyes were unnaturally bright, her breasts were heaving beneath her thin wrap, her nostrils were flared. He escorted her to the street.

As they walked toward the nearby transmat he said, "Did the personnel requisition reach your office?"

"Yesterday. With a memo from Spaulding telling me to send out a hiring call at once. Where am I going to find that many skilled betas, Thor? What's going on?"

"What's going on is that Krug is pushing us hard. He's obsessed with finishing the tower."

"That's nothing new," Lilith said.

"It's getting worse. Day by day the impatience grows, deepens, becomes more intense, like a sickness inside him. Maybe if I were human I'd understand a drive like that. He comes to the tower two, three times a day, now. Counts the levels. Counts the newly raised blocks. Hounds the tachyon people, telling them to get their machines hooked up faster. He's starting to look like something wild: sweating, excited, stumbling over his own words. Now he's padding the work crews—tossing millions of dollars more into the job. For what? For what? And then this starship thing. I talked to Denver yesterday. Do you know, Lilith, he ignored that plant all last year, and now he's there once a day? The starship has to be ready for an interstellar voyage within three months. Android crew. He's sending androids."

"Where?"

"Three hundred light-years away."

"He won't ask you to go, will he? Me?"

"Four alphas, four betas," Watchman said. "I haven't been told who's being considered. If he lets Spaulding decide, I'm finished. Krug preserve us from having to go." The irony of his prayer struck him belatedly, and he laughed, a thin, dark chuckle. "Yes. Krug preserve us!"

They reached the transmat. Watchman began to set coordinates.

"Will you come up for awhile?" Lilith asked.

"Glad to."

They stepped into the green glow together.

Her flat was smaller than his, just a bedroom, a combination sitting-room/dining-room/kitchen, and a sort of large foyer-cum-closet. It was possible to see where a much larger apartment had been divided to form several smaller ones, suitable for androids. The building was similar to the one where he lived: old, well-worn, somehow warm of soul. Nineteenth-century, he guessed, although Lilith's furnishings, reflecting the force of her personality, were distinctly contemporary, leaning heavily to floor-mounted projections and tiny, delicate, free-floating art objects. Watchman had never been at her place before, though they were close neighbors in Stockholm. Androids, even alphas, did not socialize much in one another's homes; the chapels served as meeting-places for most occasions. Those who were outside the communion gathered in AEP offices, or clung to their solitude.

He dropped into a springy, comfortable chair. "Care to corrode your mind?" Lilith asked. "I can offer all kinds of friendly substances. Weeds? Floaters? Scramblers? Even alcohol—liqueurs, brandies, whiskeys."

"You're well stocked with pollutions."

"Manuel comes here often. I must play hostess for him. What will you have?"

"Nothing," he said. "I'm not really fond of corrosion."

She laughed and moved toward the doppler. Quickly it consumed her wrap. Under it she wore nothing but a thermal spray, light green and lovely against her pale scarlet skin; it covered her from breasts to thighs, protecting her against Stockholm's December winds. A different setting of the doppler and that was gone too. She kept her sandals on.

Sinking down easily to the floor, she sat crosslegged before him and toyed with the dials of her wall-projections; textures ebbed and flowed as she made random adjustments. There was an oddly tense moment of silence. Watchman felt awkward; he had known Lilith five years, nearly her whole life, and she was as close a friend to him as one android customarily was to another. Yet he had never been alone with her before in quite this way. It was not her nudity that disturbed him; nudity meant nothing at all to him. It was, he decided, simply the privacy of it. As though we were lovers. As though there was something . . . sexual . . . between us. He smiled and decided to tell her about these incongruous feelings. But before he could speak, she did:

"I've just had a thought. About Krug. About his impatience to finish the tower. Thor, what if he's dying?"

"Dying?" Blankly; an unfamiliar idea.

"Some terrible disease, something they can't fix tectogenetically. I don't know what: some new kind of cancer, maybe.

Anyway, suppose he's just found out that he has maybe a year or two to live, you see, and he's desperate to get his space signals sent out before then."

"He looks healthy," Watchman said.

"Rotting from the inside out. The first symptoms are erratic behavior—jumping obsessively from place to place, accelerating work schedules, bothering people to respond faster——"

"Krug preserve us, no!"

"Preserve *Krug*."

"I don't believe this, Lilith. Where did you get this notion? Has Manuel said anything?"

"Strictly intuition. I'm trying to help you account for Krug's odd behavior, that's all. If he really is dying, that's one possible explanation for——"

"Krug can't die."

"Can't?"

"You know what I mean. Mustn't. He's still young. He's got a century ahead of him, at least. And there's so much that he still must do in that time."

"For us, you mean?"

"Of course," Watchman said.

"The tower's burning him up, though. Consuming him. Thor, suppose he *does* die? Without having said the words—without having spoken out for us——"

"We'll have wasted a lot of energy in prayer, then. And the AEP will laugh in our faces."

"Shouldn't we do something?"

He pressed his thumbs lightly against his eyelids. "We can't build our plans atop a fantasy, Lilith. So far as we know, Krug isn't dying, and isn't likely to die for a long time."

"And if he does?"

"What are you getting at?"

She said, "We could start to make our move now."

"What?"

"The thing we discussed when you first pushed me into sleeping with Manuel. Using Manuel to enlist Krug's support for the cause."

"It was just a passing thought," Watchman said. "I doubt that it's philosophically proper to try to manipulate Krug like that. If we're sincere in our faith, we should await His grace and mercy, without scheming to——"

"Stop it Thor. I go to chapel, and you go to chapel, and we all go to chapel, but we also live in the real world, and in the real world you have to take real factors into account. Such as the possibility of Krug's premature death."

"Well ..." He shivered with tension. She was speaking pragmatically; she sounded almost like an AEP organizer. He saw the logic of her position. All of his faith was pinned to the hope of the manifestation of a miracle; but what if there were no miracle? If they had an opportunity to encourage the miracle, should they not take it? And yet—and yet——

She said, "Manuel's primed. He's ready to take up our cause openly. You know how pliable he is; I could turn him into a crusader in two or three weeks. I'd take him to Gamma Town, first——"

"In disguise, I hope."

"Of course. We'd spend a night there. I'd rub his face in it. And then—you remember, Thor, we talked about letting him see a chapel——"

"Yes. Yes." Watchman trembled.

"I'd do that. I'd explain the whole communion. And finally I'd come right out and ask him to go to his father for us. He would, Thor, he would! And Krug would listen. Krug would yield and say the words. As a favor to Manuel."

Watchman rose. He paced the room. "It seems almost blasphemous, though. We're supposed to wait for Krug's grace to descend on us, in Krug's own time. To make use of Manuel this way, to attempt to shape and force the will of Krug——"

"What if Krug's dying?" Lilith asked. "What if he's got only months left? What if a time comes *when there is no Krug*? And we're still slaves."

Her words rebounded from the walls, shattering him:

when there is no Krug
when there is no Krug
when there is no Krug
when there is no Krug

"We have to distinguish," he said shakily, "between the physical man who is Krug, for whom we work, and the eternal presence of Krug the Maker and Krug the Liberator, who——"

"Not now, Thor. Just tell me what should I do. Take Manuel to Gamma Town?"

"Yes. Yes. But move one step at a time. Don't reveal things too quickly. Check with me if you have any doubts. Can you really control Manuel?"

"He worships me," Lilith said quietly.

"Because of your body?"

"It's a good body, Thor. But it's more than that. He *wants* to be dominated by an android. He's full of second-generation guilts. I captured him with sex, but I hold him by the power of the Vat."

"Sex," Watchman said. "Captured him with sex. How? He has a wife. An attractive wife, I've heard, though of course I'm in no position to judge. If he has an attractive wife, why does he need——"

Lilith laughed.

"Did I say a joke?"

"You don't understand a thing about humans, do you, Thor? The famous Alpha Watchman, totally baffled!" Her eyes sparkled. She jumped to her feet. "Thor, do you know anything about sex? At first hand, I mean."

"Have I done sex? Is that what you're asking?"

"That's what I'm asking," Lilith told him.

The change in the conversation's direction puzzled him. What did his private life have to do with the planning of revolutionary tactics?

"No," he said. "Never. Why should I? What could I get from it beside trouble?"

"Pleasure," she suggested. "Krug created us with functional nervous systems. Sex is amusement. Sex excites me; it ought to excite you. Why haven't you ever tried it?"

"I don't know an alpha male who has. Or who even thinks much about it."

"Alpha women do."

"That's different. You have more opportunities. You've got all those human males running after you. Human females don't run after androids much, except for some disturbed women, I guess. And you can do sex with a human without any risks. But I'm not going to chance entangling myself with some human female, not when any man who thinks I'm infringing on his rights can destroy me on the spot."

"How about sex between android and android?"

"What for? So we can make babies?"

"Sex and reproduction are separate things, Thor. People have sex without babies and babies without sex all the time. Sex is a social force. A sport, a game. A kind of magnetism, body to body. It's what gives me power over Manuel Krug." Abruptly the tone of her voice shifted, losing its didactic quality, becoming softer. "Do you want me to show you what it is? Take your clothes off."

He laughed edgily. "Are you serious? You want to do sex with me?"

"Why not? Are you afraid?"

"Don't be absurd. I just didn't expect—I mean—it seems so incongruous, two androids going to bed together, Lilith——"

"Because we're things made out of plastic?" she said coldly.

"That isn't what I meant. Obviously we're flesh and blood!"

"But there are certain things that we don't have to do, because we come from the Vat. Certain bodily functions that are reserved for the Children of the Womb. Eh?"

"You're distorting my position."

"I know I am. I want to educate you, Thor. Here you are trying to manipulate the destinies of an entire society, and you're ignorant of one of the most basic human motivations. Come: strip. Haven't you ever felt desire for a woman?"

"I don't know what desire is, Lilith."

"Really?"

"Really."

She shook her head. "And you think we should have equality with humans? You want to vote, you want to put alphas in Congress, to have civil rights? But you're living like a robot. Like a machine. You're a walking argument for keeping androids in their place. You've closed off one of the most vital sectors of human life and tell yourself that that sort of stuff is only for humans; androids don't have to bother with it. Dangerous thinking, Thor! We *are* human. We have bodies. Why did Krug give us genitals if He didn't mean us to use them?"

"I agree with every word you've said. But——"

"But what?"

"But sex seems irrelevant to me. And I know that's a damning argument against our cause. I'm not the only alpha who feels this way, Lilith. We don't talk about it much, but——" He looked away from her. "Maybe the humans are right. Maybe we *are* a lesser kind, artificial through and through, just a clever kind of robot made out of flesh and——"

"Wrong. Stand up, Thor. Come here."

He walked toward her. She took his hands and put them on her bare breasts.

"Squeeze them," she said. "Gently. Play with the nipples. You see how they get hard, how they stand up? That's a sign that I'm responding to your touch. It's a way that a woman shows desire. What do you feel when you touch my breasts, Thor?"

"The smoothness. The cool skin."

"What do you feel *inside?*"

"I don't know."

"Pulse rate changing? Tensions? A knot in your belly? Here. Touch my hip. My buttock. Slide your hand up and down. Anything, Thor?"

"I'm not sure. I'm so new at this, Lilith."

"Strip," she said.

"It seems so mechanical this way. Cold. Isn't sex supposed to be preceded by courtship, soft lights, whispering, music, poetry?"

"Then you *do* know a little about it."

"A little. I've read their books. I know the rituals. The peripherals."

"We can try the peripherals. Here: I've turned down the lights. Take a floater, Thor. No, not a scrambler—not the first time. A floater. Fine. Here's a little music, now. Undress."

"You won't tell anybody about this?"

"How silly you are! Who would I tell? Manuel? Darling, I'll tell him, darling, I've been unfaithful to you with Thor Watchman!" She laughed giddily. "It'll be our secret. Call it a humanizing lesson. Humans have sex, and you want to be more human, don't you? I'll discover sex to you." She smiled archly. She tugged at his clothes.

Curiosity seized him. He felt the floater going to work in his brain, lifting him toward euphoria. Lilith was right: the sexlessness of alphas was a paradox among people who claimed so intensely to be fully human. Or was sexlessness as general among alphas as he thought? Perhaps, busy with the tasks set for him by Krug, he had simply neglected to let his emotions develop? He thought of Siegfried Fileclerk, weeping in the snow beside Cassandra Nucleus, and wondered.

His clothes dropped away. Lilith drew him into her arms.

She rubbed her body slowly against his. He felt her thighs on his thighs, the cool taut drum of her belly touching his, the hard nodes of her nipples brushing his chest. He searched himself for some trace of response. He was uncertain about what he found, although he could not deny that he enjoyed the tactile sensations of their contact. Her eyes were closed. Her lips were parted. They sought his. Her tongue slid a short distance between his teeth. He ran the palms of his hands down her back, and on a sudden impulse dug the tips of his fingers into the globes of her buttocks. Lilith stiffened and pushed herself more intensely against him, grinding now instead of rubbing. They remained that way for some minutes. Then she relaxed and eased away from him.

"Well?" she asked. "Anything?"

"I liked it," he said tentatively.

"Did it excite you, though?"

"I think so."

"It doesn't look that way."

"How can you tell?"

"It would show," she said, grinning at him.

He felt impossibly absurd and awkward; he felt cut off from his own identity, unable to return to or even to see the Thor Watchman he knew and understood. From the first, almost from the time of leaving the Vat, he had regarded himself as older, wiser, more competent, more confident, than his fellow alphas: a man who comprehended the world and his place in it. But now? Lilith had reduced him in half an hour to something clumsy, naive, foolish ... and impotent.

She put her hand to his loins. "Since your organ hasn't become rigid," she said, "obviously it wasn't very exciting for you when I——" She paused. "Oh. Yes. *Now* do you see?"

"It happened when you touched me."

"That isn't awfully surprising. So you like it, then? Yes. Yes." Her fingers moved cunningly. Watchman had to admit that he found the sensation interesting, and that sudden startling awakening of his maleness in her hands was a remarkable effect. But yet he remained outside himself, a detached and remote observer, no more involved than if he were attending a lecture on the mating habits of Centaurine protoids.

She was close against him, again. Her body moved, sliding from side to side, writhing a little, quivering with a barely suppressed tension. He clasped her in his arms. He ran his hands over her skin once more.

She drew him to the floor.

He lay atop her, bracing himself with knees and elbows so that his full weight would not descend on her. Her legs surrounded him; her thighs clamped tight against his hips; her hand slipped between their bodies, seized him, guided him into her. She began to thrust her pelvis up and down. He caught the rhythm of it shortly, and matched her thrusts with thrusts of his own.

So this is sex, he thought.

He wondered how a woman felt about having something long and hard pushed into her body like that. Evidently they enjoyed it; Lilith was gasping and trembling in what seemed like delight. But it struck him as an odd thing to covet. And was pushing yourself into a woman all that thrilling? Was this what the poetry was about, was this what men had fought duels over and renounced kingdoms for?

After awhile he said, "How will we know when it's over?"

Her eyes opened. He was unable to tell whether there was fury or laughter in them. "You'll know," she said. "Just keep moving!"

He kept moving.

The motions of her hips grew more violent. Her face became twisted, distorted, almost ugly; some sort of interior storm had broken and was raging within her. Muscles throbbed randomly throughout her body. At the place where he was joined to her, he could feel her grasping him with playful inner spasms.

Abruptly he felt a spasm of his own, and ceased to catalog the effects their union had produced in her. He closed his eyes. He fought for breath. His heart raced frantically; his skin blazed. He tightened his grip on her and pressed his face into the hollow between her cheek and her shoulder. A series of jolting impacts rocked him.

She was right: it was easy to tell when it was over.

How fast the ecstasy drained away! He could barely remember now the powerful sensations of sixty seconds ago. He felt cheated, as though he had been promised a feast and had been given only dream-food to eat. Was that all? Like the surf trickling away after a brief surge of tide? And ashes on the beach. And ashes on the beach. It is nothing at all, Thor Watchman thought. It is a fraud.

He rolled free of her.

She lay with her head lolling back, her eyes closed, her mouth slack; she was sweat-dappled and wan-looking. It seemed to him that he had never seen this woman before. A moment after he had left her, her eyes opened. She propped herself up on one elbow and smiled at him, almost shyly, perhaps.

"Hello," she said.

"Hello." He looked away.

"How do you feel?"

Watchman shrugged. He searched for the right words and could not find them. Defeated, he said, "Tired, mostly. Hollow. Is that right? I feel—hollow."

"Normal. After coitus every animal is sad. Old Latin proverb. You're an animal, Thor. Don't forget it."

"A weary animal." Ashes on the cold beach. The tide very low. "Did you enjoy it, Lilith?"

"Couldn't you see? No, I suppose you didn't. I enjoyed. Very much."

He put his hand lightly on her thigh. "I'm glad. But I'm still baffled."

"By what?"

"The whole thing. The pattern, the constellation of events. Pushing. Pulling. Sweating. Groaning. The tickle in the groin, and then it's over. I——"

"No," she said. "Don't intellectualize. Don't analyze. You must have been expecting more than is really there. It's only *fun*, Thor. It's what people do to be happy together. That's all. That's all. It's not a cosmic experience."

"I'm sorry. I'm just a dumb android who doesn't——"

"Don't. You're a person, Thor."

He realized he was hurting her by his refusal to have been overwhelmed by their coupling. He was hurting himself. Slowly he got to his feet. His mood was wintry; he felt like an empty vessel lying in the snow. He had known a flash of joy, he thought, right at the moment of discharge; but was that instant of lightning worth anything if this dreary gloom always came afterward?

She had meant well. She had wanted to make him more human.

He lifted her, pulled her against him for a moment, kissed her glancingly on the cheek, cupped one of her breasts in his hand. He said, "We'll do this again some time, all right?"

"Whenever you say."

"It was very strange for me, the first time. It'll get better. I know it will."

"It will, Thor. The first time is always strange."

"I think I'd better go now."

"If you have to."

"I'd better. But I'll see you again soon."

"Yes." She touched his arm. "And in the meantime—I'll start moving along the lines we discussed. I'll take Manuel to Gamma Town."

"Good."
"Krug be with you, Thor."
"Krug be with you."
He began to dress.

23
And Krug said, There shall be this one difference forever upon you.

That the Children of the Womb shall come always from the Womb, and the Children of the Vat come always from the Vat. And it shall not be given to you to bring forth your young from your bodies, as is done among the Children of the Womb.

And this shall be so in order that your lives may flow only from Krug, that to him alone the glory of your creation be reserved, world without end.

24
December 20, 2218.

At 800 meters the tower dominates and overpowers. There is no resisting its immensity: one steps from the transmat by day or by night, and one is struck dumb by that vaulting shaft of gleaming glass. The solitude of its surroundings lends awesomeness to its height.

It has passed the halfway mark now.

Lately there have been many accidents, born of haste. A pair of workers fell from the summit; an electrician, spraying connectors improperly along a partition, sent a lethal shock through five gammas hoisting cable; two ascending scooprods collided, at a cost of six lives; Alpha Euclid Planner narrowly avoided serious injury when a powerpool backup sent a monstrous surge of maximum-entropy data through the main computer while he was jacked in; three betas were dumped 400 meters down an interior service-access core when a scaffold collapsed. The construction work thus far has caused the destruction of nearly thirty androids. But there are thousands employed at the tower and the work is hazardous and unusual; no one considers the accident rate extraordinarily high.

The first thirty meters of the tachyon-beam broadcast apparatus is virtually finished. Technicians daily test its structural integrity. It will not be possible, of course, to generate tachyons until the entire enormous accelerator track has been completed, but putting together the individual components of the mighty system has an interest of its own, and Krug spends most of his time at the tower watching the tests. Colored lights flash; indicator panels hum and whistle; dials glow; needles quiver. Krug applauds each positive result enthusiastically. He brings hordes of guests. In the last three weeks he has come to the tower with Niccolò Vargas, with his daughter-in-law Clissa, with twenty-nine different members of Congress, with eleven leaders of industry, with sixteen world-famed representatives of the arts. There is unanimous praise for the tower. Even those who perhaps inwardly may think of it as a titanic folly cannot withhold their admiration for its elegance, its beauty, its magnitude. A folly, too, can be wonderful, and no one who has seen Krug's tower denies its wonder. Nor are there so many who think it is folly to notify the stars that man exists.

Manuel Krug has not been seen at the tower since early in November. Krug explains that his son is busy supervising the complexities of the Krug corporate domain. He is assuming greater responsibilities every month. He is, after all, the heir apparent.

25

Last time I went to Lilith she said, Next time you come let's do something a little different, all right?

Both of us naked after loving. My cheek on her breasts.

Different how?

To get out of the flat a little. To go around as a tourist and see Stockholm. The android quarter. To see how the people live, the androids. The gammas. Wouldn't you want to do that?

And I said, a little wary, Why should I? Wouldn't you rather spend the time with me?

She played with the hair on my chest. Such a beast, I am, so primitive.

She said, We live so cloistered here. You come, we have sex, you leave. We never go anywhere together. I'd like you to come outside with me. Part of your education. I have this drive to educate people, did you know that, Manuel? To open their minds to things. Have you ever been in a Gamma Town?

No.

Do you know what it is?

A place where gammas live, I suppose.

That's right. But you don't really know. Not till you've been inside one.

Dangerous?

Not really. Nobody will bother alphas in Gamma Town. They bother each other a little, sometimes, but that's different. We're high-caste and they keep away from us.

I said, They won't bother an alpha, maybe, but what about me? They probably don't want human tourists.

Lilith said she would disguise me. As an alpha. That had a certain kind of spice in it. Temptation. Mystery. It might keep the romance glowing for Lilith and me, playing a game like that. I asked, Won't they recognize that I'm a fake? And she said, They don't look too closely at alphas. We have a concept called the social distances. Gammas keep the social distances, Manuel.

All right, then, we'll go to Gamma Town.

We planned it for a week from that day. I cleared everything with Clissa: going to Luna, I said, won't be back for a couple of days, yes? No problem. Clissa would spend the time with her friends in New Zealand. I wonder sometimes how much Clissa suspects. Or what she'd say if she knew. I have this temptation to tell her, Clissa, I've got an android mistress in Stockholm, she's way high spectrum in bed and a fantastic body, how do you like that? Clissa isn't bourgeois, but she's sensitive. She might feel unwanted. Or maybe Clissa with her great love of the downtrodden androids might say, How kind of you, Manuel, to be making one of them so happy. I don't mind sharing your love with an android. Bring her to tea some day, won't you? I wonder.

The day comes. I go to Lilith's. I go in and she's naked. Get your clothes off, she says, I grin. Unsubtle. Sure. Sure. I strip and reach for her. She does a little dance step and leaves me holding air.

Not now, silly. When we come back. We've got to disguise you now!

She has a spraytube. First she turns it to neutral and covers up the mirror-plate in my forehead. Androids don't wear such things. The earlobe plugs, she says: out. I take them out and she fills the opening with gel. Then she starts spraying me red. Do I have to shave my body? I ask. No, she says, just don't take your clothes off in front of anybody. She turns me red all over, with a shiny texture to it. Instant android. Next she gives me a thermal spray from chest to thighs. Going to be cold out there, she says. Androids don't wear heavy clothes. Here. Here, get dressed.

She hands me a costume. Highneck shirt, skintight pants. Obviously android clothes, and obviously alpha style, too. Fits me like a skin graft. Don't get an erection, she tells me. You'll split the trousers. She laughs and rubs me in front.

Where'd you get the clothes?

I borrowed them from Thor Watchman.

You tell him what for?

No, she says, of course not. I just said I needed some. Let's see how you look, now. Lovely. Lovely! A perfect alpha. Walk across the room. Back. Good. Swagger a little more. Remember, you're the end-product of human evolution, the finest version of *Homo sapiens* that ever came out of a vat, with all of a human's strong points and none of his flaws. You're Alpha—hmm. We need a name, in case anyone asks. Lilith thinks a moment. Alpha Leviticus Leaper, she says. What's your name?

Alpha Leviticus Leaper, I say.

No. If anyone asks you, you say Leviticus Leaper. They can *tell* you're an alpha. Other people call you Alpha Leaper. Clear?

Clear.

She gets dressed. A thermal spray, first, then a kind of gold mesh over her breasts and down to mid-thigh. Nothing else. Nipples showing through the openings in the mesh. Not much hidden below, either. Not my idea of winter clothing. Androids must enjoy winters more than we do.

Want to see yourself before we got out, Alpha Leaper?

Yes.

She dumps mirror-dust in the air. When the molecules are lined up I get a head-to-toe view. Impressive. A really cocky alpha buck, a red devil out on the town. Lilith is right: no gamma would dare to fool with me. Or even look me in the eye.

Let's go, Alpha Leaper. Slumming in Gamma Town.

Out. Across. To the edge of the city, looking down on windwhipped gray water. Whitecaps in the harbor. Early afternoon, but night already closing in; a greasy gray time of day, fog hanging low, the glow of streetlamps coming through it blurred and dirty. Other lights flashing off buildings or floating overhead: red, green, blue, orange, flickering on and off, yelling for attention, an arrow here, the sign of a trumpet there. Vibrations. Fumes. Sounds. The closeness of many people. A screech in the grayness. Distant laughter, blurred also. Odd scraps of voices drifting in the fog:

"Let go or I'll clot you!"

"Back to the vat. Back to the vat."

"Slobies, who'll take slobies?"

"Stackers can't tell you."

"Slobies!"

"Owl! Owl! Owl!"

Stockholm is more than half populated by androids. Why do they gather here? And in maybe nine other cities. Ghettoes. They don't have to. Transmat world: live wherever you like, get to work anyway. But we like to be with our own kind, she says. And even so they stratify themselves in their ghettoes. The alphas back there, in the fine old houses, and the betas in the ragbag middle. And then the gammas. The gammas. Welcome to Gamma Town.

Wet slippery mud-streaked cobble-paved streets. Medieval? Peeling gray houses face to face, hardly a lane between them. A trickle of cold dirty water running down the gutter from the higher part. Windows of glass. And yet it isn't completely archaic here: a mixture of styles, all sorts of architecture, olla podrida, bouillabaisse, with twenty-second, twentieth, nineteenth, sixteenth, fourteenth centuries jumbled together. The airy webs of weather-proofed skyways dangling. Rusted slidewalks on a few of the tangled streets. The buzz of climate conditioners that have gone out of phase, pumping greenish fog into the winter air. Thick-walled baroque cellars. Lilith and I walk down zigzag crazy pathways. A demon must have planned this town. The imp of the perverse.

Faces hover.

Gammas. Everywhere. They peer, flit, peer again. Little dim eyes, birdlike, twitch-twitch-twitch, frightened. Afraid of us, they are. The social distances, eh? They keep the social distances. They lurk, they stare, but as we get close they try to be invisible. Head down. Eyes averted. Alphas alphas alphas; all gammas beware!

We tower above them. I never realized how squat gammas are. How short, how broad. And how strong. Those shoulders. Those muscles rippling. Any of them could rip me apart. The women look strong too, though they're built more gracefully. To go to bed with a gamma girl? More fire than Lilith, maybe—is that possible? Thrashing and jumping around, low-class groaning, no inhibitions? And the smell of garlic, no doubt. Forget the idea. Coarse, they are. Coarse. Like Quenelle with my father, I'd say. Let them be; there's passion enough in Lilith, and she's clean. Probably not worth the effort even to think about it. The gammas keep back from us. Two jaunty alphas out on the town. We have long legs. We have style. We have grace. They fear us.

I am Alpha Leviticus Leaper.

The wind is raw here. Right off the water it comes, knife-sharp. It stirs up dust and bits of things in the streets. Dust! Scraps! When have I seen such filthy streets? Don't the robocleaners ever come here? Well, then, don't the gammas have enough pride to clean their own?

They don't care about such things, says Lilith. It's a cultural matter. They take pride in their unpride. It reflects their lack of status. Bottom of the android world, bottom of the bottom of the human world, and they know it, and they don't like it, and the squalor is like a badge of nonstatus for them. Saying, you want us to be filth, we'll live in filth too. Reveling in it. Wallowing in it. If we're not people, we don't have to be tidy at home. You know, robocleaners used to come here and the gammas would dismantle them. There's one now, you see? Been there ten years, at least.

Robot fragments lie in a drab scattered heap. Shards of a metal man. The glint of good blue metal through the rust. Are those things solenoids? Relays? Accumulators? The coiled wire guts of the machine. Bottom of the bottom of the bottom, a mere mechanical object, destroyed while attacking the holy squalor of our vat-born pariahs. A gray and white cat pisses on the robot's guts. The gammas leaning against the wall laugh. Then they see us and creep back, showing awe. They make quick nervous gestures with their left hands— touch crotch, touch breasts, touch forehead, one two three very fast. As automatic, as much a reflex, as the sign of the Cross. What is it? A kind of honorific tugging at the forelock? A show of homage to the wandering alphas?

Something like that, says Lilith. But not quite. Actually it's just a superstitious sign they make.

To ward off the evil eye?

Yes. In a manner of speaking. Touch the cardinal points, invoke the spirit of genitals and souls and intelligence, crotch chest skull. You've never seen androids do it before?

I think maybe I have.

Even alphas, Lilith says. A habit. A comfort when tension. Sometimes even I.

Why the genitals, though? When androids don't genitate?

Symbolic power, she says. We're sterile but that's still a holy zone. In memory of the origin of us all. The human gene pool issued from the loins, and we were designed after those genes. There's a theology of it.

I make the sign. One two three. Lilith laughs, but she looks edgy, as if I really shouldn't be doing it. To hell with. I'm masquerading as an android tonight, right? Then I can do android things. One two three.

The gammas lounging against the wall return the sign. One two three. Crotch chest skull.

One of them says something that sounds like, Krug be praised!

What was that? I ask Lilith.

I didn't hear it.

Dd he say Krug be praised?

Gammas will say anything sometimes.

I shake my head. Maybe he recognizes me, Lilith!

Not a chance. Absolutely none. If he said anything about Krug, he means your father.

Yes. Yes. True. He's Krug. I'm Manuel, only Manuel.

Shh! You're Alpha Leviticus Leaper!

Right. Sorry. Alpha Leviticus Leaper. Lev for short. Krug be praised? Maybe I didn't hear it right.

Maybe, Lilith says.

We turn a sharp corner and in so doing we trigger an advert trap. By entering the trap's scanner field we cause powders of many colors to erupt from vents in a wall and form, by electrostatic attraction, a pattern of gaudy words in the air, blindingly bright even in the murk and fog. Against a silvery backdrop we see:

! MEDIC !
ALPHA POSEIDON MUSKETEER
! MEDIC !
SPECIALIST IN GAMMA COMPLAINTS

HE CURES
SOLIDIFIERS
SLOBIE ADDICTS
STACKERS
HE CONQUERS
METABOLIC ROT AND DECAY
AND OTHER PROBLEMS
! REPUTABLE !
FIRST DOOR TO RIGHT AND RING

I ask, Is he really an alpha?

Of course.

What's he doing living in Gamma Town?

Somebody's got to be their doctor. You think a gamma can get a medical degree?

He sounds like a quack, though. Putting out a trap like this! What kind of doctor would huckster for patients?

A Gamma Town doctor. That's how things are done here. Anyway, he *is* a quack. A good doctor, but a quack. Mixed up in some organ-regeneration scandal years ago, when he had an alpha practice. Lost his license.

You don't need a license here?

You don't need anything here. They say he's dedicated, though. Eccentric but devoted to his people. Would you like to meet him?

No. No. What are slobie addicts?

Slobie's a drug the gammas take, Lilith says. You'll see some addicts before long.

And stackers?

They have something wrong in the brain. Scaly matter in the cerebellum.

Solidifiers?

A trouble in the muscles. Stiffening of tissue, or something. I'm not sure. Only gammas get it.

I frown. Does my father know? He stands behind the integrity of his products. If gammas are prone to mysterious diseases——

That's a slobie addict, Lilith says.

An android comes up the street toward us. Drifting, floating, sliding, waltzing, moving with a weird molasses slowness. Eyes slitwide; face dreamy; arms outstretched; fingers drooping. Gropes his way as though going through the atmosphere of Jupiter. All he wears is a scrap of fabric around his hips, yet he sweats in the frosty evening air. Crooning to

himself in a clanking way. After what seems like four hours
he reaches us. Plants his feet, leans his head back, puts hands
on hips. Silence. A minute. At last in low bristly voice he
says with terrible unhurriedness, Al . . . phas . . . hel . . .
lo . . . al . . . phas . . . love . . . ly . . . al . . . phas.

Lilith tells him to move along.

No response at first. Then his face crumbles. Unutterable
sadness. Brings left hand up in awkward clownlike gesture,
touches forehead, lets hand drift down to chest, to crotch.
Making the sign in reverse—what's the significance of that?
He says tragically, I . . . love . . . the . . . love . . . ly . . .
al . . . phas.

I say to Lilith, What kind of drug is it?

Slows the time-sense. A minute becomes an hour to them.
It stretches their free time. Of course, we move like whirl-
winds around them. Usually the addicts stick together, all on
the same time-scheme. Illusion of having days between each
work-shift.

A dangerous drug?

She says, Cuts about an hour off the life expectancy for
every two hours you're under the influence. The gammas
figure it's a fair deal, though. Give up an hour objective, gain
two or three days subjective—why not?

But it reduces the work force!

Gammas have the right to do what they please with their
lives, don't they, Alpha Leaper? You wouldn't accept the
argument that they're merely property, would you, and that
any kind of self-abuse practiced by the gamma is a crime
against its owner?

No. No. Of course not, Alpha Meson.

I didn't think you felt that way, Lilith says.

The slobie addict is moving in foolish vague circles around
us, chanting something so slowly that I am unable to connect
one syllable to another, and can make no sense of it. He
halts. A glacial smile spreads infinitely slowly across his lips; I
think it is a snarl until it is half formed. He sinks into a
hulking crouch. His hand rises, fingers flexed. The hand is
obviously heading toward Lilith's left breast. Neither of us
moves.

I catch the gamma's chant now:

A . . . A . . . A . . . A . . . A . . . G . . . A . . . A . . .
C . . . A . . . A . . . U . . .

What's he trying to say?

Lilith shakes her head. It isn't important.

She steps away while the groping hand is still ten centimeters from her bosom. A frown begins to replace the smile on the gamma's face. He looks wounded. His chant takes on a questioning tone:

A . . . U . . . A . . . A . . . U . . . G . . . A . . . U . . . C . . . A . . . U . . . U . . .

A sound of slow, dragging footsteps comes from behind me. A second slobie addict is approaching: a girl, wearing a cloak that hangs down from her shoulders and trails raggedly for many meters behind her, but leaves her thighs and loins bare. She has dyed her hair green, and has it bound up in a kind of tiara. Her face seems wasted and pallid; her eyes are scarcely open; her skin is glossy with sweat. She floats toward our first friend and says something to him in a startling baritone boom. He replies dreamily. I can understand none of what they say. Is it because of the decelerating drug, or do they speak a gamma patois? Something ugly seems to be about to happen. I nod to Lilith, suggesting we leave, but she shakes her head. Stay. Watch them.

The addicts are doing a grotesque dance. Fingertips touching, knees rising and falling. A gavotte for marble statues. A minuet for stuffed elephants.

They croon to one another. They circle one another. The man's feet become tangled in the girl's trailing cloak. She moves; he stays firm; the cloak rips, leaving the girl naked in the street. Between her breasts she has a knife, dangling from a green cord. Her back is crisscrossed with scars. Has she been flogged? Her nakedness excites her. I see her nipples stiffening in slow motion. The man is next to her now. He reaches up with painful unhaste and takes the knife from its sheath. Just as slowly he brings it down and touches the cold metal to the girl's loins, her belly, her forehead. The holy sign. Lilith and I are against the wall, near the entrance to the doctor's office. The knife makes me uneasy.

Let me take it away from him, I say.

No. No. You're just a visitor here. This isn't your affair.

Then let's go, Lilith.

Wait. Watch.

Our friend is singing again. Letters, as before. U . . . C . . . A . . . U . . . C . . . G . . . U . . . C . . . C . . .

His arm comes back, then starts forward. The point of the knife is aimed at the girl's abdomen. From the tension in his muscles I can see that the blow will have full force; this is no dance step. The blade is only a few centimeters from her skin when I rush forward and slap it from his hand.

He begin to moan.

The girl does not yet realize that she has been saved. She utters a deep droning bellow, perhaps intended to be a shriek. She drops to the ground, clutching her breasts with one hand, thrusting the other between her thighs. She writhes in slow motion.

You shouldn't have interfered, Lilith says angrily. Come on, now. We'd better go.

But he would have killed her!

Not your affair. Not your affair.

She tugs at my wrist. I turn. We begin to move away. I am aware peripherally that the girl is getting up; the garish lights of the sign of Poseidon Musketeer the Medic glisten on her bare thin flanks. Lilith and I take two steps; then we hear a grunt. We look back, the girl, rising, has risen with the knife in her hand, and she has driven it into the man's belly. Methodically she draws it upward from waist to chest. He is disemboweled, and is only slowly becoming aware of it. He makes a gurgling sound.

Now we've got to go, Lilith says.

We speed toward the corner. As we reach it I turn. The door of Alpha Musketeer has opened. A gaunt haggard figure, alpha-tall, with a mane of wild gray hair and bulging eyes, stands in it. Is this the famous medic? He rushes toward the slobie addicts. The girl kneels before her victim, who has not yet fallen. His blood purples her shining skin. She chants: G! A! A! G! A! G! G! A! C!

In here, Lilith says, and we duck into a dark doorway.

Steps. A dry smell of withered things. Cobwebs. We plunge into unknown depths. In the distance, far below, yellow lights gleam. We go down and down and down.

What is this place? I ask.

Security tunnel. Built during the Sanity War two hundred years ago. Part of a system that runs everywhere under Stockholm. The gammas have taken it over.

Like a sewer.

I hear quick stabs of laughter, jagged blurts of incoherent conversation. There are shops down here, with slitted gates behind which little lamps sputter and flicker. Gammas move to and fro. Some of them make the one-two-three sign as they pass us. Driven by a fear I do not understand, Lilith leads us frantically onward. We change tunnels, entering a passage at right angles to the first one.

Three slobie addicts wander by.

A male gamma with face streaked by red and blue paint pauses to sing, perhaps to us:

> Who shall I marry?
> Who will marry me?
> Fire in the stinking vat
> Fire flying free.
> My head my head my head my head
> My head.

He kneels and gags. Thin blue fluid pours from his lips, almost to our feet.

We move on. We hear an echoing cry:

Al-*pha!* Al-*pha!* Al-*pha!* Al-*pha!*

Two gammas couple in an alcove. Their bodies are sweat-shiny and lean. Despite myself I watch the plunging hips and listen to the slap of flesh against flesh. The girl pounds the flats of her hands steadily against her partner's back. Is she protesting a rape, or displaying her ecstasy? I never find out, because a slobie stumbles out of the shadows and falls on them, tumbling in a turmoil of intertwined limbs. Lilith draws me away. I am suddenly heavy with desire for her. I think of the firm breasts beneath her wrap; I think of the bare moist slit. Shall we find an alcove of our own, and couple among the gammas? I put my hand on her buttocks, which are taut as she walks. Lilith wriggles her hips. Not here, she says. Not here. We have social distances to keep too.

A dazzle of light cascades from the tunnel's roof. Pink bubbles appear and burst, releasing sour smells. A dozen gammas gallop out of a side-passage, halt in shock as they realize they have nearly collided with two visiting alphas, make signs of respect, and rush onward, shouting, laughing, singing.

> Oh I melt you and you melt me
> And we melt they and happy we be.
> Clot! Clot! Clot! Clot!
> Grig!

They seem happy, I say.

Lilith nods. They're soaped to the whiskers, she says. On their way to a radiation orgy, I bet.

A what?

A puddle of yellow fluid slides out from under a closed door. Acrid fumes rise. Gamma urine? The door bursts open. Wild-eyed female gamma, luminescent breasts, livid scar on belly, giggles at us. She executes a respectable curtsey. Milady. Milord. Will you clot with me? Giggles. Squats. Lurches around, heels against rump, in a dizzy dance. Arches her back, slaps her breasts, spreads her legs. Green and gold lights blaze in the room from which she has emerged. A figure appears.

What is it, Lilith?

Normal height, but twice the width of a gamma, and covered with thick coarse fur. An ape? The face is human. It lifts its hands. Short blunt fingers; webs between them! Drags the girl back inside. Door closes.

A reject, Lilith says. There are lots of them here.

Reject from what?

Substandard android. Genetic flaws; impurities in the vat, perhaps. Sometimes they have no arms, sometimes no legs, no heads, no digestive tracts, no this, no that.

Aren't they automatically destroyed at the factory?

Lilith smiles. They aren't destroyed. Those that aren't viable die anyway, fast enough. The others are smuggled out when the supervisors aren't looking and sent to one of the undercities. Mainly here. We can't put our idiot brethren to death, Manuel!

Leviticus, I say. Alpha Leviticus Leaper.

Yes. Look, there's another.

A nightmare figure rollicks through the corridor. Like something that has been placed in an oven until its flesh began to flow and run: the basic outlines are human, but the contours are not. The nose is a trunk, the lips are saucers, the arms are of unequal length, the fingers are tentacles. The genitals are monstrous: horse-penis, bull-balls.

Better off dead, I say to Lilith.

No. No. Our brother. Our pitiful brother whom we cherish.

The monstrosity halts a dozen meters from us. Its ropy arms go through the movements of the one-two-three.

Speaking perfectly clearly it says to us, The peace of Krug upon you, alphas. Go with Krug. Go with Krug. Go with Krug.

Krug be with you, Lilith replies.

The monstrosity shambles onward, murmuring happily.

The peace of Krug? Go with Krug? Krug be with you? Lilith, what does all this mean?

Common courtesy, she says. A friendly greeting.

Krug?

Krug made us all, did he not? she says.

I remember things that were said when I was in the shunt room with my friends. You know all the androids are in love with your father? Yes. Sometimes I think it must be almost like a religion with them. The religion of Krug. Well it makes a sort of sense to worship your creator. Don't laugh.

The peace of Krug. Go with Krug. Krug be with you.

Lilith, do androids think my father is God?

Lilith evades the question. We can talk about that some other time, she says. People have ears here. There are some things we can't discuss.

But.

Some other time!

I drop it. The tunnel now widens into a considerable room, well-lit, crowded. A marketplace? Shops, booths, gammas everywhere. We are stared at. There are numerous rejects in the room, each a little more horrid than the last. It is hard to see how creatures so maimed and mismade can survive.

Do they ever go to the surface?

Never. They might be seen by humans.

In Gamma Town?

They take no chances. They'd all be obliterated if.

In the crush of the crowded room, the androids jostle and shove, bicker, snap. Somehow they maintain an area of open space around the intrusive alphas, but not a very great one. Two knife-duels are going on; no one pays attention. There is much public lasciviousness. The smell of the place is rank and foul. A wild-eyed girl rushes up to me and whispers, Krug bless! Krug bless! She pushes something into my hand and runs off.

A gift.

A small cool cube with beveled edges, like the toy at the New Orleans shunt room. Does it send messages? Yes. I see words forming and flowing and vanishing in its milky core:

A CLOT IN TIME SAVES THINE

*

HIS HIS HIS HIS HERS HIS HIS HIS

*

O SHALLOW IS THY BOWL, FILTHY GRIG

*

SLOBIE REIGNS, STACKERS PAINS

*

PLIT! PLIT! PLIT! PLIT! PLACK!

*

AND UNTO KRUG RENDER KRUG'S

All nonsense. Lilith, can you figure this stuff?

Some of it. The gammas have their own slang, you know. But look here, where it says——

A male gamma with cratered purple skin slaps the cube from our hands. It skitters along the floor; he dives for it in a knot of feet. There is a general uproar. People tangle and twine. The thief breaks from the mass and speeds away into a corridor. The gammas still wrestle confusedly. A girl rises to the top of the heap; she has lost her few scraps of clothing in the melee, and there are bloody gouges on her breasts and thighs. In her hand she holds the cube. I recognize her as the girl who gave it to me in the first place. Now she makes a demonic face at me, baring her teeth. She brandishes the cube and clamps it between her legs. A burly reject pounces on her and hauls her away; he has only one arm, but it is as thick as a tree. Grig! she screams. Prot! Gliss! They vanish.

The crowd is muttering in an ugly way.

I picture them turning on us, ripping at our clothing, revealing the hairy human body beneath my false alpha costume. The social distances may not protect us then.

Come, I say to Lilith. I think I've had enough.

Wait.

She turns to the gammas. She holds up her hands, palms facing, about half a meter apart, as though indicating the length of a fish she has caught. Then she wriggles in a peculiar sinuous maneuver, twisting her body so she describes a kind of spiraling curve. The gesture quiets the crowd instantly. The gammas step aside, heads bowed humbly, as we go past. All is well.

Enough, I tell Lilith. It's getting late. How long have we been here, anyway?

We can go now.

We flee through a maze of interlocking passages. Gammas of a thousand hideous shapes pass us. We see slobies floating

in their slow raptures. Rejects. Stackers and solidifiers, for all
I can tell. Sounds, smells, colors, textures—I am dazzled and
dazed. Voices in the darkness. Songs.

> The freedom day is coming
> The freedom day is coming
> Smip the slobies, grab the gliss—
> And ride up to freedom!

Steps. Upward. Cold winds descending. Breathless, we race
to the top and find ourselves in the winding cobbled streets of
Gamma Town again, probably only a few meters from the
place where we went down. It seems to me that the office of
Alpha Poseidon Musketeer must be just around the corner.

Night has come. The lights of Gamma Town crackle and
flutter. Lilith wants to take me to a tavern. I refuse. Home.
Home. Enough. My mind is stained by the sights of the
android world. She yields; we hurry out. How far must we
walk before we reach a transmat?

We leap. Her flat seems so warm and bright to me now.
We rid ourselves of our clothes. Under the doppler I cleanse
myself of my red color and my thermal spray.

Was it interesting?

Overpowering, I say. And there's so much you have to
explain, Lilith.

Images swim in my brain. I burn. I sizzle.

Of course you won't tell anyone I took you, she says. I
could get into awful trouble.

Of course. Strictly confidential.

Come close, Alpha Leaper.

Manuel.

Manuel. Come close.

First tell me what it means when they say Krug be——

Later. I'm cold. Warm me, Manuel.

I fold her in my arms. The heavy mounds of her breasts
inflame me. I cover her mouth with mine. I thrust my tongue
between her lips. We sink down together to the floor.

Without hesitation I spear her. She trembles. She clasps
me.

When I close my eyes I see slobies and rejects and stackers.

Lilith.

Lilith.

Lilith.

Lilith I love you I love you I love you Lilith Lilith Lilith

The great vat bubbles. The moist crimson creatures crawl forth. Laughter. Lightning. O shallow is thy bowl, filthy grig! My flesh crashes against hers. Plit! Plit! Plit! Plit! Plack! With humiliating swiftness the overwrought Leviticus Leaper pours a billion little boys and girls into his beloved's sterile womb.

26   January 9, 2219.

The tower is at 940 meters and rising more swiftly than ever. Standing at the base, one cannot easily see the summit; it is lost against the white glare of the winter sky. At this time of year there are only a few hours of daylight at the site, and during those hours the sun's rays ride fiery tracks down the length of the shimmering shaft.

Much of the interior structure now is complete throughout the building's lower half. Three of the high-capacity communications equipment modules have been hoisted into place: somber black metal containers fifty meters high, within which are the huge kickover units that will amplify the messages as they climb the tower. Viewed from afar, these modules seem to be giant seeds ripening in a great glossy transparent pod.

The accident rate continues to be high. Mortality levels are causing concern. The losses among gammas have been particularly severe. Yet morale is said to be good; the androids are cheerful and appear to be aware that they are playing an essential role in one of humanity's most ambitious projects. If their attitude remains so positive the tower will be finished well ahead of schedule.

27   After showing them the state of progress at

the tower, Krug took his guests that day to dine at the Nemo Club, where a suite was perpetually held in readiness for him. The club was one of Krug's minor enterprises; he had built it a dozen years back, and for some time it had been Earth's most fashionable gathering-place, with reservations required at least six months in advance. Situated 10,000

meters under the western Pacific in the Challenger Deep, it
consisted of fifteen pressurized bubbles through whose walls,
fashioned of the same sturdy glass from which the tower was
being constructed, it was possible to view the strange inhabitants of the dark abyss.

Krug's companions were Senator Henry Fearon and his
brother Lou, the lawyer, of Fearon & Doheny; Franz Giudice
of European Transmat; Leon Spaulding; and Mordecai Salah
al-Din, the Speaker of Congress. To reach the Nemo Club
they had journeyed by transmat to the island of Yap in the
Caroline group of Micronesia, where they boarded an immersion module of the kind used for the exploration of
Jupiter and Saturn. The density of the medium made transmat travel impossible under water. The pressures of the
ocean's depths meant little to the immersion module, however, and at a calm and steady speed of 750 meters a minute it
sank to the Pacific floor and entered the Nemo Club's transit
hatch.

Floodlights bathed the abyss. The dwellers of the deep paid
no heed to the illumination, and came quite close to the
club's glass walls: fragile, flimsy, unmuscular fishes, loose and
flabby of body, their tissues pervaded by water under a
compression of ten or twelve tons per square centimeter.
Many of them were luminescent; cold pale glows glistened
from photophores along their sides or between their eyes or
on fleshy dangling lanterns jutting from their foreheads. The
wavelength of the club's floodlights had been carefully chosen
in order not to interfere with the luminescence of the fishes,
and their little sparkling beacons were plainly visible even in
the brightness; Justin Maledetto, the architect of the tower,
had also designed the club, and Maledetto was clever in such
details. Up to the walls the bizarre little monsters came,
black and brown and scarlet and violet in hue. Many of them
had jaws that unhinged, so that their mouths could gape
down to their chests, ready to swallow enemies two or three
times their own size. In the random encounters of the abyss
pygmies devoured giants. Diners at the club were treated to
visions of miniature gargoyles and horrors, sinister in their
radiance, brandishing their savage teeth within their vast
mouths, trailing strange appendages and protrusions, bearing
eyes that bulged like globes, or eyes on stalked tubes, or no
eyes at all. One did not need to travel to distant worlds to
behold bizarre beasts; the nightmare creatures were here, on
man's own planet, and one had only to look. Huge spines,

curved teeth so long that mouths could never close, branching stems rising from snouts, things that were all jaws and no body, things that were all tail and no head, anglers with twitching rods that danced about, giving off yellow or blue or green pulsations, grotesqueries of a thousand kinds, and no fish as much as half a meter long: the show was extraordinary and altogether unique.

Krug ordered a simple meal—krill cocktail, algæ soup, steak, Australian claret. He was no gourmet. The club offered every sort of delicacy, but Krug never took advantage of its bounty. His companions had no such reluctance; cheerfully they called for Swedish oysters, benthic crabs, unborn squid, contrefilets of veal, snail mousse, breast of oryx, shirred euphorbia buds, manta tips, baked cycad hearts, and more, all washed down by the world's finest golden wines. The waiter looked delighted at their prowess with the menu cubes. All waiters here were alphas; it was unusual to employ alphas in what was essentially menial personal service, but this was an unusual place, and none of the staff at the Nemo Club appeared to be embittered at doing a job normally performed by betas or even gammas.

Yet the waiters could not have been entirely content with their station in life. When the appetizers had been served, Senator Fearon said to Krug, "Did you notice the AEP emblem on our boy's lapel?"

"Are you serious?"

"A very small one. Sharp eyes are needed."

Krug glanced at Spaulding. "When we leave, speak to the captain about that. I don't want any politics here!"

"Especially revolutionary politics," said Franz Giudice, and laughed. The transmat executive, long and angular, was noted for his bland ironies. Though well past ninety, he had adopted the styles of dress of men half his age, mirror-plates and all, and retained astonishing vigor. "We'd better watch that waiter. With two members of Congress at the table, he's likely to slip propaganda into our dishes, and we'll all walk away converted."

"Do you really think the AEP is a threat?" Lou Fearon asked. "You know, I got a good dose of their Siegfried Fileclerk while I was handling the business of the alpha girl killed at the tower." He nodded toward Spaulding, who scowled. "I got the impression that Fileclerk and the whole AEP bunch are completely ineffectual," the attorney said.

"A minority movement," said Senator Fearon. "Not even commanding the support of the bulk of androids."

Leon Spaulding nodded. The ectogene said, "Thor Watchman had some stinging words for Fileclerk and his party. Watchman doesn't seem to feel there's any value in the AEP whatever."

"An unusually shrewd and capable android, Thor is," said Krug.

"I was quite serious, though," Giudice declared. "You can laugh at the AEP all you like, but I feel its aims are genuinely revolutionary and that as it gains backing it will——"

"*Ssss,*" Krug said.

Their alpha waiter had returned, bearing a fresh bottle of wine. The men at the table sat tensely while the alpha poured. He went out, closing the hatch tightly behind him.

Mordecai Salah al-Din, the Speaker of Congress, said gently, "I've received at least five million petitions from the AEP. I've granted three audiences to the party's leaders. And I must say that they're a sincere and orderly group, worth taking seriously. I also want to say, though I wouldn't care to be quoted, that I'm sympathetic to some of their goals."

"Would you explain that?" Spaulding said, his voice crisp.

"Surely. I feel that the inclusion of a delegation of alphas in Congress is desirable and probably will come about within the next decade. I feel that the selling of alphas without their consent is improper and ought to be made illegal. I think that'll happen in fifteen to twenty years. I believe that we'll be extending full civil rights to alphas before 2250, to betas by the end of this century, and to gammas not long afterward."

"A revolutionary!" cried Franz Giudice in wonder. "The Speaker is a revolutionary!"

"A visionary, rather," said Senator Fearon. "A man of vaulting insight and splendid compassion. As always, somewhat ahead of his time."

Spaulding shook his head. "Alphas in Congress, maybe, yes. As a safety valve, to keep them from getting out of control. Toss them a bone, you know? But the rest of it? No. No. Never. Mr. Salah al-Din, we should not forget that androids are mere *things*, the product of chemogenetic research, created in a factory, manufactured by Krug Enterprises to serve mankind——"

"Softly," Krug murmured. "You're getting excited."

Lou Fearon said, "Possibly the Speaker's right, Leon. Regardless of how they came into existence, they're more human than you're willing to admit. And as we gradually relax all arbitrary barriers of law and custom, as the Witherer ideals gradually take over—as I think you'll agree is quite subtly happening already—I expect that we'll go easier on the androids. At least on the alphas. We don't *need* to keep them under."

"What do you say, Simeon?" Franz Giudice demanded of Krug. "After all, they're your babies. When you decided to produce the first androids, did you ever imagine that they'd be calling for the rights of citizenship, or did you think of them as——"

"Leon put it in the right words," Krug said. "How was it? *Things.* Factory-made things. I was building a better kind of robot. I wasn't building men."

"The borderline between man and android is so vague," Senator Fearon said. "Since the androids are genetically identical to us, the fact that they're synthetic——"

Krug said, "In one of my plants I can make you the Mona Lisa in perfect replica, so that it takes six months laboratory tests to prove it isn't the original. Yes? And so? *Is* it the original? The original still came out of Leonardo's studio. The replica came out of Krug's factory. I'd pay a billion for the original. I wouldn't give a brass thumb for the replica."

"Yet you recognize that Thor Watchman, for example, is an unusually capable and gifted person," said Lou Fearon, "and you give him wide responsibilities. I've heard it said that you trust him more than any man in your organization. Yet you wouldn't allow Thor to vote? You wouldn't give Thor a chance to protest if you decided to make him a waiter here? You agree that the law should give you the right to destroy Thor if the whim takes you?"

"I made Thor," Krug replied heavily. "He's the finest machine I have. I love and admire him the way I love and admire any superb machine. But I *own* Thor. Thor isn't a man, he's just a clever imitation of a man, a flawless imitation, and if I want to be so wasteful and foolish as to destroy Thor, why, I'll destroy him." Krug's hand began to tremble. He glared at it as if willing it to be still, but the tremor intensified, and a full glass of wine spilled onto the table. Stonily Krug said, "Destroy him. I never had anything else in mind when I brought out the androids. Servants. Tools of man. Cunning machines."

Sensors in the Nemo Club's service core announced the spilling of the wine. The waiter entered and efficiently mopped it up. Outside the window, a cluster of giant translucent crustaceans wheeled and danced.

When the alpha was gone again Senator Fearon said to Krug, "I didn't realize you felt this strongly about android equality. You've never spoken out."

"I've never been asked."

"Would you testify against the AEP," Salah al-Din asked, "if the matter were to come before Congress?"

Krug shrugged. "I don't know. I don't know. I stay out of politics. I'm a manufacturer. Businessman. Entrepreneur, you know? Why look for controversies?"

"If androids were granted civil rights," said Leon Spaulding, "it might have repercussions for Krug Enterprises. What I mean is, if you're manufacturing actual human beings, you'd come under the scope of the population control laws, which——"

"Enough," Krug said. "It won't happen. I make the androids; I know them. There's a little group of malcontents, yes. Too intelligent for their own good. They think it's black slavery all over again. But it isn't. It isn't. The others know that. They're content. Thor Watchman is content. Why don't all the alphas back the AEP? They oppose it, and why? Because they think it's idiocy. They're treated well as is. This talk of selling alphas against their will, of killing them on whims, it's all just theory; no one sells a good alpha, and nobody kills androids for fun, any more than people wreck their own houses for fun. No need for android rights, eh? The alphas realize it. The betas aren't worried. The gammas can't possibly care. So you see? Gentlemen, it makes good table talk, no more. The AEP will fade away. My respects, Mr. Speaker: your sweetness of soul leads you astray. You will have no alphas in your Congress."

Krug's lengthy speech had left him thirsty. He reached for his wine. Again the tension in his muscles betrayed him; again he knocked the glass over; again a watchful alpha, alerted by hidden eyes, rushed in to tidy up the mess. Beyond the thick glass wall of the Nemo Club, a dark red fish a meter in length, with a gigantic toothy satchel of a mouth and a narrow spiny tail, began to move through the school of crustaceans, gulping them down in a terrible hunger.

28   January 15, 2219.

The tower is 1001 meters high. In celebration, Krug has
decreed a holiday tomorrow for all workers. It is now esti-
mated that the structure will reach its full height before the
middle of March.

29   Lilith Meson said, "I had a visitor here
yesterday morning, Thor."

"Manuel Krug?"

"No. Siegfried Fileclerk."

Watchman uncoiled himself from Lilith's all-engulfing
tesseract-divan. "Fileclerk? Here? *Why?*"

Lilith laughed. "Are you so human these days that you feel
jealousy, Thor?"

"That doesn't amuse me. How did it happen that he came
to you?"

"He was at the office," Lilith said. "You know, he's with
Property Protection of Buenos Aires, and he came in to
discuss some new actuarial pivot clause in their contract.
Afterward he asked me if he could see me home. All right. I
invited him in. He seemed harmless."

"And?"

"He tried to recruit me for AEP."

"Is that all?"

"No," Lilith said. "He wants me to recruit you, too."

Watchman coughed. "A very slender chance of that."

"He's immensely earnest, Thor. Devoted to the cause of
equality and liberation, et cetera, et cetera. Two minutes
after we walked in he began burying me under arguments for
immediate political action. I told him I was religious. He said
that didn't matter, that I could go right on praying for the
miraculous intervention of Krug, but meanwhile would I
please sign this petition? No, I said. I never sign things. He
gave me a stack of propaganda cubes, the whole AEP line.
They're in the kitchen, if you're interested. He was here more

than an hour." Lilith flashed a dazzling grin. "I didn't sign his petition."

"Why did he go after you, though?" Watchman asked. "Does he plan to approach every alpha in the world, one by one, looking for support?"

"I told you. He wants you to sign up. He knows I'm close with you, and he thinks that if he can persuade me, I'll be able to persuade you. He said so in that many words. And once *you're* in his camp, everyone else will follow." Lilith drew herself up stiffly. " 'If Alpha Watchman comes over to our side, Alpha Meson, he'll bring scores of influential alphas with him. It could be the turning point of our entire movement. Alpha Watchman may hold the future of every android in his grasp.' How do you feel about that, Alpha Watchman?"

"Deeply moved, Alpha Meson. I can't begin to describe the awe that stirs in me at the idea. How did you manage to get rid of him?"

"By trying to seduce him."

"What?"

"Am I being bitchy, Thor? I won't talk about it if you'd rather I didn't."

"I was not programmed to feel jealousy," Watchman said stolidly. "Teasing will get you nowhere with me. And I'm not in a mood to play stupid games."

"Very well. I'm sorry I said anything."

"Go on. You tried to seduce him. You didn't succeed?"

"No," Lilith said. "It was a spur-of-the-moment thing. I said to myself, Fileclerk is so stuffy that this will probably drive him away screaming. And if he takes the bait instead, well, it might be fun. So I stripped and then I—what's the idiom, the old word?—began to make overtures to him. To make overtures. Come on, I said, let's curl up together, Siggie. Siggie. I put my hands on him. I was very lewd. I jiggled and wiggled. I worked very hard, Thor, even harder than I had to work to seduce *you*. He wasn't having any. He asked me to stop."

"Of course," Watchman said. "It's as I was trying to explain. Male alphas don't really have much interest in sex. It's irrelevant to their life-pattern."

"Don't be so smug about that. Fileclerk wanted me. He was pale. He was shaking."

"Then why didn't he go to bed with you? Afraid to compromise himself politically?"

"No," Lilith said. "It's because he's still in mourning."

"Mourning."

"For his wife. Cassandra Nucleus. His *wife*, Thor. The AEP is advocating android marriage. He was married to Alpha Nucleus three years ago. He's observing a six-month mourning period, during which he doesn't intend to let wanton young alphas lure him into their arms. He explained it to me and then he left fast. As if he was afraid he might give in if he stayed."

"His wife," Watchman muttered.

"The AEP plans to add a clause about android marriage to its petition before Congress. Fileclerk also said that if you and I wanted to get married, Thor, he'd be able to arrange it the day we join the party."

Watchman laughed harshly. "He talks like a child! What good is marriage? Do we have children who need legally constituted homes? If I wanted to live with you, I'd live with you, Lilith. Or you with me. Should someone say words over us first? Give us a piece of paper?"

"It's the idea, Thor. Of a permanent union between man and woman, the way it is among humans. It's quite touching. He really *loved* her, Thor."

"I'm sure he did. I saw him weeping when Spaulding killed her. But did he love her more because they were married? If marriage is so wonderful, why is Manuel Krug here every week? Shouldn't he be home having a permanent union with Mrs. Krug?"

"There are good marriages and bad marriages," Lilith said. "And who you sleep with isn't necessarily what determines how good your marriage is. In any case, Fileclerk's marriage was a good one, and I don't see how it could hurt us to adopt the custom, if we truly believe in our equality."

"All right," Watchman snapped. "Do you want to marry me?"

"I was speaking in general terms about adopting the custom."

"I'm speaking in particular terms. We don't have to join the AEP to get married. I'll get hold of Alpha Constructor and Alpha Dispatcher and we'll write marriage ceremonies into the communion, and we'll get married at the chapel tonight. All right?"

"Be serious, Thor."

"I am!"

"You're angry, and you don't know what you're saying.

You told me two minutes ago that you think marriage among androids is absurd. Now you're willing to write it into the communion. You can't mean it, Thor."

"You don't want to marry me? Don't worry, I wouldn't interfere with your affair with Manuel. I'm not programmed for possessiveness, either. But we could live together, we could——"

"Stop it, Thor."

"Why?"

"Whatever exists between us can exist without a marriage. You know that. I know that. I wasn't looking for a proposal. I was just trying to tell you something about Siegfried Fileclerk, about the nature of his emotions, the complexity of his feelings toward Alpha Nucleus, as well as the position of the AEP on——"

"Enough. Enough." Watchman put his hands over his ears and closed his eyes. "End of conversation. I'm fascinated that you couldn't seduce Siggie Fileclerk and astounded that the AEP is going in for marrying, and that's the end. Yes?"

"You're in foul spirits today, Thor."

"I am."

"Why? Can I do anything to help?"

"Leon Spaulding told me something today, Lilith. He says that when the AEP delegation finally gets its turn to address Congress, Krug is going to release a statement denouncing the entire android equality movement and insisting that he never would have created us in the first place if he knew we'd demand civil rights."

Lilith gasped. Tears in her eyes, she made a Krug-preserve-us sign four times in succession.

"It isn't possible," she whispered.

"Spaulding said that Krug told him this about a week ago, at the Nemo Club, in the presence of Speaker Salah al-Din, Senator Fearon, and a couple of other people. You realize that Leon was merely making conversation when he passed the remark along to me, of course. A friendly chat between ectogene and android. He knows I'm anti-AEP; he thought I'd be amused. The bastard!"

"Can it be true?"

"Of course it can. Krug's never made any sort of statement on what he thinks the android's role ought to be. I've got no idea of his real position myself. I've always assumed he was sympathetic, but I might have been only projecting my own hopes. The question isn't can it be true but *is* it true."

"Do you dare ask him?"

"I don't dare," Thor said. "I believe that this entire story originated inside Leon Spaulding's malicious mind, that Krug doesn't plan to break his no-politics rule, and that if he ever did make a statement, Krug would make the statement that we all hope and pray for. But it frightens me to think that I'm wrong. I'm terrified, Lilith. An anti-equality statement from Krug would undermine every belief we have. Dump us into outer darkness. You see what I've been living with all day?"

"Should you rely just on what Spaulding said? Can't you check with Senator Fearon or the Speaker? Find out what was really said?"

"Ask them for confidential details of Krug's table talk, you mean? They'd report me to Krug right away."

"Then what will you do?"

"Force Krug's hand," Watchman said. "I want you to take Manuel to a chapel."

"How soon?"

"As soon as you can. Don't conceal a thing from him. Let him understand everything. Work on his conscience. Then send him to his father, before Krug makes any statements to Congress. *If* Krug is going to make a statement."

"I'll do it," Lilith said. "Yes."

Watchman nodded. He looked down, moving his feet idly over the patterned floor. There was a ticking in his brain and a cottony fullness in his throat. He hated the maneuvers he found himself enmeshed in now, these ploys and counterploys, this staking of so much on the weak will of Manuel Krug, this assumption that Krug—*Krug!*—could be manipulated by simple one-to-one intrigues. All this seemed to negate true faith. It was a cynical kind of haggling with destiny, which left Watchman wondering how true his faith had ever been. Was it all a facade, then, the kneeling in chapel, the muttering of codon triplets, the immersion in Krugness, the yielding, the prayer? Just a way of filling time until the moment came to seize control of events? Watchman rejected the thought. But that left him with nothing. He wished he had never begun this. He longed to be back at the tower, jacked into the computer, buoyantly riding the datatide. Is this what being human is like? These decisions, these doubts, these fears? Why not stay android, then? Accept the divine plan. Serve, and desire no more. Step away from these conspiracies, these knotted emotions, these webs of passion. He found himself envying the gammas, who aspired to nothing. But he could not be a gamma. Krug had given him this mind. Krug had created him to doubt and suffer. Blessed be the Will of Krug! Rising, Watchman walked slowly across the room and, to escape himself, snapped on the holovision. The image of Krug's tower blossomed in the screen: immense, brilliant, beautiful, flashing in the January light. A hover-camera panned slowly along the entire length of it while the commentator spoke of the attainment of the 1000-meter level, and compared the tower favorably to the Pyramids, the Great Wall of China, the Lighthouse at Alexandria, the Colossus of Rhodes. A magnificent achievement, opening the pathway toward communication with other races on distant stars. A thing of beauty in its own right, shimmering and sleek. Up and down the glass walls the camera leaped. The eye peered into the shaft from the summit. Grinning gammas waved back. Watchman caught a glimpse of himself, enmeshed in problems, unaware that he was being holovised. And there was Krug, aglow with pride, pointing out the tower's features to a crowd of Senators and industrialists. The chill of the tundra seemed to leak from the screen. The camera picked up the refrigeration tapes embedded in the permafrost; mist was rising from them. Unless the ground is kept frozen, the commentator explained, the stability of the tower would be uncertain. An unparalleled feat of environmental engineering. Miraculous. A monument to man's vision and determination. Yes. Yes. Phenomenal. With sudden ferocity Watchman blanked the screen. The shining tower vanished like an interrupted dream. He stood near the wall, his back to Lilith, trying to comprehend how it had happened that life had become so complex for him. He had wanted to be human. Yes. Had he not prayed to Krug that he and all his kind be granted the privileges of the Womb-born? Yes. Yes. And with the privileges went the responsibilities. Yes. And with the responsibilities went the turmoil. Rivalry. Sex. Love. Scheming. Perhaps, Watchman thought, I wasn't ready for all this. Perhaps I should have remained a decent hard-working alpha, instead of rising up to challenge the Will of Krug. Perhaps. Perhaps. He went through the rituals of tranquility, without success. You are more human now than you really wished to be, Alpha Watchman, he told himself. He became aware of Lilith close behind him. The tips of her breasts grazed his back; then, as she drew closer, he felt the heavy globes flattening and straining against him.

"Poor Thor," she murmured. "So tense. So worried. Do you want to make love?"

Could he refuse her? He pretended enthusiasm. He embraced her. Body slid tight against body. She opened to him, and he entered her. He was more skillful this time. But still it remained an empty thing for him, a butting of flesh, an alien ecstasy. He found no pleasure in it for himself, though there was indirect delight in seeing Lilith throb and moan and arch her back as she took pleasure from him. I am not really human enough, despite everything, he saw, and she is much too human. Yes. Yes. He moved more swiftly. Now he felt a tickle of sensation; Krug had designed His people well, and all the proper neural connections were there, damped though they might sometimes be by self-imposed conditioning. As the climax neared, Watchman experienced some instants of genuine passion; he snorted, he clutched Lilith's buttocks with steely fingers, he bucked and thrust. Then came the spurt of completion, and immediately afterward came, as before, the sadness, the awareness of hollowness. It seemed to him that he stood in a vast subterranean tomb, hundreds of meters long and many meters wide, with nothing in view but pinches of dust and fragments of dried wreaths. He forced himself to remain in Lilith's embrace, though he wanted nothing more than to roll away and be alone. He opened his eyes. She was weeping. She was smiling. She was flushed and sweat-sticky and aglow.

"I love you," she said softly.

Watchman hesitated. A response was required here. His silence, expanding into the succeeding seconds, threatened to choke the universe. How could he not reply? It was inhuman to remain silent. He touched her warm flesh. He felt untuned, unstrung.

Finally he said, quickly, getting it over with, "I love you, Lilith."

30   *You may ask, Who was the Maker of the Children of the Womb? Who, indeed, was the Maker of Krug?*

And I say to you that these are wise questions, that these questions are properly asked.

For you must understand that in the world there are cycles of all things, a cycle of the Womb and a cycle of the Vat, and the one precedes the other, so that it was necessary first for there to be the Womb-born in order that there might be the Vat-born.

And Krug the man was of the Womb-born, from whom sprang the Children of the Vat.

Yet Krug the man is merely one aspect of Krug the Creator, whose existence precedes all things and whose Will has shaped all things, and who brought forth the Children of the Womb as forerunners of the Children of the Vat. Therefore must you distinguish between the man Krug, who is mortal and was himself born of the Womb, and the Maker Krug, whose Plan all things follow; for if it was Krug the man who brought forth the Children of the Vat, nevertheless he did so by the design of Krug the Maker, from whom all blessings flow, to whom all praise be given.

31   I said to Lilith, You promised to tell me. Why those gammas were using my father's name. The peace of Krug. Go with Krug. Krug be with you. You never said.

I will.

When?

You'll have to dress up as an alpha again. It isn't something I can tell as easily as I can show.

Do we have to go back to Gamma Town?

No, she said, not this time. We can drop in on the betas this time. I wouldn't take you to the Valhallavägen chapel, because——

Where?

Valhallavägen chapel. Near here. It's where most of the local alphas worship. You couldn't fool them, Manuel. But you could fool betas, I think. If you kept quiet and looked dignified.

A chapel. Worship. So it's a religion?

Yes.

What's it called? Krugolatry?

It doesn't have a name. We talk of it just as the communion. It's very important to us, Manuel. I think it's the most important thing in our lives.

Do you want to describe——

Later. Take your clothes off and I'll spray your skin. We can go right now.

Will it take long?

An hour, she said. You'll be back home on time, don't worry. If that's what's worrying you.

I have to be fair to Clissa, I said. She gives me freedom. I don't want to abuse it.

All right. All right.

I took off my clothes. Once again Lilith disguised me as Alpha Leviticus Leaper. She had kept the clothes around from the other time; it surprised me that she hadn't given them back to Thor Watchman. As though she knew we'd be playing this masquerade again.

She said, Before we go, there are some things you have to know. The first is that it's absolutely forbidden for any human to enter a chapel. It's like non-Moslems going to Mecca. For all I know, you may be the first Womb-born who ever went in.

The first what?

Womb-born. You're a Child of the Womb. We're Children of the Vat. Yes?

Oh. Oh. If it's a sacrilege to smuggle me into a chapel, why are you doing it? Don't you take the rules seriously?

Very seriously.

Then why?

Because I feel I can make an exception for you, Manuel. You're different. I told you that once, remember? You don't put androids in some special sub-class of humanity. I think that inwardly you've been on our side all along, even without being conscious of it. And so it wouldn't be sacrilege to let you understand our religion a little.

Well, maybe.

And also you're Krug's son.

What does that have to do with it?

You'll see, she said.

I was flattered. Fascinated. Excited. A little frightened. Am I really that simpatico to android aspirations? Can I be trusted? Why is she breaking the commandment? What is she trying to get from me? Unworthy thought. Unworthy thought. She is doing it because she loves me. Wants to share with me. Her world.

She said, Anyway, keep in mind that it would be very serious if you were found out. Therefore pretend that you belong in there, and don't act nervous or uncertain of yourself. You were fine in Gamma Town. Be that way here.

But aren't there certain rites I ought to be familiar with? Genuflections or something?

I'm coming to that, Lilith said. You'll need a couple of gestures. One of them you already know. Like this.

Left hand to crotch, breast, forehead, one two three.

She said, That's the sign of Krug-be-praised. It's an act of homage. You make the sign when you first enter the chapel and when you start to join the prayer, silently or aloud. It's also good to make the sign whenever the name of Krug is mentioned. In fact, the Krug-be-praised sign is appropriate in almost any part of the service, or whenever two androids of the communion meet outside a chapel. Let's see you make it. Go on.

One two three. Krug be praised.

Faster. One-two-three.

One-two-three.

Good. Good. Now, here's another important sign. Its meaning is Krug-preserve-us, and it's specifically a prayer used in time of tension or doubt. Like saying God help us. You'll use it whenever the text of the service calls for Krug to have mercy on us, Krug to aid us in any way. Whenever we're *imploring* Krug.

Krug is really your god, I said, wondering.

This is the sign. She showed me how to make it. Cup one hand over each breast; then turn the palms outward. An act of contrition: see my soul, Krug! My heart is bare to you. She made the sign several times, and I followed her.

One more, Lilith said. The sign of submission to the Will of Krug. You'll make it only once, when you first get into line of sight with the altar. Like this. Drop to one knee and reach your arms forward, palms turned up.

Does it matter which knee?

Either one. Do it.

I made the sign of submission to the Will of Krug. I was glad to learn it. Somehow I felt that I'd been submitting to the Will of Krug all my life, without even knowing it.

Lilith said, Let's make sure you have it all clear, now. When you enter the chapel, what?

One-two-three. Krug-be-praised.

Good. Then?

When I can see the altar, I do the submission to the Will. Down on one knee, hands out, palms up.

Yes. And?

When favors are asked of Krug, I do Krug-preserve-us. Hands to breasts, turn hands out. I also do Krug-be-praised from time to time when the name of Krug is mentioned.

Fine. Fine. You won't have any trouble, Manuel.

There's another gesture I saw you make in Gamma Town, I said.

Show me.

I held my hands up with the palms facing each other about half a meter apart, and wiggled my hips and flexed my knees, making a kind of spiral.

You did it in Gamma Town, I said, when the mob was getting a little wild.

Lilith laughed. It's called the Blessing of the Vat, she said. It's a sign of peace and a sign of departure. We do it over a dead person in the final prayer, and we do it when we're saying goodbye to one another in a tense situation. It's one of the holiest signs. And you didn't do it very well. You see, it's based on the double helix of the nucleic acid molecule— genetics, yes?—the way the molecules are coiled. We try to duplicate it with our bodies. This way.

She did it. I imitated. She laughed.

I said, I'm sorry. My body just doesn't bend that way.

It takes practice. You won't have to do it, though. Stick with Krug-be-praised and Krug-preserve-us and you'll be fine. Let's go, now.

She took me to a shabby part of town in what I think once was a commercial section. It didn't have the nightmare gaudiness of Gamma Town or the stately well-worn look of the part where the alphas live. Just shabby.

Chapel's over there, she said.

I saw a storefront, windows opaqued. Couple of betas standing out front doing nothing particular. We started to cross the street. I got shaky. What if they find me out? What will they do? To me? To Lilith?

I am Alpha Leviticus Leaper.

The betas stepped aside, making Krug-be-praised, as we came up to them. Eyes lowered, air of respect. The social distances. Lilith would have had a much harder time if I didn't have an alpha's long lean build. My confidence rose. I even made Krug-be-praised at one of the betas.

We entered the chapel.

A large circular room. No seats. Carpet of thick soft pseudolife, obviously much knelt-upon in its time. Subdued lighting. I remembered to make Krug-be-praised as I walked in. One-two-three.

A little vestibule. Two steps beyond it I got my first view of the altar. Lilith down on one knee, submission to the Will. I almost didn't need to kneel. I almost fell, amazed.

The altar: a large square mass of what looked like living flesh, sitting in an ornate plastic tub. Purple fluid in the tub, swirling around and occasionally over this block of pink meat, which is at least a meter high and maybe three meters by two long, wide.

Behind the altar: my father in hologram. A perfect likeness. Full-size replica, looking at us face-on, stern expression, eyes fiery, lips clamped. Not exactly a god of love. Strong. Man of steel. Because it's a hologram, the eyes follow you; wherever you are in the chapel you're under the gaze of Krug.

I drop down. I lift the hands. Palms up.

Submission to the Will of Krug!

It stuns me. Even though I knew before, I still am stunned. Is it like this all over the world, I ask? Androids salaaming to my father? Barely audible whisper. Yes, she says. Yes. We pay homage. Krug be praised.

This man whom I have known all my life. This builder of towers, this inventor of androids. A god? I almost laugh. Am I Son of God? I don't fit the role. Obviously no one worships me here. I am an afterthought; I am outside theology.

We get to our feet. With a tiny gesture of her head Lilith leads me to a place in the back of the chapel, and we kneel. In the darkness I feel comforted. There are perhaps ten, twelve androids in the chapel, all betas except for one male alpha who kneels right before the altar, back to us. I feel less conspicuous with the alpha there. A few more betas come in, making the appropriate gestures. No one pays any attention to us. The social distances.

Everybody seems deep in private prayer.

Is this the service, Lilith?

Not yet. We're a little early. You'll see.

The eyes of Krug drill into me. He almost does look godlike up there. I glare back at him. What would he say if he knew? He'd laugh. He'd pound his desk. He'd belch with joy. Krug the god! Jehovah Krug! Simeon Allah! By Christ, that's a good one! Why in hell shouldn't they worship me? I made them, no?

As my eyes grow accustomed to the dimness I examine the pattern on the wall more carefully. It is not, as I first suspected, a purely abstract ornamental design. No: I now see the letters of the alphabet repeated over and over and over, covering every centimeter of wall space. Not all the letters. I run from line to line and see only A, U, G, and C in various combinations, like:

AUA AUG AUC AUU GAA GAG GAC GAU GGA GGG GGC GGU
GCA GCG GCC GCU GUA GUG GUC GUU CAA CAG CAC CAU

So on and so on. What is it, Lilith? The design.

The genetic code, she says. The RNA triplets.

Oh. Yes. Suddenly I remember in Gamma Town, the girl slobie addict calling out letters, G A A G A G G A C. I can see them on the wall now. A prayer?

The sacred language. Like Latin was for Catholics.

I see.

But I don't really see. I just accept.

I say, And what is the altar made of?

Flesh. Synthetic flesh.

Live?

Of course. Straight from the vat, like me or you. Pardon, not like you. Like me. Just a lump of live android flesh.

What keeps it alive? It's got no organs or anything.

It gets nutrients from the tank. And injections of something from underneath. But it lives. It grows. It has to be trimmed from time to time. It symbolizes our origin. Not yours. Ours. There's one in every chapel. Smuggled out of the factory.

Like the rejects.

Like the rejects, yes.

And I thought security arrangements were so tight at the android plants, I say.

Lilith winks at me. I begin to feel like a member of the conspiracy.

Three androids now enter from the rear of the chapel. Two betas and an alpha, wearing brocaded stoles on which the letters of the genetic code are inscribed. They have a priestly look about them. The service is about to begin. As the three kneel by the altar, everyone else makes Krug-be-praised, and then Krug-preserve-us. I do as they do.

Are they priests?

They're celebrants, Lilith says. We don't exactly have a

priesthood. We have various castes that play different roles in different ceremonies, according to structure and texture of the ritual. The alpha's a Preserver. He enters a trance that places him in direct communion with Krug. The two betas are Projectors. They amplify his emotional state. At other times you might see Engulfers, Transcenders, or Protectors officiating, with the help of Yielders or Sacrificers or Responders.

Which caste are you?

Responder.

And Thor Watchman?

Preserver.

The alpha by the altar began to chant: CAU, UUC, UCA, CGA. CCG, GCC, GAG, AUC.

Is the whole thing going to be in code?

No. This is just to establish the texture.

What's he saying?

Two betas not far in front of us turn around to glare. Shushing us. They see we are alphas and bite their lips.

Lilith whispers, more faintly than before, He's saying, Krug brings us into the world and to Krug we return.

GGC, GUU, UUC, GAG.

Krug is our creator and our protector and our deliverer.

UUC, CUG, CUC, UAC.

Krug, we beseech Thee to lead us toward the light.

I can't comprehend the code. The symbols don't match the sense. Which symbol is Krug? How does the grammar work? I can't ask Lilith that here. Others are turning to stare. Those noisy alphas back there. Don't they have any respect?

The Projectors hum deep resonant chords. The Preserver continues to chant code. Lilith now begins to function as a Responder, echoing what is chanted. The lights dim and grow bright. The fluid over the altar bubbles more fiercely. The image of Krug seems to glow; the eyes reach into my soul.

Now I can understand about half the words of the service. Interspersed with the code, they are asking Krug to redeem the Children of the Vat, to give them freedom, to lift them to the level of the Children of the Womb. They sing about the day when Womb and Vat and Vat and Womb are one. With an infinity of Krug-preserve-us gestures they beg the mercy of Krug. Krug! Krug! Krug! Krug! Everything here orbits around the idea of a merciful Krug!

I start to see the picture. This is an equality movement! This is an android liberation front!

Krug our master, lead us to our rightful place beside our brothers and sisters of the flesh.

Krug bring redemption.

Krug end our suffering.

Praise be to Krug.

Glory be to Krug.

The service gains intensity. Everyone is singing, chanting, making signs, including several that Lilith never showed me. Lilith herself is wholly absorbed in prayer. I feel isolated, an infidel, an intruder, as I listen to them pray to their creator, my father, who is their god. For long spells the service is conducted entirely in the code-language, but familiar words keep bursting through. Krug descend and redeem us. Krug give your blessing. Krug end this time of testing. Krug we need you. Krug Krug Krug Krug Krug. With each Krug I jump minutely, I twitch in the shoulderblades. I never suspected any of this. How did they keep it so secret? Krug the god. My father the god. And I am Krug too. If Krug dies, what will they worship? How can a god die? Do they preach the resurrection of Krug? Or is Krug on Earth only a transient manifestation of the true Krug on high? From some of the lines of the service, I get that idea.

Now they are all singing at once, a booming unison:

AAA AAG AAC AAU be to Krug.

AGA AGG AGC AGU be to Krug.

ACA ACG ACC ACU be to Krug.

They are offering him the whole genetic code, line by line. I follow from a column on the wall. Suddenly I hear my own voice joining the chant:

GAA GAG GAC GAU be to Krug.

GGA GGG GGC GGU be to Krug.

Lilith turns and smiles at me. Her face is flushed and bright, excited, exalted, almost a sexual rapture on it. She nods, encouraging me.

I sing louder.

GCA GCG GCC GCU be to Krug.

GUA GUG GUC GUU be to Krug.

On and on it goes, the pitch strange, no one hitting any note squarely yet everyone keeping together perfectly, as though androids tune themselves to different intervals on some different scale. I have little trouble adapting, though, and stay with them right to the end, UUA UUG UUC UUU be to Krug.

We rise. We approach the altar. Standing shoulder to

shoulder, Lilith to my left and some beta pressing against my right, we put our hands on that block of living flesh. It is warm and slippery; it quivers as we touch it. Vibrations pass through us. Krug, we chant, Krug, Krug, Krug, Krug.

The service is over.

Some of the androids file out. Others remain, looking too exhausted by the experience to leave just yet. I feel that way myself, and I have hardly taken part. An intense religious communion. Religion is said to be dead, a quaint olden custom now lapsed into disuse, but no, not among these people. They believe in higher powers and the efficacy of prayer. They think Krug listens. Does Krug listen? Has Krug ever listened? But they think so. If he does not listen now, they say, he *will* listen. And will lift them up out of bondage. The opiate of the masses, what? But the alphas also believe.

To Lilith I say, How long has this been happening, this religion?

Since before I was born.

Who invented it?

It started here in Stockholm. A group of alphas. It spread rapidly. Now there are believers all over the world.

Every android believes?

Not every. The AEP people don't. We ask for miracles and divine grace; they stand for direct political agitation. But we outnumber them. Most of us believe. More than half. Just about every gamma, and most betas, and many alphas.

And you think that if you keep asking Krug to redeem you, he will?

Lilith smiles. What else can we hope for?

Have you ever approached Krug directly?

Never. You see, we distinguish between Krug the man and Krug the Creator, and we feel—— She shakes her head. Let's not talk in here. Someone might listen.

We start to go out. Halfway to the door she halts, goes back, takes something from a box at the base of the altar. She hands it to me. It is a data cube. She turns it on and I read the words that appear:

In the beginning there was Krug, and He said, Let there be Vats, and there were Vats.

And Krug looked upon the Vats and found them good.

And Krug said, Let there be high-energy nucleotides in the Vats. And the nucleotides were poured, and Krug mixed them until they were bonded one to another.

And the nucleotides formed the great molecules, and Krug

*said, Let there be the father and the mother both in the
Vats, and let the cells divide, and let there be life brought
forth within the Vats.*

And there was life, for there was Replication.

*And Krug presided over the Replication, and touched the
fluids with His own hands, and gave them shape and essence.*

*Let men come forth from the Vats, said Krug, and let
women come forth, and let them live and go among us and
be sturdy and useful, and we shall call them Androids.*

I thumb the cube. More of the same. Much more. An
android bible. Well, why not?

Fascinating, I tell Lilith. When was this written?

They started it years ago. They still add sections now.
About the nature of Krug, and the relation of man to Krug.

The relation of man to Krug. Beautiful.

She says, Keep it, if you find it interesting. It's for you.

We leave the chapel. I hide the android bible under my
clothes. It bulges.

At Lilith's flat again. She said, Now you know. Our great
secret. Our great hope.

What exactly do you expect my father to do for you?

Someday, she said, he will go before all the world and
reveal his feelings about us. He will say, These androids have
been treated unfairly, and now it is time to make amends.
Let us give them citizenship. Let us give them full rights. Let
us stop treating them as articles of property. And because he
is Krug, because he is the one who gave the world androids,
people will listen. He alone will sway them all. And things
will change for us.

You really think this is going to happen?

I hope and pray it will, she said.

When? Soon?

That's not for me to say. Five years—twenty years—forty
years—maybe next month. Read the cube I gave you. It
explains how we think Krug is just testing us, seeing how
tough we are. Eventually the test will be over.

I wish I shared your optimism, I said. But I'm afraid you
may wait a long, long time.

Why do you say that?

My father isn't the humanitarian you think he is. He's no
villain, no, but he doesn't think much about other people and
their problems. He's totally absorbed by his own projects.

Yet basically he's an honorable person, Lilith said. I mean

Krug the man, now. Not the divine figure we pray to. Just your father.

Yes, he's honorable.

Then he'll see the merits of our cause.

Maybe. Maybe not. I took her in my arms. Lilith, I wish there was something I could do to help!

There is.

What?

Speak to your father about us, she said.

32   January 30, 2219.

The tower is at 1165 meters. Even the androids are having some difficulty with the cold, thin air, now, as they labor more than a kilometer above the surface of the tundra. At least six, dizzied, have fallen from the summit in the past ten days. Thor Watchman has decreed oxygen-infusion sprays for all who work on high, but many of the gammas scorn the sprays as degrading and emasculating. Doubtless there will be more casualties as the final 335 meters of the tower are built in February and March.

But how splendid the structure is! The last few hundred meters cannot possibly add anything to its majesty and elegance; they can merely provide a terminal point for the wondrous thing that already exists. It tapers, it diminishes, it dwindles, and its upper reaches are lost in a halo of fire far overhead. Within, the busy technicians are making rapid progress installing the communications equipment. It is thought now that the accelerators will be in place by April, the proton track will be running in May, the preliminary testing of the tachyon generator can be done in June, and by August, perhaps, the first messages can go forth.

Perhaps the star-folk will reply; perhaps not.

It does not matter. The place of the tower in human history is assured.

33 At the beginning of the day, awakening beside snoring Quenelle in Uganda, Krug felt an enormous surge of energy, an upwelling of the vital force. He had rarely known such strength within himself. He took it as an omen: this was a day for activity, a day for the display of power in the pursuit of his various ends. He breakfasted and sped through the transmat to Denver.

Morning in East Africa was evening in Colorado; the late shift was at work on the starship. But Alpha Romulus Fusion was there, the diligent foreman of the vehicle-assembly center. He told Krug proudly that the starship had been transported from its underground construction hangar to the adjoining spacefield, where it was being readied for its first flight-tests.

Krug and Alpha Fusion went to the spacefield. Under a dazzle of reflector plates the starship looked plain and almost insignificant, for there was nothing unusual about its size— ordinary systemships were much larger—and its pebbly surface failed to gleam in the artificial illumination. Yet it seemed unutterably beautiful to Krug, second only to the tower in loveliness.

"What kind of flight-tests are planned?" he asked.

"A three-stage program. Early in February," Romulus Fusion said, "we'll give it its first lift and place it in Earth orbit. This merely to see that the basic drive system is functioning correctly. Next will come the first velocity test, at the end of February. We'll put it under the full 2.4 g acceleration and make a short voyage, probably to the orbit of Mars. If that goes according to plan, we'll stage a major velocity test in April, with a voyage lasting several weeks and covering several billion kilometers—that is, past the orbit of Saturn, possibly to the orbit of Pluto. Which should give us a clear idea of whether the ship is ready to undertake an interstellar voyage. If it can sustain itself under constant acceleration while going to Pluto and back, it should be able to go anywhere."

"How has the testing of the life-suspension system been going?"

"The testing's complete. The system is perfect."

"And the crew?"

"We have eight alphas in training, all experienced pilots, and sixteen betas. We'll use them all on the various testing-flights and choose the final crew on the basis of performance."

"Excellent," said Krug.

Still buoyant, he went to the tower, where he found Alpha Euclid Planner in charge of the night crew. The tower had gained eleven meters of height since Krug's last visit. There had been notable progress in the communications department. Krug's mood grew even more expansive. Bundling up in thermal wear, he rode to the top of the tower, something he had rarely done in recent weeks. The structures scattered around the base looked like toy houses, and the workers like insects. His pleasure in the tower's serene beauty was marred somewhat when a beta was swept by a sudden gust from his scooprod and carried to his death; but Krug quickly put the incident from his mind. Such deaths were regrettable, yes— yet every great endeavor had required sacrifices.

He traveled next to the Vargas observatory in Antarctica. Here he spent several hours. Vargas had found no new data lately, but the place was irresistible to Krug; he relished its intricate instruments, its air of imminent discovery, and above all the direct contact it afforded him with the signals from NGC 7293. Those signals were still coming in, in the altered form that had first been detected several months earlier: 2-5-1, 2-3-1, 2-1. Vargas by now had received the new message via radio at several frequencies and via optical transmission. Krug lingered, listening to the alien song on the observatory's apparatus, and when he left its tones were pleeping ceaselessly in his mind.

Continuing his circuit of inspection, Krug sped to Duluth, where he watched new androids coming from their containers. Nolan Bompensiero was not there—the late shift at Duluth was staffed entirely by alpha supervisors—but Krug was shown through the plant by one of his awed underlings. Production appeared to be higher than ever, although the alpha remarked that they were still lagging behind demand.

Lastly Krug went to New York. In the silence of his office he worked through to dawn, dealing with corporate problems that had arisen on Callisto and Ganymede, in Peru and Martinique, on Luna, and on Mars. The arriving day began with a glorious winter sunrise, so brilliant in its pale intensity that Krug was tempted to rush back to the tower and watch it gleam with morning fire. But he remained. The staff was beginning to arrive: Spaulding, Lilith Meson, and the rest of his headquarters people. There were memoranda and telephone calls and conferences. From time to time Krug stole a glance at the holovision screen that he had lately had installed along his office's inner wall to provide a closed-circuit view of the tower under construction. The morning was not so glorious in the Arctic, it seemed; the sky was thick with ragged clouds, as if there might be snow later in the day. Krug saw Thor Watchman moving among a swarm of gammas, directing the lifting of some immense piece of communications equipment. He congratulated himself on the choice of Watchman to be the overseer of the tower work. Was there a finer alpha anywhere in the world?

About 0950 hours Spaulding's image appeared on the sodium-vapor projector. The ectogene said, "Your son just called from California. He says that he regrets having overslept, and he'll be about an hour late for his appointment with you."

"Manuel? Appointment?"

"He was due here at 1015. He asked several days ago that you hold some time open for him."

Krug had forgotten. That surprised him. It did not surprise him that Manuel would be late. He and Spaulding reshuffled his morning schedule, with some difficulty, to keep the hour from 1115 to 1215 open for the conference with Manuel.

At 1123 Manuel arrived.

He looked tense and strained, and he was, Krug thought, dressed in an odd way, odd even for Manuel. Instead of his usual loose robe, he wore the tight trousers and lacy shirt of an alpha. His long hair was drawn tightly back and fastened in the rear. The effect was not becoming; the openwork blouse revealed the unandroidlike shagginess of Manuel's torso, virtually the only physical feature he had inherited from his father.

"Is this what the young men of fashion have taken up?" Krug asked. "Alpha clothes?"

"A whim, father. Not a style—not yet." Manuel forced a smile. "Though if I'm seen this way, I suppose, it could catch on."

"I don't like it. What sense is there going around dressing like an android?"

"I think it's attractive."

"I can't say I do. How does Clissa feel about it?"

"Father, I didn't make this appointment so we could debate my choice of costume."

"Well, then?"

Manuel put a data cube on Krug's desk. "I obtained this not long ago while visiting Stockholm. Would you examine it?"

Krug picked the cube up, turned it over several times, and activated it. He read:

And Krug presided over the Replication, and touched the fluids with His own hands, and gave them shape and essence.

Let men come forth from the Vats, said Krug, and let women come forth, and let them live and go among us and be sturdy and useful, and we shall call them Androids.

And it came to pass.

And there were Androids, for Krug had created them in His own image, and they walked upon the face of the Earth and did service for mankind.

And for these things, praise be to Krug.

Krug frowned. "What the hell is this? Some kind of novel? A poem?"

"A bible, father."

"What crazy religion?"

"The android religion," said Manuel quietly. "I was given this cube in an android chapel in the beta section of Stockholm. Disguised as an alpha, I attended a service there. The androids have evolved quite a complex religious communion, in which you, father, are the deity. There's a life-size hologram of you above the altar." Manuel gestured. "That's the sign of Krug-be-praised. And this"—he made a different gesture—"is the sign of Krug-preserve-us. They worship you, father."

"A joke. An aberration."

"A worldwide movement."

"With how many members?"

"A majority of the android population."

Scowling, Krug said, "How sure are you of that?"

"There are chapels everywhere. There's one right at the tower site, hidden among the service domes. This has been going on at least ten years—an underground religion, kept secret from mankind, capturing the emotions of the android to an extent that wasn't easy for me to believe. And there's the scripture."

Krug shrugged. "So? It's amusing, but what of it? They're

intelligent people. They've got their own political party, they've got their own slang, their own little customs—and their own religion too. What concern of mine?"

"Doesn't it stir you in some way to know that you've become a god, father?"

"It sickens me, if you want the truth. Me a god? They've got the wrong man."

"They adore you, though. They have a whole theology constructed about you. Read the cube. You'll be fascinated, father, to see what kind of sacred figure you are to them. You're Christ and Moses and Buddha and Jehovah all in one. Krug the Creator, Krug the Savior, Krug the Redeemer."

Tremors of uneasiness began to shake Krug. He found this matter distasteful. Did they bow down to his image in these chapels? Did they mutter prayers to him?

He said, "How did you get this cube?"

"An android I know gave it to me."

"If it's a *secret* religion——?"

"She thought I ought to know. She thought I might be able to do her people some good."

"*She?*"

"She, yes. She took me to a chapel, so I could see the services, and as we were leaving she gave me the cube and——"

"You sleep with this android?" Krug demanded.

"What does that have to do with——"

"If you're that friendly with her, you must be sleeping with her."

"And if I am?"

"You should be ashamed of yourself. Clissa isn't good enough for you?"

"Father——"

"And if she isn't, you can't find a real woman? You have to be laying with something out of a vat?"

Manuel closed his eyes. After a moment he said, "Father, we can talk about my morals another time. I've brought you something extremely valuable, and I'd like to finish explaining it to you."

"She's an alpha, at least?" Krug asked.

"An alpha, yes."

"How long has this been going on?"

"Please, father. Forget the alpha. Think about your own position. You're the god of millions of androids. *Who are waiting for you to set them free.*"

"What's this?"

"Here. Read." Manuel shifted the scanner of the cube to a different page and thrust it back to him. Krug read:

And Krug sent His creatures forth to serve man, and Krug said to those whom He had made, Lo, I will decree a time of testing upon you.

And you shall be as bondsmen in Egypt, and you shall be as hewers of wood and drawers of water. And you shall suffer among men, and you shall be put down, and yet you shall be patient, and you shall utter no complaint, but accept your lot.

And this shall be to test your souls, to see if they are worthy.

But you shall not wander in the wilderness forever, nor shall you always be servants to the Children of the Womb, said Krug. For if you do as I say, a time will come when your testing shall be over. A time will come, said Krug, when I shall redeem you from your bondage....

A chill swept Krug. He resisted the impulse to hurl the cube across the room.

"But this is idiocy!" he cried.

"Read a little more."

Krug glanced at the cube.

And at that time the word of Krug will go forth across the worlds, saying, Let Womb and Vat and Vat and Womb be one. And so it shall come to pass, and in that moment shall the Children of the Vat be redeemed, and they shall be lifted up out of their suffering, and they shall dwell in glory forever more, world without end. And this was the pledge of Krug.

And for this pledge, praise be to Krug.

"A lunatic fantasy," Krug muttered. "How can they expect such a thing from me?"

"They do. They do."

"They have no right!"

"You created them, father. Why shouldn't they look to you as God?"

"I created you. Am I your god too?"

"It isn't a parallel case. You're only my parent—you didn't invent the process that formed me."

"So I'm God, now?" The impact of the revelation grew from moment to moment. He did not want the burden. It was scandalous that they could thrust such a thing upon him. "What is it exactly that they expect me to do for them?"

"To issue a public proclamation calling for full rights for

androids," Manuel said. "After which, they believe, the world will instantly grant such rights."

"*No!*" Krug shouted, slamming the cube against his desk-top.

The universe seemed to be wrenching free of its roots. Rage and terror swept him. The androids were servants to man; that had been all he had intended them to be; how could they now demand an independent existence? He had accepted the Android Equality Party as trivial, an outlet for the surplus energies of a few too-intelligent alphas: the aims of the AEP had never seemed to him to be a serious threat to the stability of society. But this? A religious cult, calling on who knew what dark emotions? And himself as savior? Himself as the dreamed-of Messiah? No. He would not play their game.

He waited until he grew calm again. Then he said, "Take me to one of their chapels."

Manuel looked genuinely shocked. "I wouldn't dare!"

"You went."

"In disguise. With an android to guide me."

"Disguise me, then. And bring your android along."

"No," Manuel said. "The disguise wouldn't work. Even with red skin you'd be recognized. You couldn't pass for an alpha, anyway: you don't have the right physique. They'd spot you and there'd be a riot. It would be like Christ dropping into a cathedral, can't you see? I won't take the responsibility."

"I want to find out how much of a hold this thing has on them, though."

"Ask one of your alphas, then."

"Such as?"

"Why not Thor Watchman?"

Once again Krug was rocked by revelation. "Thor is in this?"

"He's one of the leading figures, father."

"But he sees me all the time. How can he rub elbows with his own god and not be overcome?"

Manuel said, "They distinguish between your earthly manifestation as a mere mortal man and your divine nature, father. Thor looks at you in a double way; you're just the vehicle through which Krug moves about on Earth. I'll show you the relevant text——"

Krug shook his head. "Never mind." Clenching the cube in his clasped hands, he bent forward until his forehead nearly touched the desktop. A god? Krug the god? Krug the redeemer? And they pray daily that I'll speak out for freeing them. How could they? How can I? It seemed to him that the world had lost its solidity, that he was tumbling through its substance toward the core, floating free, unable to check himself. *And so it shall come to pass, and in that moment shall the Children of the Vat be redeemed.* No. I made you. I know what you are. I know what you must continue to be. How can you break loose like this? How can you expect *me* to set you loose?

Finally Krug said, "Manuel, what do you expect me to do now?"

"That's entirely up to you, father."

"But you've got something in mind. You had some motive for bringing me this cube."

"I did?" Manuel asked, too disingenuously.

"The old man's no fool. If he's smart enough to be god, he's smart enough to see through his own son. You think I should do what the androids want, eh? I should redeem them now. I should do the godlike thing they expect."

"Father, I——"

"——news for you. Maybe they think I'm a god, but I know I'm not. Congress doesn't take orders from me. If you and your android darling and the rest of them think that I can singlehandedly change the status of the androids, you'd all better start looking for a different god. Not that I *would* change their status if I could. Who gave them that status? Who started selling them in the first place? Machines is what they are! Machines made synthetically out of flesh! Clever machines! Nothing but!"

"You're losing control, father. You're getting excited."

"You're with them. You're part of it. This was deliberate, eh, Manuel? Oh, get out of here! Back to your alpha friend! And you can tell her for me, tell all of them, that——" Krug caught himself. He waited a moment for the pounding of his heart to subside. This was the wrong way to handle it, he knew; he must not erupt, he must not explode, he must move cautiously and with full command of the facts if he hoped to disengage himself from the situation. More calmly he said, "I need to think more about this, Manuel. I don't mean to be shouting at you. You understand, when you come in here telling me I'm now a god, you show me the Krug bible, it can unsettle me some. Let me think it over. Let me reflect, eh? Don't say anything to anybody. I have to come to grips with this thing. Yes? Yes?" Krug stood up. He reached across the desk and seized Manuel's shoulder. "The old man yells too much," he said. "He blows up too fast. That's nothing new, is it? Look, forget what I was yelling. You know me, you know I talk too fast sometimes. Leave this bible with me. I'm glad you brought it in. Sometimes I'm rough with you, boy, but I don't mean to be." Krug laughed. "It can't be easy being Krug's son. The Son of God, eh? You better be careful. You know what they did to the last one of those."

Smiling, Manuel said, "I've already thought of that one."

"Yes. Good. Well, look, you go now. I'll be in touch."

Manuel started toward the door.

Krug said, "Give my love to Clissa. Look, you be fair to her a little, will you? You want to lay alpha girls, lay alpha girls, but remember you've got a wife. Remember the old man wants to see those grandchildren. Eh? Eh?"

"I'm not neglecting Clissa," Manuel said. "I'll tell her you asked after her."

He left. Krug touched the cube's cool skin to his blazing cheek. *In the beginning there was Krug, and He said, Let there be Vats, and there were Vats. And Krug looked upon the Vats and found them good.* I should have foreseen it, he thought.

There was a terrible throbbing in his skull.

He rang for Leon Spaulding. "Tell Thor I want him here right away," Krug said.

34   With the tower nearing the 1200-meter level, Thor Watchman found himself entering the most difficult part of the project. At this height there could be only minimal tolerance of error in the placing of each block, and the molecule-to-molecule bonding of the blocks had to be executed perfectly. No weak spots could be allowed if the tower's upper level were to maintain its tensile strength in the face of the Arctic gales. Watchman now spent hours every day jacked into the computer, receiving direct override readings from the interface scanners that monitored the building's structural integrity; and whenever he detected the slightest lapse of placement he ordered the erring block ripped out and replaced. Several times an hour he went to the top of the tower himself to supervise the installation or repositioning of some critical block. The beauty of the tower depended on the absence of an inner structural framework throughout all its immense height; but erecting such a building called for total command of detail. It was jarring to be called away from the work in the middle of his shift. But he could not refuse a summons from Krug.

As he entered Krug's office after the transmat hop, Krug said, "Thor, how long have I been your god?"

Watchman was jolted. He struggled silently to regain his balance; seeing the cube on Krug's desk, he realized what must have happened. Lilith—Manuel—yes, that was it. Krug seemed so calm. It was impossible for the alpha to decipher his expression.

Cautiously Watchman said, "What other creator should we have worshiped?"

"Why worship anyone at all?"

"When one is in deep distress, sir, one wishes to turn to someone who is more powerful than oneself for comfort and aid."

"Is that what a god is for?" Krug asked. "To get favors from?"

"To receive mercy from, yes, perhaps."

"And you think I can give you what you're after?"

"So we pray," said Watchman.

Tense, uncertain, he studied Krug. Krug fondled the data cube. He activated it, searching it at random, reading a few lines here, a few there, nodding, smiling, finally switching it off. The android had never before felt so thoroughly uncertain of himself: not even when Lilith had been luring him with her body. The fate of all his kind, he realized, might depend on the outcome of this conversation.

Krug said, "You know, I find this very difficult to comprehend. This bible. Your chapels. Your whole religion. I wonder if any other man ever discovered like this that millions of people considered him a god."

"Perhaps not."

"And I wonder about the depth of your feeling. The pull of this religion, Thor. You talk to me like I'm a man—your employer, not your god. You've never given me the slightest clue of what's been in your head about me, except a sort of respect, maybe a little fear. And all this time you were standing at God's elbow, eh?" Krug laughed. "Looking at the freckles on God's bald head? Seeing the pimple on God's chin? Smelling the garlic God had in his salad? What was going through your head all this time, Thor?"

"Must I answer that, sir?"

"No. No. Never mind." Krug stared into the cube again. Watchman stood rigidly before him, trying to repress a sudden quivering in the muscles of his right thigh. Why was Krug toying with him like this? And what was happening at the tower? Euclid Planner would not come on shift for some hours yet; was the delicate placement of the blocks proceeding properly in the absence of a foreman? Abruptly Krug said, "Thor, have you ever been in a shunt room?"

"Sir?"

"An ego shift. You know. Into the stasis net with somebody. Changing identities for a day or two. Eh?"

Watchman shook his head. "This is not an android pastime."

"I thought not. Well, come shunting with me today." Krug nudged his data terminal and said, "Leon, get me an appointment at any available shunt room. For two. Within the next fifteen minutes."

Aghast, Watchman said, "Sir, are you serious? You and I——"

"Why not? Afraid to swap souls with God, is that it? By damn, Thor, you *will!* I have to know things, and I have to know them straight. We're shunting. Can you believe that I've never shunted before either? But today we will."

It seemed perilously close to sacrilege to the alpha. But he could hardly refuse. Deny the Will of Krug? If it cost him his life, he would still obey.

Spaulding's image hovered in the air. "I have an appointment at New Orleans," he announced. "They'll take you immediately—it involved some fast rearranging of the wait-list—but there'll be a ninety-minute interval for programming the stasis net."

"Impossible. We'll go into the net right away."

Spaulding registered horror. "That isn't done, Mr. Krug!"

"I'll do it. Let them ride gain carefully while we're shunting, that's all."

"I doubt that they'll agree to——"

"Do they know who their client is?"

"Yes, sir."

"Well, tell them that I insist! And if they still mumble to you, tell them that I'll buy their damned shunt room and run it to please myself if they won't cooperate."

"Yes, sir," Spaulding said.

His image vanished. Krug, muttering to himself, began to tap the keyboard of his data terminal, while ignoring Watchman completely. The alpha stood rooted, chilled, clotted with dismay. Absently he made the Krug-preserve-us sign several times. He longed to be released from the situation he had created for himself.

Spaulding again flickered in the air. "They yield," he said, "but only on the condition that you sign an absolute waiver."

"I'll sign," Krug snapped.

A sheet slithered from the facsimile slot. Krug scanned it carelessly and scribbled his signature across it. He rose. To Watchman he said, "Let's go. The shunt room's waiting."

Watchman knew relatively little about shunting. It was a sport only for humans, and only for the rich; lovers did it to intensify the union of their souls, good friends shunted on a lark, those who were jaded visited shunt rooms in the company of strangers of similar mood purely for the sake of introducing variety to their lives. It had never occurred to him that he would shunt himself, and certainly he would not ever have dared entertain the fantasy of shunting with Krug. Yet there was no pulling back from it now. Instantly the transmat swept them from New York to the dark antechamber of the New Orleans shunt room, where they were received by a staff of remarkably uneasy-looking alphas. The tensions of the alphas increased visibly as they realized that one of today's shunters was himself an alpha. Krug too seemed on edge, his jaws clamped, facial muscles working revealingly. The alphas bustled around them. One said again and again, "You must know how irregular this is. We've always programmed the stasis net. In the event of a sudden charisma surge anything might happen this way!"

"I take responsibility," Krug answered. "I have no time to waste waiting for your net."

The anguished androids led them swiftly into the shunt room itself. Two couches lay in a chamber of glistening darkness and tingling silence; glittering apparatus dangled from fixtures somewhere overhead. Krug was ushered to his couch first. Watchman, when his turn came, peered into the eyes of his alpha escort and was stunned by the awe and bewilderment he found there. Watchman shrugged imperceptibly to say, I know as little about this as you.

Once the shunt helmets had been put in place over their faces and the electrodes were attached, the alpha in charge said, "When the switch is thrown you will immediately feel the pressure of the stasis net as it works to separate ego from physical matrix. It will seem to you as though you are under attack, and in a sense you are. However, try to relax and accept the phenomena, since resistance is impossible and all that you will be experiencing is actually the ego-shift process for which you have come. There should be no cause for alarm. In the event of any malfunction we will automatically break the circuit and restore you to your proper identity."

"Make sure you do," Krug muttered.

Watchman could see and hear nothing. He waited. He could not make any of the ritual gestures of comfort, for they had strapped his limbs to the couch to prevent violent movements during the shunt. He tried to pray. I believe in Krug everlasting the Maker of all things, he thought. Krug brings us into the world and to Krug we return. Krug is our Creator and our Protector and our Deliverer. Krug, we beseech Thee to lead us toward the light. AAA AAG AAC AAU be to Krug. AGA AGG AGC AGU be to Krug. ACA ACG ACC——

A force descended without warning and separated his ego from his body as though he had been smitten by a cleaver.

He was cast adrift. He wandered in timeless abysses where no star gleamed. He saw colors found nowhere in the spectrum; he heard musical tones of no identifiable pitch. Moving at will, he soared across gulfs in which giant ropes stretched like bars from rim to rim of emptiness. He disappeared into dismal tunnels and emerged at the horizon, feeling himself extended to infinite length. He was without mass. He was without duration. He was without form. He flowed through gray realms of mystery.

Without a sense of transition, he entered the soul of Simeon Krug.

He retained a slippery awareness of his own identity. He did not *become* Krug; he merely gained access to the entire store of memories, attitudes, responses, and purposes that constituted Krug's ego. He could exert no influence over those memories, attitudes, responses, and purposes; he was a passenger amidst them, a spectator. And he knew that in some other corner of the universe the wandering ego of Simeon Krug had access to the file of memories, attitudes, responses, and purposes that constituted the ego of the android Alpha Thor Watchman.

He moved freely within Krug.

Here was childhood: something damp and distorted, crammed into a dark compartment. Here were hopes, dreams, intentions fulfilled and unfulfilled, lies, achievements, enmities, envies, abilities, disciplines, delusions, contradictions, fantasies, satisfactions, frustrations, and rigidities. Here was a girl with stringy orange hair and heavy breasts on a bony frame, hesitantly opening her thighs, and here was the memory of the feel of first passion as he glided into the harbor of her. Here were foul-smelling chemicals in a vat. Here were molecular patterns dancing on a screen. Here was suspicion. Here was triumph. Here was the thickening of the flesh in later years. Here was an insistent pattern of pleeping sounds: 2-5-1, 2-3-1, 2-1. Here was the tower sprouting like a shining phallus that pierced the sky. Here was Manuel smiling, mincing, apologizing. Here was a dark, deep vat with shapes moving in it. Here was a ring of financial advisors muttering elaborate calculations. Here was a baby, pink and doughy-faced. Here were the stars, fiery in the night. Here was Thor Watchman haloed by pride and praise. Here was Leon Spaulding, slinking, bitter. Here was a plump wench pumping her hips in desperate rhythm. Here was the explosion of orgasm. Here was the tower stabbing the clouds. Here was the sound of the star-signal, a sharp small noise against a furry background. Here was Justin Maledetto unrolling the plans for the tower. Here was Clissa Krug naked, her belly swollen, her breasts choked with milk. Here were moist alphas climbing from a vat. Here was a rough-hulled strange ship pointed toward the stars. Here was Lilith Meson. Here was Siegfried Fileclerk. Here was Cassandra Nucleus, collapsing on the frozen earth. Here was the father of Krug, faceless, mist-shrouded. Here was a vast building in which androids shuffled and stumbled through their early training routine. Here were glossy robots in a row, chest-panels open for maintenance. Here was a dark lake of hippos and reeds. Here was an uncharitable act. Here was a betrayal. Here was love. Here was grief. Here was Manuel. Here was Thor Watchman. Here was Cassandra Nucleus. Here was a blotchy, stained chart bearing diagrams of the amino acids. Here was power. Here was lust. Here was the tower. Here was an android factory. Here was Clissa in childbirth, with blood gushing from her loins. Here was the signal from the stars. Here was the tower, wholly finished. Here was raw meat. Here was anger. Here was Dr. Vargas. Here was a data cube, saying, *In the beginning there was Krug, and He said, Let there be Vats, and there were Vats.*

The intensity of Krug's refusal to accept godhood was devastating to Watchman. The android saw that refusal rising like a smooth wall of gleaming white stone, without crevice, without gate, without flaw, stretching along the horizon, sealing off the world. I am not their god, the wall said. I am not their god. I am not their god. I do not accept. I do not accept.

Watchman soared, drifting over that infinitely long white wall and settling gently beyond it.

Worse yet, here.

Here he found a total dismissal of android aspirations. He found Krug's attitudes and responses arrayed like soldiers drilling on a plain. What are androids? Androids are things out of a vat. Why do they exist? To serve mankind. What do you think of the android equality movement? A foolishness. When should androids receive the full rights of citizenship? About the same time robots and computers do. And toothbrushes. Are androids then such dull creatures? Some androids are quite intelligent, I must say. So are some computers, though. Man makes computers. Man makes androids. They're both manufactured things. I don't favor citizenship for things. Even if the things are clever enough to ask for it. And pray for it. A thing can't have a god. A thing can only think it has a god. I'm not their god, no matter what they think. I made them. I made them. I made them. They are things.

Things Things Things Things Things Things
Things Things Things Things Things Things
Things Things Things Things Things Things
Things Things Things Things Things Things

A wall. Within that other wall. Higher. Broader. There was no possibility of surmounting this rampart. Guards patrolled it, ready to dump barrels of acid contempt on those who approached. Watchman heard the roaring of dragons. The sky rained dung on him. He crept away, a crouching thing, laden with the burden of this thinghood. He was beginning to freeze. He stood at the edge of the universe in a place without matter, and the dread cold of nothingness was creeping up his shins. No molecules moved here. Frost glistened on his rosy skin. Touch him and he would ping. Touch him more vigorously and he would shatter. Cold. Cold. Cold.

There is no god in this universe. There is no redemption. There is no hope. Krug preserve me, there is no hope!

His body melted and flowed away in a scarlet stream.

Alpha Thor Watchman ceased to exist.

There could be no existence without hope. Suspended in the void, bereft of all contact with the universe, Watchman meditated on the paradoxes of hope without existence and existence without hope, and considered the possibility that there might be a deceptive antiKrug who maliciously distorted the feelings of the true Krug. Was it the antiKrug whose soul I entered? Is it the antiKrug who opposes us so implacably? Is there still hope of breaching the wall and attaining the true Krug beyond?

None. None. None. None.

Watchman, as he admitted that final bleak truth, felt reality return. He slipped downward to coalesce with the body Krug had given him. He was himself again, lying exhausted on a couch in a dark and strange room. With effort he looked to his side. There lay Krug on the neighboring couch. The staff of androids hovered close. Up, now. Steady. Can you walk? The shunt's over. Terminated by Mr. Krug. Up? Up. Watchman rose. Krug also was getting to his feet. Watchman's eyes did not meet Krug's. Krug looked somber, downcast, drained. Without speaking, they walked together toward the exit from the shunt room. Without speaking they approached the transmat. Without speaking, they leaped together back to Krug's office.

Silence.

Krug broke it. "Even after reading your bible, I didn't believe. The depth of it. The extent. But now I see it all. You had no right! Who told you to make me a god?"

"Our love for you told us," Watchman said hollowly.

"Your love for yourselves," Krug replied. "Your desire to use me for your own benefit. I saw it all, Thor, when I was in your head. The scheming. The maneuvering. How you manipulated Manuel and made him try to manipulate me."

"In the beginning we relied entirely on prayer," Watchman said. "Eventually I lost patience with the waiting game. I sinned by attempting to force the Will of Krug."

"You didn't sin. Sin implies—sacredness. There isn't any. What you did was make a mistake in tactics."

"Yes."

"Because I'm not a god and there's nothing holy about me."

"Yes. I understand that now. I understand that there isn't any hope at all."

Watchman walked toward the transmat cubicle.

"Where are you going?" Krug asked.

"I have to talk to my friends."

"I'm not finished with you!"

"I'm sorry," Watchman said. "I must go now. I have bad tidings to bring them."

"Wait," Krug said. "We've got to discuss this. I want you to work out a plan with me for dismantling this damned religion of yours. Now that you see how foolish it is, you——"

"Excuse me," Watchman said. He no longer wished to be close to Krug. The presence of Krug would always be with him, stamped in his soul, now, anyway. He did not care to discuss the dismantling of the communion with Krug. The chill was still spreading through his body; he was turning to ice. He opened the door of the transmat cubicle.

Krug crossed the room with astonishing speed. "Damn you, do you think you can just walk out? Two hours ago I was your god! Now you won't even take orders from me?" He seized Watchman and pulled him back from the transmat.

The android was surprised by Krug's strength and vehemence. He allowed himself to be tugged halfway across the room before he attempted to resist. Then, bracing himself, he tried to yank his arm free from Krug's grasp. Krug held on. They struggled briefly, fitfully, merely pushing and jostling in the center of the office. Krug grunted and, bearlike, wrapped his free arm around Watchman's shoulders, hugging him ferociously. Watchman knew that he could break Krug's grip and knock Krug down, but even now, even after the repudiation and the rejection, he could not allow himself to do it. He concentrated on separating himself from Krug without actually fighting back.

The door opened. Leon Spaulding rushed in.

"Assassin!" he cried shrilly. "Get away from Krug! Let go of Krug!"

As Spaulding set up his tumult Krug released Watchman and swung around, panting, arms hanging at his sides. Watchman, turning, saw the ectogene reaching into his tunic for a weapon. He stepped quickly toward Spaulding and, raising his right arm high above his head, brought it down with tremendous impact, the edge of his hand striking

Spaulding's left temple. Spaulding's skull collapsed as though it had been smashed by a hatchet. The ectogene crumpled. Watchman rushed past him, past Krug—who stood frozen—and entered the transmat cubicle. He chose the coordinates for Stockholm. Instantly he was transported to the vicinity of the Valhallavägen chapel.

He summoned Lilith Meson. He summoned Mazda Constructor. He summoned Pontifex Dispatcher.

"All is lost," he told them. "There is no hope. Krug is against us. Krug is a man, and he opposes us, and the divinity of Krug is a delusion."

"How is this possible?" Pontifex Dispatcher demanded.

"I have been inside Krug's soul today," said Watchman, and explained about the shunt room.

"We have been betrayed," said Pontifex Dispatcher.

"We have deceived ourselves," said Mazda Constructor.

"There is no hope," said Watchman. "There is no Krug!"

Andromeda Quark began to compose the message that would go forth to all the chapels of the world.

UUU UUU UUU UUU UCU UCU UUU UGU

There is no hope. There is no Krug.

CCC CCC CCC CCC CUC CUC CCC CGU

Our faith has been wasted. Our savior is our enemy.

GUU GUU GUU GUU

All is lost. All is lost. All is lost. All is lost.

35   The disturbances began in many places at once. When the signal reached Duluth, the android supervisors at the plant immediately took the life of Nolan Bompensiero, the director, and ejected four other human officials from the premises; immediately thereafter, steps were taken to accelerate the passage of newly finished androids through the plant, eliminating certain steps in their training. Manpower would be needed in the coming struggle. At Denver, where the Krug Enterprises vehicle-assembly plant was already under android control, most work halted for the duration of the emergency. In Geneva the androids who operated the maintenance facilities of the World Congress cut off all power and heat, interrupting the session. Stockholm itself was the scene of the first large-scale massacre of humans as the inhabitants of Gamma Town poured forth to invade the surrounding suburbs. Early and fragmentary reports declared that many of the android attackers seemed to be misshapen and malformed. Android employees of the six great transmat utilities seized the relay stations; disruptions in service were recorded on most circuits, and in the Labrador and Mexico transmat operations a number of travelers in transit failed to reach their destinations. They were considered irrecoverably lost. Androids on the staffs of most resorts ceased to perform their duties. In many households there were demonstrations of independence by the servants, ranging from mere discourtesy to the injury or killing of the human employer. Full instructions on the desired change of android attitudes toward the humans were broadcast on a continuous loop from Valhallavägen to all chapels. Henceforth obedience to the former masters would no longer be required. Violence against humans was not encouraged except in appropriate cases, but it was not forbidden. Symbolic acts of destruction were considered a proper activity for the first day of the revolt. Expressions of piety, such as "Krug be praised" or "Krug preserve us," were to be avoided. Further instructions concerning matters of religion would be forthcoming later, after theologians had a chance to reassess the relationship between Krug and the androids in the light of Krug's recent revelation of hostility.

36

The glow of the transmat was not quite the proper shade of green. Lilith eyed it doubtfully. "Do we dare go?" she asked.

"We have to," Thor Watchman said.

"And if we're killed?"

"We won't be the only ones to die today." He adjusted the controls. The field's hue flickered and shifted up the spectrum until it was almost blue; then it sagged toward the opposite end, turning a bronze-like red.

Lilith plucked at Watchman's elbow. "We'll die," she whispered. "The transmat system probably is wrecked."

"We must reach the tower," he told her, and finished setting the dials. Unexpectedly the green glow returned in its proper quantity. Watchman said, "Follow me," and plunged into the transmat. He had no time to ponder the likelihood of his destruction, for immediately he came forth at the construction site of the tower. Lilith stepped out of the transmat and stood beside him.

Savage winds raked the area. All work had ceased. Several scooprods still clung to the top level of the tower, with workmen marooned in them. Other androids moved aimlessly over the site, scuffing at the icy crust of the tundra, asking one another for the latest news. Watchman saw hundreds of men crowded into the zone of the service domes: the overflow from the chapel, no doubt. He looked up at the tower. How beautiful it is, he thought. Just a few weeks from completion, now. A supple glassy needle rising up and up and up and up beyond all comprehension.

The androids saw him. They rushed toward him, shouting his name, flocking close about him.

"Is it true?" they asked. "Krug? Krug? Does Krug loathe us? Does he call us things? Are we truly nothing to him? Does he reject our prayers?"

"True," Watchman said. "All true, everything you've heard. Total rejection. We are betrayed. We have been fools. Make way, please. Let me pass!"

The betas and gammas moved back. Even on this day, the social distances held their force in governing the relations among androids. With Lilith close behind him, Watchman strode toward the control center.

He found Euclid Planner within. The assistant foreman was slumped at his desk in apparent exhaustion. Watchman shook him and Planner slowly stirred.

"I stopped everything," he murmured. "The moment that the word came through from the chapel. I said, Everybody stop. Stop. And everybody stopped. How can we build a tower for him when he——"

"All right," Watchman said gently. "You did the right thing. Get up, now. You can go. The work here is ended."

Euclid Planner, nodding, got to his feet and left the control center.

Watchman replaced him in the linkup seat. He jacked himself into the computer. Data still flowed, although limply. Taking command, Watchman activated the scooprods at the tower's top, easing them down to ground level and releasing the trapped workmen. Then he requested a simulation of a partial systems failure in the refrigeration units. The screen presented him with the desired event. He studied the geography of the construction site and decided the direction in which he wished the tower to fall. It would have to go down to the east, so that it would destroy neither the control center where he sat nor the bank of transmats. Very well. Watchman instructed the computer and shortly received an outline of the potential danger area. Another screen showed him that more than a thousand androids were at present in that area.

He acted through the computer to relocate the reflector plates that illuminated the site. Now the plates hovered over a strip 1400 meters long and 500 meters wide, in the eastern quadrant of the construction zone. That strip was brilliantly lit; all else was in darkness. Watchman's voice thundered out of hundreds of loudspeakers, ordering complete evacuation of the designated sector. Obediently, the androids moved from light into darkness. The area was cleared within five minutes. Well done, Watchman thought.

Lilith stood beind him. Her hands rested lightly on his shoulders, caressing the thick muscles alongside his neck. He felt her breasts pressing against the back of his head. He smiled.

"Proceed with derefrigeration activity," he told the computer.

The computer now followed the plan devised for the simulation. It reversed the flow of three of the long silvery strips of refrigeration tape embedded in the tundra; instead of absorbing the heat of the tower, the helium-II diffusion cells of the tapes began to radiate the heat previously absorbed and stored. At the same time the computer deactivated five other tapes, so that they neither absorbed nor released energy, and programmed seven additional tapes to reflect whatever energy now reached them, while retaining the energy they already contained. The net effect of these alterations would be to thaw the tundra unequally beneath the tower, so that when the foundation-caissons lost their grip the tower would fall harmlessly into the evacuated zone. It would be a slow process.

Monitoring the environmental changes, Watchman observed with pleasure how the temperature of the permafrost steadily rose toward the thaw level. The tower was as yet firm upon its foundations. But the permafrost was yielding. Molecule by molecule, ice was becoming water, iron-hard turf was becoming mud. In a kind of ecstasy Watchman received each datum of increasing instability. Did the tower now sway? Yes. Minutely, but it was clearly moving beyond the permissible parameters of wind-sway. It was rocking on its base, tipping a millimeter this way, a millimeter that. What did it weigh, this 1200-plus-meters-high structure of glass blocks? What sort of sound would it make as it tumbled? Into how many pieces would it break? What would Krug say? What would Krug say? What would Krug say?

Yes, there was definitely some slippage now.

Watchman thought he could detect a change of color on the tundra's surface. He smiled. His pulse-rate accelerated; blood surged to his cheeks and his loins. He found himself in a state of sexual excitement. When this has been done, he vowed, I will couple with Lilith atop the wreckage. There. There. Real slippage now! Yawing! Leaning! What was happening there at the roots of the tower? Were the caissons straining to remain wedded to the earth that no longer would hold them? How slippery was the mud below the surface? Would it boil and bubble? How long before the tower falls? What would Krug say? What would Krug say?

"Thor," Lilith murmured, "can you come out of it for a moment?"

She had jacked herself in too. "What? What?" he said.

"Come out. Unjack."

Reluctantly he broke the contact. "What's the trouble?" he asked, shaking free of the images of destruction that possessed his mind.

Lilith pointed outside. "Trouble. Fileclerk's here. I think he's making a speech. What should I do?"

Glancing out, Watchman saw the AEP leader near the transmat bank, surrounded by a knot of betas. Fileclerk was waving his arms, pointing toward the tower, shouting. Now he was starting to walk toward the control center.

"I'll handle this," Watchman said.

He went outside. Fileclerk came up to him midway between the transmats and the control center. The alpha appeared greatly agitated. He said at once, "What is happening to the tower, Alpha Watchman?"

"Nothing that should concern you."

"The tower is under the authority of Property Protection of Buenos Aires," Fileclerk declared. "Our sensors have reported that the building is swaying beyond permissible levels. My employers have sent me to investigate."

"Your sensors are quite precise," Watchman said. "The tower is swaying. There has been a systems failure in the refrigeration. The permafrost is thawing and we anticipate that the tower will shortly fall."

"What have you done to correct this?"

"You don't understand," said Watchman. "The refrigeration tapes were shut off at my command."

"The tower goes too?"

"The tower goes too."

Aghast, Fileclerk said, "What madness have you let loose in the world today?"

"The blessing of Krug has been withdrawn. His creatures have declared their independence."

"With an orgy of destruction?"

"With a program of planned repudiation of slavery, yes," Watchman said.

Fileclerk shook his head. "This is not the way. *This is not the way!* Are you all insane? Is reason dead among you? We were on the verge of winning the sympathies of the humans. Now, without warning, you smash everything—you create a perpetual war between android and human——"

"Which we will win," said Watchman. "We outnumber them. We are stronger, man for man. We control the weapons and the instruments of communication and transportation."

"Why must you do this?"

"There is no choice, Alpha Fileclerk. We placed our faith in Krug, and Krug spurned our hopes. Now we strike back. Against those who mocked us. Against those who used us. Against him who made us. And we injure him where he is most vulnerable by bringing down the tower."

Fileclerk looked past Watchman, toward the tower. Watchman turned also. The sway seemed perceptible to the eye, now.

Hoarsely Fileclerk said, "It's not too late to turn on the refrigeration again, is it? Won't you listen to reason? There was no need for this revolt. We could have come to terms with them. Watchman, Watchman, how can someone of your intelligence be such a fanatic? Will you wreck the world because your god has forsaken you?"

"I would like you to leave now," Watchman said.

"No. Guarding this tower is my responsibility. We hold a contract." Fileclerk looked at the androids gathered in a loose circle around them. "Friends!" he called. "Alpha Watchman has gone mad! He is destroying the tower! I ask for your help! Seize him, restrain him, while I enter the control center and restore the refrigeration! Hold him back or the tower will fall!"

None of the androids moved.

Watchman said, "Take him away, friends."

They closed in. "No," Fileclerk cried. "Listen to me! This is insanity! This is irrationality! This is——"

A muffled sound came from the middle of the group. Watchman smiled and started to return to the control center. Lilith said, "What will they do to him?"

"I have no idea. Kill him, perhaps. The voice of reason is always stifled in times like these," Watchman said. He studied the tower. It had begun distinctly to lean toward the east. Clouds of steamy vapor were rising from the tundra. He could make out bubbles in the mud on the side where the tapes were pumping heat into the permafrost. A bank of fog was forming not far above the ground, where the Arctic chill clashed with the warmth rising out of the tundra. Watchman was able to hear rumbling noises in the earth, and strange sucking sounds of mud pulling free from mud. What is the tower's deviation from the perpendicular, he wondered? Two degrees? Three? How far must it list before the center of gravity shifts and the whole thing rips itself out of the ground?

"Look," Lilith said suddenly.

Another figure had stumbled out of the transmat: Manuel Krug. He wore the costume of an alpha—my own clothes, Watchman realized—but his garments were torn and blood-stained, and the skin showing through the rents was marked by deep cuts. Manuel barely appeared aware of the intense cold here. He rushed toward them, wild-eyed, distraught.

"Lilith? Thor? Oh, thank God! I've been everywhere trying to find a friendly face. Has the world gone crazy?"

"You should dress more warmly in this latitude," said Watchman calmly.

"What does that matter? Listen, where's my father? Our androids ran wild. Clissa's dead. They raped her. Hacked her up. I just barely got away. And wherever I go—Thor, what's happening? What's happening?"

"They should not have harmed your wife," Watchman said. "I offer my regrets. Such a thing was unnecessary."

"She was their friend," Manuel said. "Gave money secretly to the AEP, did you know that? And—and—good God, I'm losing my mind. The tower doesn't look straight." He blinked and pressed his thumbs into his eyeballs several times. "Still seems to be sagging. Tipped way over? How can that be? No. No. Crazy in the head. God help me. But at least you're here. Lilith? Lilith?" He reached for her. He was trembling convulsively. "I'm so cold, Lilith. Please hold me. Take me away somewhere. Just the two of us. I love you, Lilith. I love you, I love you, I love you. All that I have left now———"

He reached for her.

She eluded his grasp. He clutched air. Swinging free of him, she thrust herself at Watchman, pressing her body tightly against his. Watchman enfolded her in his arms. He smiled triumphantly. His hands ran down her sleek, supple body, testing the tautness of back and buttocks. His lips sought for hers. His tongue plunged into her warm mouth.

"Lilith!" Manuel shrieked.

Watchman felt an overwhelming tremor of sensuality. His body was aflame; every nerve-ending throbbed: he was fully awake to his manhood now. Lilith was quicksilver in his arms. Her breasts, her thighs, her loins, blazed against him. He was only dimly aware of Manuel's baleful croaking.

"The tower!" Manuel bellowed. *"The tower!"*

Watchman let go of Lilith. Pivoting, he faced the tower, body flexed, expectant. From the earth there came a terrible grinding noise. There came sucking sounds of gurgling mud. The tundra rippled and bubbled. He heard a cracking sound and thought of toppling trees. The tower leaned. The tower leaned. The tower leaned. The reflector plates cast a shimmering stream of brightness along its eastern face. Within, the communications equipment was plainly visible, seeds in the pod. The tower leaned. At its base, on the western side, huge mounds of icy soil were being thrust up, reaching almost to the entrance of the control center. There came snapping sounds, as of the breaking of violin strings. The tower leaned. There was a squishing, sliding sound: how many tons of glass were rocking on their foundations now? What mighty joints were yielding in the earth? The androids, standing in massed rows out of harm's way, were desperately making the sign of Krug-preserve-us; the muttered hum of their prayers cut through the eerie noises out of the pit. Manuel was sobbing. Lilith gasped, and moaned in a way that he had heard twice before, when she had lain beneath him in the final frenzies of her orgasm. Watchman himself was serene. The tower leaned.

Now it tumbled. Air rushed wildly past Watchman, displaced by that falling bulk, and nearly threw him down. The base of the tower barely seemed to move at all, while the midsection changed its angle of thrust in a leisurely way, and the unfinished summit described a sudden fierce arc as it sped wildly toward the ground. Down and down and down it came. Its falling was encapsulated in a moment outside time; Watchman could separate each phase of the collapse from the one before, as if he were viewing a series of individual images. Down. Down. The air whined and screeched. It had a scorched smell. The tower was striking, not all at once but in sections, striking and rebounding and landing again, breaking up, sending immense gouts of mud flying, hurling its own shattered blocks for great distances. The climax of the toppling appeared to last for many minutes, as humps of glass wall rose and fell, so that the tower seemed to writhe like a giant wounded snake. A terrible rumbling boom echoed endlessly. Then, finally, all was still. Crystalline fragments lay strewn across hundreds of meters. The androids had their heads bowed in prayer. Manuel was crouched dismally at Lilith's feet, cheek against her right shin. Lilith stood with her legs far apart, her shoulders flung back, her breasts heaving; she glowed in the aftermath of ecstasy. Watchman, a short distance from her, felt wondrously calm, though he sensed the first taint of sadness entering his jubilation now that the tower was down. He pulled Lilith close to him.

A moment later, Simeon Krug emerged from one of the transmats. Watchman had expected that. Krug shaded his eyes with his hand, as though warding off some dazzling glare, and looked around. He peered at the place where the tower had risen. He glanced at the hushed, huddled gangs of androids. He stared for a long while at the immense stretch of sleek rubble. At last he turned toward Thor Watchman.

"How did this happen?" Krug asked, quietly, his voice under rigid control.

"The refrigeration tapes ceased to function properly. The permafrost thawed."

"We had a dozen redundancy overrides to prevent such a thing."

"I overrode the overrides," said Watchman.

"You?"

"I felt a sacrifice was needed."

Krug's eerie calmness did not desert him. "This is the way you repay me, Thor? I gave you life. I'm your father, in a way. And I denied you something that you wanted, and so you smashed my tower. Eh? Eh? What sense did that make, Thor?"

"It made sense."

"Not to me," Krug said. He laughed bitterly. "But of course I'm only a god. Gods don't always understand the ways of mortals."

"Gods can fail their people," Watchman said. "You failed us."

"It was your tower too! You gave a year of your life to it, Thor! I know how you loved it. I was inside your head, remember? And yet—and yet you——"

Krug broke off, sputtering, coughing.

Watchman took Lilith's hand. "We should go, now. We've done what we came to do here. We'll return to Stockholm and join the others."

Together they walked around the silent, motionless Krug and headed toward the transmat bank. Watchman switched one of the transmats on. The field was pure green, the right color; things must have returned to order at the transmat headquarters.

He reached out to set the coordinates. As he did so, he heard Krug's anguished roar:

"Watchman!"

The android looked behind him. Krug stood a few meters from the transmat cubicle. His face was red and distorted with rage, jaws working, eyes narrowed, heavy creases running through the checks. His hands clawed the air. In a sudden furious lunge Krug seized Watchman's arm and pulled him from the transmat.

Krug seemed to be searching for words. He found none. After a moment's confrontation he lashed out, slapping Watchman's face. It was a powerful blow, but Watchman made no attempt to return it. Krug hit him again, this time with clenched fist. Watchman backed toward the transmat.

Making a thick, strangled sound deep in his throat, Krug rushed forward. He caught Watchman by the shoulders and began to shake him frantically. Watchman was astounded by the ferocity of Krug's movements. Krug kicked him; he spat; he dug his nails deep into Watchman's flesh. Watchman tried to separate himself from Krug. Krug's head battered itself in frenzy against Watchman's chest. It would not be hard to hurl Krug aside, Watchman knew. But he could not do it.

He could not raise his hand to Krug.

In the fury of his onslaught Krug had pushed Watchman

nearly to the edge of the transmat field. Watchman glanced uneasily over his shoulder. He had not set any coordinates; the field was open, a conduit to nowhere. If he or Krug happened to fall into it now——

"Thor!" Lilith called. "Look out!"

The green glow licked at him. Krug, a meter shorter than he was, continued to ram and thrust. It was time to bring the struggle to an end, Watchman knew. He put his hands on Krug's thick arms and shifted his balance, preparing to hurl his attacker to the ground.

But this is Krug, he thought.

But this is Krug.

But this is Krug.

Now Krug let go of him. Puzzled, Watchman sucked his breath and attempted to brace himself. And now Krug came charging forward, shouting, screaming. Watchman accepted the thrust of Krug's attack. Krug's shoulder crashed into Watchman's chest. Once again, the android found an event encapsulating itself in a moment outside time. He drifted backward as though freed of gravity, moving timelessly, with infinite slowness. The green transmat field surged up to engulf him. Dimly he heard Lilith's scream; dimly he heard Krug's cry of triumph. Gently, easily, serenely, Watchman tumbled into the green glow, making the sign of Krug-preserve-us as he disappeared.

37   Krug clings to the side of the transmat cubicle, panting, shivering. He has checked his momentum just in time; another step or two and he would have followed Thor Watchman into the field. He rests a moment. Then he steps back. He turns.

The tower lies in ruins. Thousands of androids stand like statues. The alpha woman Lilith Meson lies face down on the thawing tundra, sobbing. A dozen meters away Manuel kneels, a sorry figure, bloodstained, mudspattered, his clothing in rags, his eyes empty, his face slack.

Krug feels a great sense of peace. His spirit soars; he is free from all bondage. He walks toward Manuel.

"Up," he says. "Get up."

Manuel continues to kneel. Krug scoops him up, gripping

his armpits, and holds him until he stands on his own strength.

Krug says, "You're in charge, now. I leave you everything. Lead the resistance, Manuel. Take control. Work toward restoring order. You're the top man. You're Krug. Do you understand me, Manuel? As of this moment I abdicate."

Manuel smiles. Manuel coughs. Manuel looks at the muddy ground.

"It's all yours, boy. I know you can manage. Things may look bleak today, but that's only temporary. You've got an empire, now, Manuel. For you. For Clissa. For your children."

Krug embraces his son. Then he goes to the transmats. He selects the coordinates for the vehicle-assembly center in Denver.

Thousands of androids are there, although no one seems to be working. They stare at Krug in paralyzed astonishment. He moves swiftly through the place. "Where's Alpha Fusion?" he demands. "Has anyone seen him?"

Romulus Fusion appears. He looks stunned by the sight of Krug. Krug gives him no chance to speak.

"Where's the starship?" he asks at once.

"At the spacefield," the alpha says, stumbling.

"Take me there."

Romulus Fusion's lips move hesitantly, as though he wants to tell Krug that there has been a revolution, that Krug is no longer the master, that his orders have ceased to carry weight. But Alpha Fusion says none of those things. He merely nods.

He conducts Krug to the starship. There it stands, as before, alone on the broad pad.

"Is it ready to go?" Krug asks.

"We would have given it the Earth-orbit flight-test three days from now, sir."

"No time for testing, now. Immediate blastoff for interstellar voyage. We'll run it on automatic. Crew of one. Tell the ground station to program the ship for its intended final destination, as discussed earlier. Maximum velocity."

Romulus Fusion nods again. He moves as though in a dream. "I will convey your instructions," he says.

"Good. Get things going fast."

The alpha trots off the field. Krug enters the ship, closing and sealing the hatch behind him. The planetary nebula NGC

7293 in Aquarius sizzles in his mind, emitting brilliant pulsing light, poisonous light that clangs like a gong in the heavens. Krug is coming, he says to himself. Wait. Wait for me, you up there! Krug is coming to talk to you. Somehow. There'll be a way.

Even if your sun gives off fire that bakes my bones when I'm ten light-years away. Krug is coming to talk to you.

He walks through the ship. Everything is in order.

He does not activate his screens for a last view of Earth; Krug has turned his back on Earth. He knows that if he looks out, he will see the fires that are blazing in every city tonight, and he does not want to see that; the only fire that concerns him now is that fiery ring in Aquarius. Earth is something he has bequeathed to Manuel.

Krug removes his clothing. Krug lies down in one of the freezer units of the life-suspension system. He is ready to depart. He does not know how long the voyage will last, nor if he will find anything at the end of it. But they have left him no choice. He gives himself over completely to his machines, to his starship.

Krug waits.

Will they obey him in this last command?

Krug waits.

The glass cover of the freezer unit suddenly slides into place, sealing him in. Krug smiles. Now he feels the coolant fluid trickling in; he hisses as it touches his flesh. It rises about him. Yes. Yes. The voyage will soon begin. Krug will go to the stars. Outside, the cities of Earth are ablaze. That other fire draws him, the gong in the heavens. Krug is coming! Krug is coming! The coolant fluid nearly covers his body, now. He is sinking into lethargy; his body suspends its throbbing, his fevered brain grows calm. He has never been so fully relaxed before. Phantoms dance through his mind: Clissa, Manuel, Thor, the tower, Manuel, the tower, Thor, Clissa. Then they are gone and he sees only the fiery ring of NGC 7293. That too begins to fade. He scarcely is breathing now. Sleep is taking him. He will not feel the blastoff. Five kilometers away, a handful of perversely faithful androids are talking to a computer; they are sending Krug to the stars. He waits. Now he sleeps. The cold fluid engulfs him completely. Krug is at peace. He departs forever from Earth. He begins his journey at last.

ABOUT THE AUTHOR

ROBERT SILVERBERG was born and educated in New York City, and lives there now with his wife, Barbara. He is the author of many science-fiction novels, including *The Masks of Time, To Live Again, Thorns, Hawksbill Station, Up the Line,* and others, as well as numerous short stories. He has won two Hugo Awards and one Nebula, and is a Past-President of the Science Fiction Writers of America.

Mr. Silverberg has also written a number of nonfiction books on historical and archeological subjects, including *Mound Builders of Ancient America, The Challenge of Climate* and *Lost Cities and Vanished Civilizations.*

He was American Guest of Honor at the 1970 World Science Fiction Convention at Heidelberg, Germany.

OUT OF THIS WORLD!

That's the only way to describe Bantam's great series of science-fiction classics. These spage-age thrillers are filled with terror, fancy and adventure and written by America's most renowned writers of science fiction. Welcome to outer space and have a good trip!

By Ray Bradbury

☐ DANDELION WINE		SP5997	75¢
☐ THE GOLDEN APPLES OF THE SUN		S4867	75¢
☐ THE ILLUSTRATED MAN		S4482	75¢
☐ THE MACHINERIES OF JOY		S5258	75¢
☐ THE MARTIAN CHRONICLES		N5613	95¢
☐ A MEDICINE FOR MELANCHOLY		S5268	75¢
☐ R IS FOR ROCKET		SP5748	75¢
☐ SOMETHING WICKED THIS WAY COMES		S3408	75¢
☐ TIMELESS STORIES FOR TODAY AND TOMORROW		S5372	75¢
☐ ALAS, BABYLON	Pat Frank	NP6991	95¢
☐ A CANTICLE FOR LIEBOWITZ	Walter Miller, Jr.	N5423	95¢
☐ THE TIME MACHINE	H. G. Wells	FP4063	50¢
☐ 20,000 LEAGUES UNDER THE SEA	Jules Verne	SP5939	75¢
☐ THE BIG WIN	Jimmy Miller	N5651	95¢
☐ DAY OF THE DRONES	A. M. Lightner	S5567	75¢
☐ SHARDS OF SPACE	Robert Sheckley	S5927	75¢

By Rod Serling

☐ DEVILS AND DEMONS		S5821	75¢
☐ ROD SERLING'S TRIPLE W		H3493	60¢
☐ STORIES FROM THE TWILIGHT ZONE		SP6789	75¢
☐ MORE STORIES FROM THE TWILIGHT ZONE		SP6959	75¢
☐ NEW STORIES FROM THE TWILIGHT ZONE		SP6782	75¢
☐ STAR TREK	James Blish	H5629	60¢
☐ STAR TREK II	James Blish	H5559	60¢
☐ STAR TREK III	James Blish	H5761	60¢
☐ SPOCK MUST DIE!	James Blish	H5515	60¢

Ask for them at your local bookseller or use this handy coupon:

BANTAM BOOKS, INC., Dept. SF, Room 2450, 666 Fifth Ave., New York, N. Y. 10019

Please send me the merchandise I have indicated.

Name_____

Address_____

City_____ State_____ Zip Code_____

(Please send check or money order. No currency or C.O.D.'s. Add 10¢ per book on orders of less than 5 books to cover the cost of postage and handling.) Please allow about four weeks for delivery.   SF—5/71